A Heart to Betray

– MICHAEL LIMMER –

An environmentally friendly book printed and bound in England by
www.printondemand-worldwide.com

Mixed Sources
Product group from well-managed
forests, and other controlled sources
www.fsc.org Cert no. TT-COC-002641
© 1996 Forest Stewardship Council

FSC

PEFC
PEFC/16-33-415

PEFC Certified

This product is
from sustainably
managed forests
and controlled
sources

www.pefc.org

This book is made entirely of chain-of-custody materials

A HEART TO BETRAY
Copyright © Michael Limmer 2015

A catalogue record for this book is available from the British Library

ISBN 978-178456-176-5

First published 2015 by
FASTPRINT PUBLISHING
Peterborough, England.

..if I turn my eyes upon myself,
I find myself a traitor with the rest.
Shakespeare: Richard II, IV:1

Prologue: London, 1942

"Oh, for crying out loud, where *is* that girl?" The landlady of the Three Bells surveyed the crowd at the bar with a sinking heart. "Just when you need some help!" She stormed along to the end of the bar and bellowed up the stairs. "Peggy, will you come down *this minute*. We're busy."

"Most likely tarting herself up for some soldier boy," a voice grunted at her elbow.

"Sam!"

"That's me. Looks like you need a hand, Stella."

"A gift sent from heaven, Sam, that's you."

"Let's get to it, then." Sam Perkins peeled off his jacket and tossed it under the bar. Then he pitched into his work, pulling pint after pint to slake the thirst of the clientèle. He reckoned everyone must have got a forty-eight-hour pass at the same time: Army, RAF, WAAF, Navy, Wrens, you name it, they were there.

Stella worked tirelessly alongside him, but Sam knew she wasn't red-faced just with the effort. His mate Bill Briggs had warned him that when he'd popped in earlier, before the pub got busy, Stella had been in a fine old taking. Sam grimaced. He was glad he was the right side of her and didn't give much for Peggy's chances when she came clickety-clacking through in her tight skirt and high heels.

"She's going," Stella snarled, as if reading his mind. "Next time she shows her painted face in here, I'll pitch her out, and that's a fact."

Sam shrugged impartially. "She's young," he said. "There's men by the wagon-load in the smoke these days. You can hardly blame her for liking the attention."

"And she's pretty," Stella added sourly. "Oh, you men are all the same, Sam Perkins. And that crafty little minx'll pull the wool over anybody's eyes. I watched her the other day through the crack in her bedroom door. Counting out the notes, she was, and there were a lot of them. Peggy Neal, I said to myself, you never came by all of that honestly."

"Black market, I s'pose," Sam said. "There's a lot of 'em at it."

"Oi, missus!" a voice boomed out. "Over here, will ya? I'm dying of flippin' thirst."

Stella looked up in annoyance. An RAF sergeant at the far end of the bar was waving vigorously to claim her attention.

"You wait your turn like everyone else," she snapped back.

Sam threw her a grin. "That's put him in his place. Loud-mouthed blighter." He lowered his voice. "And if we're talking black market, I reckon he's your boy. Don't come much shiftier 'n him."

Stella switched the sergeant a glance. He was in his thirties, red-faced and balding, with a permanent sneer on his face which he'd probably reckon was a smile. She'd seen him in the Bells before and didn't like him: pushy, offensive, always with some scheme on the go. But he suddenly seemed to have forgotten his thirst. A young WAAF had joined him, trim in her blue uniform. The sergeant was appraising her greedily, but what shocked Stella as she caught sight of the girl's face were the attractive features distorted by fear, the rivulets of recent tears on her cheeks.

"Let's have some service, missus!" Stella's attention was quickly reclaimed, and she went back to working alongside Sam.

* * *

"Wotcher, gorgeous!" The sergeant couldn't believe his eyes. "What can I do you for, then? And what you been upsetting yourself over? Spoil them pretty looks. Here, pop upstairs with me, and I'll soon put the smile back on your face."

The girl seemed oblivious to the crude chat-up lines. "You're the one they call Sarge, aren't you?" she asked tentatively.

"Yep. The one and only Sarge, that's me. Good times guaranteed. Threepence a go."

"Is *he* with you?"

"Who? Oh – *him*. Swipe me, just my ruddy luck. Yes, darling, he's with me. Well, not exactly *with* me, you understand. But he's here, large as bloomin' life. Come on, cop hold. Let's roust him out."

Sarge took the girl's hand in his meaty grasp and led her out into the passageway that ran at right angles to the bar.

"Where you off to, Sarge?" a wag chirped up, as they shouldered their way through the press. "Struck it lucky, then?"

"Nark it, will ya?" Sarge growled. Once in the passageway, he stole a glance along the bar, where the landlady and barman were fully occupied and likely to be for a while. The stairs creaked as they began to climb, and the WAAF tried to pull away from him.

"Come on, now," he chided. "Ain't gonna eat you. Though I dare say you'd make quite a feast."

"Sarge?" An anxious voice called from beyond the landing. "Sarge, that you?"

"It's me, sir. Everything okay?"

"Got a bit of a problem here."

"Right-o. With you in a jiffy."

"Is there someone with you?"

"Yep. But she won't give us no trouble. I'll look after her, you can guarantee it."

As he turned and leered at the fidgeting girl, she broke free and ran off down the stairs. Swearing violently, Sarge bounded after her and caught her up as she struggled to push open the pub's side door.

She made to scream, but he clamped a vicious hand over her mouth. Her eyes dilated with fear.

Sarge held her there for a few moments, waited until he was satisfied no-one had heard them.

"Now you just calm yourself down and come along o' me, miss," he murmured. "Nothing to worry about, you'll see." He chuckled crudely. "Be daft to let a tasty morsel like you slip through my grasp so easy now, wouldn't it?"

1

There were no flies on Madge Ventnor, ever watchful where her husband and other women were concerned. She'd probably not thought it pure chance when they'd bumped into Eve Ransom during one of their regular forays up to London. And could it really have been the first time Tony had seen her since the war? All right, she'd allow him that, but she knew exactly what had been going through his mind when he'd suggested the three of them meet for dinner the following week.

Madge had got in quickly. "Oh, how divine! And why don't we make it a foursome, Tony? Let's invite along that friend of yours – the nice, shy man who runs the bookshop in the High Street..."

Alan Cawley grinned. Trust Madge to think of him: Madge, ever brassy beneath the county veneer. There'd been a couple of occasions when, rocking with too much gin and too little tonic, she'd hazarded certain suggestions. Perhaps she'd simply been playing Tony at his own game, maybe hoping that Alan would take her seriously. Anyway, what did he care? She'd successfully spiked her husband's guns and done Alan the most wonderful service into the bargain. She'd introduced him to Eve.

They'd spent a pleasant evening. But he'd learned very little about Eve and hadn't imparted too much about himself. Not that there was much to tell and in any case, with both Ventnors in full spate, getting a word in edgeways had been quite an achievement.

And Tony hadn't given up, earning himself a withering glare from his wife. "You must come down to us in the country, my dear. Come and stay over the weekend. We've bags of room."

Madge, of course, could do nothing but smile sweetly and endorse the invitation. And to Alan's surprise, Eve came. Madge made sure to invite him too, her insurance policy, and he went for a long walk with Eve on the Sunday at her suggestion. He supposed she wanted it understood that whatever might have happened in the past, she didn't want to be part of a triangle in the present.

He showed her round the sleepy market town of Durleyford, practically deserted on a Sunday afternoon, his bookshop in the High Street and his tiny cottage down a lane on the edge of town.

It was no more than friendship and, attractive as Eve was, Alan was reluctant to push the boundaries. But it was he who issued the next invitation, suggesting she return in a fortnight's time for an outing in the Cotswolds, an area with which she was unfamiliar, and offering to book her in at Mrs Darvill's guest house in River Street. She'd given this a few moments' consideration before accepting. He'd been elevated to cloud nine.

That had been back in the spring, and that summer of 1961 found him still there. Still there on a balmy July evening, waiting in the vestibule of Durleyford Hall, the country residence of newly-elected MP Kelvin Guilfoyle, as Eve powdered her nose in the ladies' room and sought to enhance what in Alan's eyes was already perfect.

His usually serious face lit up as the door swung open and she came towards him.

She was in her late thirties, a year or so younger than him. No longer a girl, and yet there was something effervescently girlish about her: the lightly freckled face, delightfully turned-up nose and laughing brown eyes.

Her frock was quite simple: white with blue polka dots. A pale blue shawl, fastened with a silver brooch, covered her slim shoulders.

She wasn't tall, her head, even with her honey-blonde hair worn up, barely above his shoulder, and yet there was nothing insignificant about her. Alan was biased, believing her to be a beautiful woman: although her beauty was, perhaps deliberately, understated.

Her gaze met his, and she smiled. Alan had already termed this her 'secret' smile, as if she could read what was on his mind.

"Sorry if I was a long time," she apologised lightly. "There was quite a crush in there, and a lot of chatter."

"I hadn't given up on you," he replied, smiling back. "Well? Shall we go in?" He offered his arm, and she took it.

"Going in is always the worst part, isn't it?" Eve's tone was sympathetic. She'd soon perceived that he was a private individual, awkward in a crowd. But it must have been ten times worse for her, a stranger. At least he had the advantage of some sort of acquaintance with everyone present.

He wanted to say that having her on his arm made a world of difference, but he lacked the courage. "The worst'll soon be past," he countered stoically and steered her towards the ballroom.

It was an imposing room, long and airy with three huge chandeliers suspended from the ornate ceiling. To the left, three sets of French windows opened on to a wide terrace bathed in evening sunlight, where people had gathered to smoke, chat and admire the views of the rolling countryside. Others sat inside, gossiping and laughing around the white-clothed tables, the women in bright frocks and jewellery, the men in flannels and open-neck shirts or linen suits.

To the right, several trestle tables groaned under the weight of a sumptuous buffet, to which the busy Mrs Foster, in constant demand as the best cook in Durleyford, was putting the finishing touches, aided by a smart yet serious young woman, whom Alan recognised as a recent recruit to the Corner House Café which was situated at the bottom end of the High Street.

Manners, Kelvin Guilfoyle's aptly-named manservant, was dispensing drinks from a silver tray, whatever he might have been thinking decently veiled by his bland expression. Guilfoyle himself, erect, broad-shouldered, his dark hair lightly tinged with grey, also lent a hand with the drinks, chatting affably with florid Colonel Prendergast and his tennis-playing, man-eating daughters, Gussie and Fliss.

Alan was gratified by the turning of several male heads and the grudging appraisal of their spouses as he progressed down the room with Eve. Gerald Carbury, the well-groomed estate agent, accorded her a beaming smile and Alan an appreciative nod, before succumbing to an eloquent tug on his sleeve from Jane, his dowdy and constantly ailing wife. Poor Gerald, Alan thought: a personable man, yet so transparent. There'd be hell to pay later.

Alan steered Eve over towards the farthest window where Madge and Tony Ventnor sat, their first beverages of the evening in their hands, the rim of Madge's glass already smeared with lipstick.

She glanced up mischievously. "We understand that the two of you would rather be alone, but it's a bit antisocial abandoning us to take refuge in alcohol, wouldn't you say?"

Alan liked Madge. She never disguised the fact that her blondeness was of the bottled variety, and although she was often made up to the nines she was, in her early forties, a handsome woman who'd maintained her figure. She rarely disguised that either, and tonight was no exception, the low neckline of her dress advertising the generous swell of her breasts.

And Madge liked him. A little too much, he feared, and he didn't think she'd taken too readily to his obvious attraction to Eve, particularly as she'd introduced them in the first place.

He wondered if that might be why she often teased him. Occasionally she'd succeed in embarrassing him, but not tonight: tonight he was prepared for the onslaught.

"You poor, shrinking violets," he gave back. "Eve, we must apologise."

"We shan't accept it." Tony Ventnor stirred in his seat, having just finished running his practised gaze over every woman in the room. He was short and stocky, in his mid-forties, a snappy dresser with a perpetually roving eye. His taste for the high life had bequeathed him a noticeable paunch, belying the quick and active mind, the persuasive salesman in him. It was farm machinery these days, and before that pre-fabs, television sets and insurance.

Tony had been a flier in the war, decorated with an array of medals for bravery, and he didn't mind who knew it. But he'd been the first to befriend Alan on his arrival in Durleyford and introduced him to various people. Alan had never forgotten that, even though in character and outlook they were poles apart.

"Actually," Tony went on, his lively gaze on Eve, "we've been whiling away the time admiring our gracious host's property. Makes our little homestead seem like a labourer's hovel. Wouldn't you agree, old girl?"

Alan grinned at yet one more of Tony's exaggerations. Bayes Wood, where the Ventnors lived, was a rambling old house of four reception rooms and six bedrooms. He didn't think the Hall could be much bigger.

"And my goodness, what a spread." Madge was studying the buffet. "Back to war rations after this blow-out, husband dear." She leaned forward to expertly whisk a second glass from the tray offered by the passing Manners.

Alan took drinks for himself and Eve and set them down before pulling out a chair for her and sitting beside her. He glanced round as Manners moved on and saw that Guilfoyle was heading their way, first pausing to greet James Kedwell, the local solicitor, his wife Cicely, and Teddy, their slightly gauche offspring who'd just been made a junior partner in his father's firm. He also had a word with the already giggling Misses Pomfrets, who were making deep inroads into his supplies of Amontillado.

"Ah!" he greeted them. "The virtuous Ventnors."

Madge snorted, and Tony raised his glass in a toast. "Here's mud in your eye, Guilfoyle. Dashed decent of you to invite us."

The MP chuckled. "Well, I took care to invite only the cream of Durleyford society."

Tony sniggered, and Madge cackled with amusement. "Oh, Kelvin, you'll have us in stitches. But what a lovely occasion, and trust you to bag such glorious weather! They say the devil looks after his own. This'll be bound to catch you a few votes."

Guilfoyle took the ribbing with practised ease. "Votes be blowed, Madge. Mac's set for a good run, and there'll be no election in the foreseeable. Ah, good evening, Cawley. I'm relieved to find I invited someone with intelligence."

"Oh, for Pete's sake, you're not going to talk about books?" Madge complained. "I swear Alan will turn into a book before long."

"We hope to enlighten you one day, Madge," Guilfoyle replied smoothly. He turned towards Eve. "And this young lady? I don't believe we've met?"

Alan sensed his blush beneath Madge's vicious grin, not helped by her *sotto voce* "Not that young." He suspected no-one else heard, certainly not Tony, who'd taken the opportunity to ogle Eve quite openly.

He rushed to drown out the comment with his own stammering introduction. "I —um, a friend of ours, Miss Ransom. Eve, our host, Kelvin Guilfoyle."

Eve offered a hand, which Guilfoyle clasped. "Charmed," he smiled, with a polite little bow. "I'm assuming you don't live locally, Miss Ransom?"

"I live in London," Eve replied. "I teach English to overseas students at a college close to Regent's Park."

"Eve and Alan get together most weekends," Madge put in wickedly.

Alan could tell that Eve was uncomfortable, for it was a long way off the truth. He'd been to London once, when they'd met for the theatre, and this was only her third visit to Durleyford. He started to intervene, but Guilfoyle was ahead of him, effortlessly dispelling the unease.

"Lovely to make your acquaintance, Miss Ransom. The first time of many, I trust. I think the buffet's about to kick off. Ah yes, here's old Manners with the gong – he loves this bit. Mrs Foster has done us proud – thanks for your recommendation, Madge."

The gong sounded, and their host strode to the middle of the floor. "Ladies and gentlemen, supper is served. Please do grab a plate and dig in."

Chairs scraped back, and an orderly stampede ensued. Unsurprisingly, the Ventnors manoeuvred themselves to the head of the queue. Eve and Alan exchanged grins, as he took her arm and steered her along in their wake. Tony's voice exclaimed from a little way ahead of them: "Done us proud? I'll echo that."

The reason for his enthusiasm was the young woman helping Mrs Foster serve the buffet. She'd not been in Durleyford more than a couple of weeks, and Alan didn't know her name.

She was above medium height, neat in her waitress' uniform and pinafore, her blonde hair drawn back in a pony-tail to reveal finely sculpted features. Alan didn't think she could be much above twenty, but she had about her a serious air which made her seem older. It might have been down to shyness, for she could scarcely have known anyone there; but when she smiled, it was no more than fleeting and only done, he felt, out of a sense of duty.

Madge raised her eyebrows in exasperation. "Down, boy. She's half your age."

Tony paid no heed, leaning across the table so that his head was almost touching the girl's. "I'll have some of the veal pie, my dear. You're new, aren't you? I've noticed you in the Corner House a couple of times in passing. I'll make sure not to pass next time. I'm Tony, by the way. Wing Commander Tony Ventnor, to give you the lot."

The girl didn't waver, calmly slicing the pie and depositing a portion on Ventnor's proffered plate; neither did she make eye contact. "Thank you, sir. Yes, madam?"

Madge gave the girl her order and her husband a smirk. "You're getting a bit old for this, aren't you, *Wing Commander*? They can spot a lecherous middle-aged man a mile off, rank or no rank."

But Tony was unmoved, shuffling obediently along the line to where the dumpy, smiling Mrs Foster was doling out vegetables with a practised hand.

"Hello, Mrs. F. I say, what a spread. And a useful little helper you have along there, I must add. What did you say her name was? Tania? What a delightful name. Thank you, Tania," he called back at the girl, who went on serving, head bent over her work.

"Delightful?" Madge muttered caustically. "Sounds like a ruddy circus elephant. And for heaven's sake, Tony, do move *along*."

Tables had been laid at the lower end of the ballroom and, once they'd been served, Eve and Alan joined the Ventnors there, making room for the subsequent arrival of the Kedwell family. Alan was pleased that Eve was seated next to Cicely, a matronly and sensible woman, able to converse on any number of subjects.

James Kedwell ended up next to Madge and Tony, and Alan couldn't help feeling a little sorry for him. But to his credit, James was a good listener.

That left Alan with young Teddy, in his early twenties and brimful of hope and innocence, reminding him a little of himself before the war. Teddy was an avid reader, keen on American crime fiction, and they quickly launched into the respective merits of Hammett and Chandler, and how

Ross MacDonald's detective Lew Archer shaped up against Chandler's excellent Philip Marlowe.

They busied themselves with food and conversation while Manners and his master came round to each table to pour wine. Everyone was into their dessert course by the time the doorbell pealed, its plea only just audible above the hubbub in the room. Manners set down his bottles and walked through to the vestibule in his unhurried fashion.

From where they sat, Alan had a clear view of the front door as Manners hauled it open to reveal a red-faced, balding man of middle years dressed in a rumpled blue suit. He was mopping his face with a large handkerchief and wore no tie, presumably on account of the warm evening. Alan wondered if he might be a late arrival, but he'd never seen him before and the man didn't seem to fit into the ranks of cosy, middle-class Durleyford.

"Step inside a moment, sir," he heard Manners say, a touch coolly. "I shall inquire."

The manservant returned to the ballroom, and the caller walked in, glancing around at the dark oil paintings which adorned the vestibule and panelled staircase.

Then he looked through into the ballroom. Alan, who'd been studying him, prepared to look away, but the man was looking past him, an impudent smile lighting up his face. He didn't appear a pleasant man, and the smile was certainly not in that category.

Manners had reached their table where Kelvin Guilfoyle stood conversing amiably with James Kedwell. He addressed him in a confidential tone, but Alan caught the words "asking for you."

Guilfoyle frowned as his gaze rested on the caller. Excusing himself to Kedwell and the rest, he followed

Manners out into the hallway and strode up to the visitor. "How can I help, Mr -?" he began.

But Alan heard no more, for by then Manners had pulled the connecting doors shut and returned to his duties in the ballroom.

Alan resumed his conversation with Teddy Kedwell, to be distracted minutes later by the sight of the blue-suited man walking past the terrace on his way back down the drive. He seemed well pleased, for he still wore the ugly grin and was patting his breast pocket in satisfaction.

Alan suddenly became aware of Eve watching him. She smiled, he thought a trifle nervously, but then her attention was claimed by Cicely, and he turned back to concentrate on Teddy's views regarding Chandler's final novel, *Playback*. He noticed that the Ventnors weren't stopping to draw breath, and James was nodding and exclaiming in all the right places. He wondered if Eve had noticed the blue-suited man too; he was pretty sure no-one else had.

The door to the hallway clicked shut, and Guilfoyle came back into the room. He nodded affably at Alan and moved across to another table to regale the Misses Pomfrets, the mild-mannered vicar, Reverend Paston, and his disapproving wife Mildred, whose half-glass of dry white wine *(Oh, whoa, Mr Manners! Whoa!")* seemed to have made her sociable to the point of volubility.

Once the buffet was finished, and the amiable Mrs Foster and Manners were clearing away plates and cutlery, her young helper served coffee, receiving several admiring glances as she did so.

Tony Ventnor was in his element. "May I introduce Tania, ladies and gentlemen? I'm sure we all appreciate everything she's done for us this evening." He held her lightly by the waist, although Madge, engrossed in her wine and no doubt aching for a gin and tonic, was in no position to see what was going on. The girl seemed unfazed by Ventnor's attentions, politely carrying on with her work and moving to the next table as soon as she decently could. Alan silently applauded her composure.

Soon afterwards the younger people gathered at the far end of the room, where Guilfoyle had thoughtfully placed a gramophone. No disappointment was registered at the fact that his tastes didn't run to rock'n'roll or jazz, and one or two couples soon began performing a slow, steady waltz, with Teddy in keen pursuit of the younger Prendergast girl, Fliss. "She'll eat him for breakfast," was Madge's cynical comment. She'd collared Manners and got him to bring her a gin and tonic. Alan somehow didn't think she'd stop at one.

A number of people were dividing into groups for whist. Eve tapped him on the arm. "I don't play whist. Do you?" she whispered.

He did, but was more than willing to miss out. "Me neither."

"Do you mind if we stretch our legs outside? Otherwise I fear I shall be stuck with Madge, and she's beginning to get a bit loud."

"A capital suggestion." He couldn't help feeling sorry for Madge, but it seemed she wasn't to be left alone. Gussie Prendergast was making her slightly unsteady way over, the colonel and Tony having succumbed to whist. The main topic of conversation was bound to be men; and it would be lively.

They excused themselves, Alan striving to distance himself from Madge's lewd wink, and went out on to the terrace.

They walked its length, down the steps on to the gravel forecourt and round to the rear of the house. Here the closely-mown lawn swept down to gardens where gravelled paths weaved a passage through a colourful jungle of summer shrubs and flowers. It was a shaded, peaceful place, and Alan was glad to be away from the babble of the ballroom. He pulled a silver cigarette case from his pocket, offered it to Eve.

She shook her head. "Only at times of stress." Her face broke into a cautious smile. "This isn't one of them. But you go ahead."

He dropped the case back in his pocket and grinned. "I hardly ever bother."

They slowed to a halt, and he pointed out the little town of Durleyford nestling in the valley, its roofs sparkling in the evening sunlight; and beyond it the delightful Cotswold countryside, where they'd head the following day.

As they resumed walking, Eve slipped her hand through his arm, and he wondered if this might be the moment to kiss her. But somehow he lacked the boldness: typical of him, not wanting to embarrass or offend.

They made their way back towards the house. His limp was hardly apparent these days, unless he had to break into a run. He suspected, however, that Eve must have noticed it and was too polite to remark upon it, probably putting it down to an injury he'd picked up in the war. In a sense, he supposed he had.

"Well, Eve," he remarked, as they drew near the terrace steps. "Tonight you've rubbed shoulders with the movers and shakers of Durleyford society. We're a pretty average bunch, I should reckon. But everyone rubs along reasonably well together."

"It's been an enjoyable evening," she replied readily. "Mr Guilfoyle's a generous host. I think he likes you very much."

"The feeling's reciprocated. He's one of my best customers." He grinned. They'd jaw on for hours about books, even shy Alan Cawley at ease in the MP's company. He felt valued; although not only by Guilfoyle. He got on well with such local *alumni* as Gerald Carbury and James Kedwell. Reverend Paston too, although at first suspicious of his Methodist roots; and of course the irrepressible Tony and openly flirtatious Madge. They'd helped him establish an identity, a purpose he never felt he'd achieve once he'd come through the war. And he believed there was an even greater purpose now that he'd met Eve.

He'd enjoyed the evening too, simply being with her. But as they reached the terrace, Eve tugged at his arm, held him back.

"Alan?"

They'd been conversing quite easily, but as he looked at her now, he sensed an anxiety, a tension about her.

"Eve? Is something wrong?"

She shook her head, smiled. "Oh no. Just that – well, if you wouldn't mind taking me back to Mrs Darvill's now, I was finding it a bit stuffy in there..."

He understood. Stuffy, and with the gin now flowing, Madge and Gussie in particular would be getting a tad unbearable. "Of course. I've had about enough myself."

Back inside, he could have predicted what it would be like. Tony Ventnor, glass in hand, was chatting up Tania as she folded and stored away the table cloths. She replied in monosyllables and was probably relieved that escape was imminent.

Colonel Prendergast was boring the polite Carburys to death with some jungle tale of long ago. Even Gerald's eye had given up roving, although Jane still clutched his arm in a vice-like grip, as they nodded and agreed in unison, stifled yawns.

James and Cicely Kedwell conversed with Reverend and Mrs Paston; Teddy, red-faced and emboldened with wine, still pursued the coquettish Fliss, the dancing having fizzled out, and Manners was fetching shawls for the Misses Pomfrets. It seemed as if one or two others had already left.

Madge and Gussie lolled on a sofa, gin-laden, each with a cigarette in a holder as they eagerly compared the merits of Charlton Heston, Rock Hudson and Troy Donahue.

"An early night, Mr Cawley?" Madge teased, as Alan confided their intention to leave. "Eve, your mother should have warned you. And there was I hoping against hope that he'd come to carry me away."

"Me too," Gussie giggled, brandishing a smile which might have graced an advertisement for Gibbs' SR.

They waved their farewells to the preoccupied Tony and thanked Guilfoyle, who came over to join them in the doorway.

"My pleasure. Here, let me walk out to your car with you."

"Our apologies for leaving early," said Eve. "It's down to me, I'm afraid. A bit of a headache. But it's been such an enjoyable evening."

"Please don't apologise," Guilfoyle reassured her. "Things are starting to wind down now, or at least I hope they are. I certainly don't want Madge and the Prendergast girls dossing on my sofas. Poor Manners would have forty fits. He's very correct, you know."

He escorted them round to the side of the house, where Alan had parked his Morris Minor in front of the stable block. He took Eve's hand, bowed politely over it and shook Alan's heartily.

"So good to meet you, Miss Ransom. You must get Cawley to bring you again before long. And Cawley, could you order the latest volume in Snow's *Strangers and Brothers* sequence? It's for a nephew of mine whose birthday I simply must not forget this year. I'll pop in on Wednesday anyhow, when old Fullarton arrives to sign his books for you." He turned to Eve and grinned. "Piers Fullarton," he explained.

"Oh, the poet?"

"That's him. Capital fellow. He was my fag at Harrow in the early thirties. Suffered terribly during the war, but his poetry is stirring stuff. Straight from the heart. Well, if you'll excuse me, I must return to the fray."

He waved to them as they drove off down the tree-lined avenue. On the short journey back to Durleyford, Eve apologised again.

"Alan, I feel so guilty dragging you away."

"Don't be. I'm pretty useless at these social gatherings and besides, Mr Guilfoyle would rather it wound down about now. His supplies of gin must be seriously depleted."

Darkness was falling as they pulled up outside the Willow Tree Guest House in River Street.

"Thank you for a lovely evening, Alan." Her hand closed over his, and a *frisson* of expectation shivered through him, dashed in the next moment. "But I'd better not ask you in. Mrs Darvill seems a little prudish where gentlemen callers are concerned."

"Well, you can always stay at my place." To his own hearing, he sounded unusually bold; certainly not because of anything he'd drunk. And he was glad of the semi-darkness, because he could sense himself blushing furiously. "I mean – I've got a spare room."

"Perhaps another time." He could see she was smiling, and he smiled back, hoping she meant that.

Alan saw her to the door, reminding her that he'd pick her up at eleven in the morning.

"Thank you, Alan. I'm looking forward to it."

He was preparing to take his leave when, for no reason, he remembered the shabby, blue-suited visitor. The man had looked into the ballroom and grinned unpleasantly. Had he recognised someone? Alan had looked at Eve soon afterwards, and she'd seemed a little taken aback. He tried to dismiss the thought, but it wouldn't go away.

"Eve?"

"Yes?"

"Was everything all right back there? At the Hall, I mean?"

"Oh, Alan, you're a worrier. Yes, it was. Just that, well, I came over a bit tired, that's all." She reached up and planted a kiss on his cheek. "Goodnight. Sleep well, my dear."

She'd turned and disappeared into the house before he could respond, and all that was left to him was to make his way home.

2

As he lay awake during the night, and as he dressed and breakfasted the following morning, Alan Cawley thought long and hard about Eve Ransom. What did he know about her? She'd told him very little. But then, he'd not been exactly forthcoming about himself. Should he have mentioned Dorothy? If their relationship was to progress beyond friendship, he knew he'd have to before long.

They'd both been open enough regarding the present, although this had been her third visit to Durleyford, and she seemed hesitant about inviting him up to London. They'd met there just once, to see *The Mousetrap*, and he'd insisted on getting her a taxi home. The wished-for invitation to accompany her hadn't materialised.

He knew that she taught part-time at Parkway Language College in a cul-de-sac off Regent Street and that she lived on the second floor of a tenement in Stepney. He got the impression it wasn't that which bothered her so much as her mother, who lived with her. And that Mrs Ransom was the likely reason why he hadn't been asked back.

"My mother never takes kindly to the fact that I may have a gentleman friend," Eve had explained. "She seems to think I'm still eighteen, not thirty-eight. She gets terribly confused over the simplest things, but she's very dear and really quite harmless. Still, the last couple of years haven't been easy."

Eve had been born in France to a French mother (Estelle had soon been anglicized to Stella) and an English father. He'd settled there after the Great War, but they'd moved to London in the late 1920s, when Hubert Ransom had taken over his father's public house in Bethnal Green. Hubert had died just before the Second World War, leaving Stella to run the pub and Eve to help her, before she'd enlisted in the WAAF.

That was about all she'd told him; but how much or little of himself had he given away? The bare minimum, really. He'd had a sheltered upbringing, the only child of parents well advanced in years. His father had been a Methodist minister, a gentle, compassionate man, and his mother a stalwart support in that ministry. They were both dead now, and Alan couldn't help feeling he'd been a disappointment to them, even though they'd never so much as hinted at that.

A quiet, bookish boy, he'd gone to university to read English Literature but had had his education scuppered by the war. He felt Percival Cawley had hoped he'd follow him into the ministry, but Alan knew he lacked the commitment. And with the war over, he didn't return to his studies. Once he'd recovered from the accident, once he was back in touch with life again, he took up a career in bookselling, serving his apprenticeship with Foyle's, then Hatchard's. With the small sum of money left him by his parents, he moved to the peaceful market town of Durleyford on the edge of the Cotswolds, close to where his father had held a stipend when Alan was a boy.

There he'd opened his bookshop, and there he was now, three years on. It was where he'd intended to stay, quietly mouldering among his books. Except, miracle upon miracles, Alan Cawley had fallen in love and would move to the ends of the earth if Eve told him she loved him too; and if that was where she wanted to go.

That day, Sunday, was another blessed with beautiful weather. He called for Eve at eleven, and she emerged, relaxed and smiling, in blouse, cardigan and pleated skirt, her hair let down over her shoulders.

She'd admitted that, since living in England, she'd rarely ventured beyond London, and this part of the country was new to her. They lunched at Evesham, strolled along the river bank and called in at Broadway for a cream tea on their journey home. The villages, fields and hedgerows were bursting with vigour and Eve, when the conversation lapsed, when they weren't laughing together, was keenly observing all around her; perhaps, he hoped, comparing it favourably to life in London.

She made no allusion to the previous evening, except once to mention what a lovely time she'd had, and what a nice woman Cicely Kedwell was. Perhaps he'd read too much into it, but Alan couldn't dismiss the feeling that the blue-suited man had recognised someone in the room. Why was he so worried that it might have been Eve? It might have been anyone – or even no-one.

They arrived back in Durleyford late in the afternoon, picked up Eve's suitcase from Mrs Darvill's and drove down to the station. They held hands as they walked out on to the platform.

"It seems a pity that I have to go back," Eve sighed.

"I was thinking the same."

As her train rumbled into the station, Eve turned towards him, and he set down her suitcase and took her in his arms, the first time he'd done so, and it seemed such a natural thing to do.

"Alan, thank you for this weekend. It's been so different – so special."

"It's been special for me too."

She reached up and kissed him. He sought to tighten his grip on her, but she eluded him and turned towards the carriage door, leaving him no option but to reach past her, open the door and place her suitcase inside. She stepped up into the carriage, leaned out of the window as the guard blew on his whistle.

"I'll phone during the week."

He took hold of her hand, kissed it. "Eve – please – come down again next weekend."

The train hissed and shuddered into motion. She smiled wistfully at the plea in his voice. Did she understand the unspoken words behind that plea? *Don't go – stay here with me.*

"There's an arrangement I can't cancel on Saturday."

"Then come down in the evening. We'll go for another drive on Sunday."

The train started to move off. He had to let go her hand but jogged along beside the carriage, aching for her answer.

"Then, yes. Yes, I will. Saturday afternoon. We'll speak during the week."

He ran out of platform, stood and returned her wave until the train had rumbled out of sight.

* * *

The next morning, Alan walked the short distance from his cottage to the shop. On sunny, cloudless days like these, he always relished the view awaiting him as he emerged from Blackbird Lane. The buildings, all of Cotswold stone, with their bright shop fronts. their window boxes and hanging baskets overflowing with colour, spilled down the hill towards the cattle market at the bottom; while above the rooftops rose the squat tower of the town's Norman church and beyond it, stretching far into the distance, a patchwork of fields of pasture, corn and barley.

The modest frontage of 'Durleyford Books' stood across the road a little way down the hill. Alan's subject knowledge was extensive, so he maintained a small stock of most subjects. The Durleyford public loved its books, ranging from Kelvin Guilfoyle's tastes in biography, history and politics to old Miss Timmins' penchant for hard-boiled thrillers. The tidy living Alan made was no less than his hard work and devotion merited.

He was also fortunate in his choice of assistant. Ariadne Gray, a maiden lady of some fifty years and a former librarian, shared his love of books and was willing to help out in the shop whenever needed.

Miss Gray was a stickler for order and method, a manic duster of display tables, who would make endless tours around the shelves, knocking books together with a gentle thud to displace any offending dust. The Everyman Library was maintained in strict numerical order, the Teach Yourself series in alphabetical order of title; and if an errant customer should return a title to the wrong place, Miss Gray would quickly rectify it with a disdainful *"Tut!"*

This morning she was awaiting him at the shop door. He was glad he wasn't late, for he noticed that she checked her watch as he strolled across the road. He greeted her cheerfully, unlocked the door and stood aside to allow her to bustle in ahead of him. She was already in the little stock room by the time he'd switched on the lights.

"The Fullarton stock should be here by mid-morning, Ariadne," he called out.

"Oh, good," she trilled back. "I must say I'm *so* looking forward to meeting him. Did I hear you say he was a friend of yours, Mr Cawley?"

"I'm afraid I've never had the pleasure of meeting him. No, he's an old school friend of Mr Guilfoyle's."

Piers Fullarton had won several awards for his poetry, and Alan had always kept his more recent titles in stock. On one of his many visits to the shop, Guilfoyle had noticed them and, as Fullarton was due to bring out another slim volume, inquired if Alan would appreciate the poet calling in to sign copies of his books and meet some of his adoring public.

Alan had jumped at the chance. Durleyford numbered a Poetry Circle among its various societies, and Piers Fullarton would be a prize catch. Guilfoyle had contacted Fullarton, who contacted his publisher, who telephoned Alan; and a visit was arranged for Wednesday of that week.

In consequence, that Monday was such a busy day as to preclude his daydreaming about Eve. Not only did the Fullarton stock arrive and require unpacking, checking off and arranging in a lovingly prepared display in the middle of the shop floor, but the previous Saturday had yielded a score of customer orders which had to be typed out and posted off to the relevant publisher.

However, as it was Monday there were few customers and Alan, for once, was grateful for that. By the time he closed the shop for lunch, they'd made decent progress. Ariadne Gray tripped off to the churchyard to consume her prim sandwiches and lose herself in a torturous biography of Charlotte Brontë, while Alan, aware of his assistant's mild disapproval, crossed the road to the Coach & Horses for a half-pint of best, a chat about the weather and cricket with Tom Badger the hearty landlord and a couple of regulars, and a round of Badger's thick-hewn ham and mustard sandwiches, the size of which would have quite startled Miss Gray.

The afternoon was quiet, allowing Alan time to sort out his Book Token returns, while Ariadne fussed around the order of her subject alphabet and shelved the newly-arrived stock.

After a while, Alan became aware of her standing in the doorway of the tiny stock room which doubled as his office and trying to claim his attention with a polite cough.

As he looked up, Miss Gray threw a nervous glance over her shoulder and stole into the office.

"There's a man over in the corner by the window," she whispered. "I want to sort out the Penguins, but he's in the way. He's been there over twenty minutes, and I feel sure he means to steal something. Besides, he reeks of beer." The latter was in itself an indictable offence in Ariadne's eyes.

Alan nodded and pushed back his chair. Satisfied that he'd deal with the problem, Miss Gray took herself off to the opposite end of the shop and started on some unnecessary rearrangement, all the while darting spiky glances in the direction of the unwanted intrusion.

Alan sighed as he stepped out of the office. He'd experienced a fair amount of shoplifting during his time in London and supposed it would only be a matter of time before Durleyford Books fell victim. Miss Timmins had made off with a James Hadley Chase the week before, but that had been absent-mindedness: she'd come back and paid for it the following morning, terribly embarrassed.

As soon as he caught sight of the man's back, Alan recognised him. The rumpled blue suit and balding head could only belong to the unexpected visitor to Durleyford Hall the previous Saturday evening.

He had no alternative but to approach, for if the man had been there as long as Miss Gray reckoned, he was unlikely to leave in a hurry. And there was always the possibility that when he did, he'd try to decamp with one or two books. Alan guessed that wouldn't be the case, but neither did he wish to leave it to chance.

The man swung round, grinning insolently, almost as if his purpose had been for Alan to accost him. "Just having a butcher's, thanks, squire. Decent stock of thrillers, I must say." Charteris, Cheyney, Creasey, to name a few: the stock bore Miss Timmins' seal of approval, which was no mean recommendation. But Alan was suspicious: the man didn't strike him as any kind of reader.

"I'll leave you to browse, then. I'm just over there, if you need some advice."

Alan was happy to withdraw. The man smelt like a brewery, and his suit at close quarters looked shabbier than it had on Saturday night. If he was up to no good, at least he could be in no doubt that Alan had rumbled him.

But the man seemed reluctant to return to the books. The smile hadn't left his face. He was several inches shorter than Alan and so was looking up at him, his eyes black and shifty, cheeks purple-veined and his teeth uneven and nicotine-stained.

"Half a mo'. Didn't I see you up at old Guilfoyle's place Sat'day night?"

"You did." Alan stared back steadily. "Because I recall seeing you there."

"'S right. I was in the area on business and thought I'd drop by and say hello to the great MP. We were both in the RAF, see. Done okay for himself, ain't he? Nah, I remember you 'cos you were sitting next to a real smasher. She your missus?"

Alan began to feel uncomfortable, and not just because Miss Gray, working silently in the far corner, was straining every sinew to listen in. Those fleeting anxieties of Saturday evening were back to trouble him. Might it after all have been Eve whom the man had recognised?

He tried to keep his tone light. "Oh no. Just a friend who was visiting."

The man's smile widened. "Then I reckon I'd be visiting her back pretty darn sharpish, squire. No feller in his right mind'd want to be away from a woman like that for too long."

Alan found the man distasteful and offensive. He'd been riled, and his tormentor knew it. It seemed to add to his amusement.

Just then the shop door pinged open and Alan, glancing up, was relieved to encounter the pleasant, smiling face of James Kedwell.

"If you'll excuse me," Alan addressed his unwanted visitor. "I have a customer." And he moved away, confident that the solicitor had come in to order a book he'd mentioned in conversation on Saturday evening.

The blue-suited man returned to the crime thriller section, picked over a couple of titles without much interest and left the shop without another word.

Kedwell stared after him. "Didn't I see that fellow up at the Hall the other night?"

"Yes, you did. I said as much to him, and he told me that he'd called in to say hullo to Mr Guilfoyle."

"Can't see they'd have a lot in common," the solicitor remarked drily. "Chap looks on his uppers. I dare say his sole purpose was to touch Guilfoyle for a couple of quid."

Alan agreed, but was convinced in his own mind that the man's visit to the Hall had had a more sinister purpose. He was glad that Kedwell had arrived so opportunely and, having made a note of the title he wished to order, fell into conversation with him until closing time. But somehow he couldn't chase away the blue-suited man's image.

Once Miss Gray and Kedwell had left, Alan bolted the shop door and returned to the office to complete his Book Token returns. By the time he'd finished, it was early evening and he thought he might allow himself a pint at the Coach & Horses before returning home to sort out some supper and put his feet up with a book.

It wasn't long past opening time, and the atmosphere was lively. A small group of men from the canning factory down the lane behind the pub were playing darts. Unsurprisingly Tony Ventnor was with them; and as so often was contributing gamely to the high spirits.

Tony was dressed smartly in a summer-weight beige suit and tie, and Alan guessed he'd called in on his way back from seeing a client. Alan wondered how long the job in farm machinery sales would last, for Ventnor never remained in one for too long. Not that he needed to work, because his parents had left him comfortably off, but Tony needed to have people around him, otherwise he was of the type who'd have gone to seed – and to drink – very quickly.

The darts match was in full flow, and Alan got his pint and leaned on the bar alongside Badger to watch. There were some wild throws, the factory hands letting off steam having just come off a nine-hour shift, and Tony rarely needed much encouragement. One of his darts flew off to the side of the board and buried its nose in Badger's calendar, more specifically in the generous breast of the bikini-clad blonde on the July page.

There was a blast of uproarious laughter. "Blimey, you been and punctured her good and proper, Wing Commander."

Soon afterwards the game ended, and Tony led his merry band across to the bar. "My round, boys," he proclaimed exuberantly. "Set 'em up, Badger, my good man, and one for yourself. Ah, my dear friend Al. Get you a drink?"

"I'm fine, thanks, Tony. Had a good day?"

"Top-hole, old sport. Talked my way into a good sale down Cirencester way this morning, hence the celebratory mood. I take it you enjoyed much pleasure with the beautiful Eve in the surrounding countryside yesterday? Smashing weather, wasn't it?"

"Yes, we had a lovely day."

"Cautious blighter, aren't you? Lucky dog into the bargain. Spare a thought for those of us forced to spend the whole day with our wives."

"Madge is a handsome woman, Tony."

"So I keep being told. Oh, but Al, the woman has a vicious tongue. No wonder a fellow's driven to take refuge in drink. Cheers!" He hoisted his tankard, swallowed a draught and wiped his mouth with the back of his hand. "I hear you've got Fullarton coming to the shop on Wednesday. Should result in a decent day's takings. Might even stroll by and pick up a copy myself – although I hear he's a bit intense. Still, the arty-farty set'll be there in droves. Bottoms up, young Cawley!"

They conversed with Badger on the latest news and, equally importantly, cricket and the weather, taking on board another pint of beer before Tony decided to push for home. Alan was also ready to leave, declining his friend's offer of a lift as he preferred to walk back to the cottage on such a beautiful evening.

As he left the pub and turned up the hill, he chuckled to himself as the thought struck him that he might be growing decadent. Twice to the pub in the same day. He visualised his father, a lifelong teetotaller, watching over him and shaking his head in smiling disapproval.

The next day was uneventful, although Tuesdays were often quiet, and Miss Gray had the day off. Alan hoped it would be the calm before tomorrow's storm, when the shop would be packed out. He worked conscientiously, only breaking off at lunch-time for a sandwich, a half of bitter and fifteen minutes of Badger's company.

Eve's phone call lifted him from the torpor.

"My, you sound pleased to hear from me."

"I *am* pleased. The day has suddenly become bright."

"Does that mean it wasn't bright before I called?"

"Nowhere near." He explained about it having been a quiet day with no more than half a dozen people coming into the shop. "Eve, we spoke about you coming down this weekend. Can you?"

She told him about the arrangement she'd made for Saturday. Two of her students were returning to France in the evening and had asked if she would have lunch and show them some of the London sights they'd yet to see.

"So it won't be before late afternoon at best," Eve said. "Will you be able to book me in at Mrs Darvill's?"

If only she'd known, he'd have crawled there on all fours at that very moment! "Leave it to me. Eve, I can't say how much I'm looking forward to Saturday. It can't come soon enough."

"Nor for me. Goodbye, my dear. I hope tomorrow goes well."

Nor for me. How his heart had leapt at those words! The receiver remained pressed to his ear long after she'd rung off. If only it could be that she felt the same way about him...

He was sliding luxuriously into the world of dreams when the accursed *ping* of the shop door bell dragged him back to reality. He rose to greet the incoming customer: Gerald Carbury. The talk would revolve around cricket, golf, horse racing and books relevant to those sports. Alan was confident that an order would come from it, but Saturday evening seemed an awfully long way away.

3

The following morning Piers Fullarton arrived at the shop a few minutes before the appointed time. People had already started to gather and Alan, in conversation with Teddy Kedwell, happened to look up and encounter a man hovering uncertainly in the doorway and glancing anxiously around.

Alan immediately recognised him from the photograph on the dust-jacket of his most recent volume. He was tall and gangling, casually dressed in a white open-neck shirt, dark corduroy trousers and scuffed suede shoes. His features were pleasant, fair hair flopping uncontrollably over one eye and a nervous hand forever sweeping it back. There was something boyish about the gesture and about him, but he wore too a gauntness, a hunted look, which Alan knew was a legacy from the war. He understood Fullarton to be two or three years older than himself, but his suffering had aged if not crippled him. He'd been shot down, captured, interrogated and tortured, one of the few who'd survived Dachau at the end of the war, a shadow of their former selves.

As a consequence, his verse echoed that suffering. But over the past dozen years it had captured the public's imagination and inspired what was, for the majority, the hope and prayer that the world would never again subject itself to such a war.

Excusing himself from Teddy, Alan approached the newcomer.

"Mr Fullarton?"

The man's face broke into a huge, relieved grin. "Ah, you must be Mr Cawley." He flung out a hand, and the two men shook firmly.

"I can't thank you enough for coming down," Alan enthused. "Quite a moment for our little town."

"Oh, I don't know about that." Alan saw that Fullarton was blushing slightly and immediately warmed to him. "But I couldn't disappoint old Guilfoyle. He'd never have forgiven me."

As soon as a date for Fullarton's visit had been arranged, Alan had set to work. He'd prepared flyers which he'd posted around the town and sent to interested societies in the county. And he'd submitted an article on Fullarton and his work to the editor of the *Durleyford Advertiser*, which the paper had included the week before. By the time the great day arrived, everyone who might be interested knew about it.

Alan escorted the still uneasy Fullarton to a small desk in the shop's far corner where he installed him behind two tall piles of his recent work and thrust a pen into his hand. On cue, Ariadne Gray brought a cup of coffee from the office, lovingly crafted in her late mother's best china. Bearing it as if it were the Holy Grail, she carefully set it down in front of him. "Such a pleasure to have you with us, Mr Fullarton," she exhaled reverently. For a moment, Alan feared she might curtsey.

The Durleyford public had responded magnificently, as Alan had hoped they might. At one point the queue snaked out through the doorway, past the window and fifteen yards or so down the hill. Fullarton was kept busy. He was more relaxed by now and chatted comfortably with the customers for whom he signed and dedicated copies of *Buried Alive*.

If conversation flagged, Alan was there to help things along, for he knew every customer at least by sight. And the businessman in him was soothed by the reassuring *thunk* of the little Lamson Paragon till drawer opening and closing with regularity as Miss Gray took payment, and the rustle of paper bags and cheerful snap of sticky tape as she wrapped purchases.

Kelvin Guilfoyle brought up the rear of the queue, and Fullarton rose to greet him, his face flushed with delight. The two men clasped hands firmly.

"Fullars, my dear chap. It's been an age. Too long, too long."

The poet grinned at Alan. "Mr Cawley, you'll never know how much I looked up to this man."

Guilfoyle laughed. "What utter rot! I was in the Sixth, and poor old Fullars' unhappy lot was to be my fag. He may have looked up to me, but only literally, because I was twice as big as him."

"And you know exactly what I mean," Fullarton chided him good-naturedly. "Mr Cawley, I declare there never was born a man of such modesty as this."

Guilfoyle clapped him on the shoulder. "That's enough. Sit, my good fellow, and dedicate this book to me. In fact I'll take three copies. You'll put them down to me, won't you, Cawley? And then I suggest we adjourn across the road for lunch. The place'll be bursting at the seams, but I'm sure Badger will manage to squeeze us in."

Alan had fully intended to stand Fullarton lunch and said as much, including Guilfoyle in his invitation.

The MP waved it aside. "Bless you, Cawley, I'll stand you both. It'll be my pleasure. Shall we say one-thirty?"

Guilfoyle had other business in the town and, as things quietened down in the shop, Alan and Fullarton lapsed into conversation. Fullarton knew the area well: he'd been brought up by an uncle in a village west of Stow-on-the-Wold. After the war he'd adopted London as his base but, as had been the case with Alan, was experiencing the need to escape. It was a straight choice between the Cotswolds and the Dorset coast, both which he'd loved since a boy. He was going to motor down to Dorset the following week. "Gilly invited me to put up with him for a few days, and I thought I'd better accept. It'll delay Dorset, but it'll be a tonic to jaw with the old boy about schooldays. Harrow, you know. I was a particularly weedy specimen but, my goodness, how that man looked out for me. Whatever self-confidence I have, he helped put there."

They met with Guilfoyle in the Coach & Horses at the appointed time. It was market day, and the bar was cluttered with farmers and farm-hands, the air choked with pipe-smoke and thick with hoarse laughter, the merry din of excited conversation and rich burr of dialect. Alice and Beryl, Badger's buxom, rosy-cheeked daughters, bustled back and forth with orders for food and drink.

The MP was greeted warmly with much doffing of crumpled caps and hats. "Arternoon, Master Guilfoyle, sir." And he was both quick and cheerful in his response. Somehow the obliging landlord had shoe-horned an extra table into the little snug, and the three of them were soon sampling an excellent steak-and-kidney pie and tankards of the pub's best bitter.

Fullarton mentioned to Guilfoyle about his forthcoming trip to Dorset. "I dare say I'll keep hold of the Bloomsbury flat, but as I've told Mr Cawley, I've a hankering to be out in the open air."

"My sentiments exactly," Guilfoyle replied. "I have to remain in Westminster when we're in session, but since I bought the Hall, this is where my spirit's been. Which reminds me: I've decided to hold a bit of a shoot up there this Saturday. One of my tenant farmers is plagued with wood pigeons, and it's high time we whittled down the population. I'll provide the weaponry, so how about it, Cawley? Ventnor tells me you shoot, and he and his lady wife'll be there. You can follow up your literary tittle-tattle with Fullars here – he's my guest over the weekend."

Fullarton grinned ruefully. "Very grateful and all that, Gilly. But I hope you'll leave me out of any shooting. I've not handled a gun since the war. You won't mind, will you?"

Alan was close enough to witness the sympathy on the MP's face. He felt then, indeed it was something he'd pondered before, that Guilfoyle was a man of deep compassion. Piers Fullarton had suffered horribly in his time at Dachau and had emerged from that place of death emaciated in body and broken in spirit. Only now, sixteen years on, was he getting to grips with life again.

Guilfoyle gave his shoulder a friendly pat. "Of course, my dear old man. I understand." He turned to Alan, a little subdued. "Oh, and Cawley, do feel free to bring Miss Ransom along."

Alan thanked him but explained that Eve had an appointment in London and wouldn't be down before early evening. The subject was quickly changed, and Guilfoyle and Alan gave Fullarton their impressions of Durleyford and its surroundings.

With lunch over, the two friends headed up to the Hall. Alan thanked them both and returned to the shop. The efficient Miss Gray had made an inventory of the number of copies sold: the event had been worth all the preparation.

The afternoon was as quiet as the morning had been busy, and Alan was glad of the opportunity to hide away in the office and catch up on the routine work. Ariadne Gray, with much tut-tutting, set about ensuring that every title was restored to its rightful place on the shelves and stock on the display tables set to rights.

Once again, Alan worked until well after she'd left. Ariadne had given him some idea of what they'd taken, but even so the sum total came as a pleasant surprise: more than a week's takings. He totted it up, mostly cash but a number of cheques, and went down to deposit it in the bank's night safe. There was still plenty of the evening left, and he decided to make for home, prepare some supper and wash it down with a glass of beer while sitting on the lawn and relaxing with a well-thumbed modern classic – he rather fancied Maugham's *Cakes And Ale* – until the sun went down.

He'd reached the top of the street and was about to cross over towards the mouth of Blackbird Lane when he heard someone call his name. He turned instinctively, and when he caught sight of the person who'd hailed him, rather wished he'd kept walking.

Sitting on a wooden bench outside the Star was the blue-suited man. The pint glass welded in his pudgy grip was three-quarters empty, although the pub couldn't long have opened its doors. The suit was looking more creased and shabby than on the previous day, and Alan wondered if the man possessed any other clothes. He felt like ignoring him altogether, turning on his heel and pressing for home. But if he avoided him tonight, he supposed the man would only show up again somewhere the following day; more likely in the shop, and Alan could do without that.

Reluctantly he made his way over. It had been a warm day, and the man's face was red, but his smile was as insolent as Alan remembered. He observed too a certain slyness about it, as if the man possessed information which he might be willing to impart, but probably at a price. Alan felt that somehow he'd been singled out. He didn't know why, but lurking at the back of his mind was the fear that it might have something to do with Eve.

"Join me for a bevy?"

"I don't think we've been introduced, Mr -?"

The grin stretched wider, and the man's small black eyes twinkled mischievously. "Let's say Jones. After all, Smith's so common a name, don't you think? Probably why I don't use it these days."

His voice was slurred, and Alan wondered if he'd been drinking for most of the day. The man annoyed him, particularly with his superior air of I-know-something-you-don't. But Alan understood that if he let his annoyance show, the opportunity to discover what, if anything, the man knew, would be lost.

"On your way home then, Mr Cawley? After a long day in the shop, I thought you could do with a jar. Top mine up too, while you're at it. Or perhaps you're in a belting hurry to get back to your lovely lady friend. Can't say I blame you there."

Alan strove to keep his voice level. "Is there something you'd like to say to me, Mr – Jones?"

The smile died, and of a sudden the man's eyes were cold and hard. He sensed Alan's contempt, and this was his reaction. For his part, Alan felt relieved, seeing the man who called himself Jones in his true light.

Jones nodded down the hill towards the cosy sprawl of Durleyford, his thick lips curling. "Don't reckon much to this town of yours, Mr Cawley. Toffee-nosed lot, I'd say, the people who live in it. Well, get this straight, squire. Me, I'm an observer. And there's people here wrapped oh-so-smug in their safe little lives, and hoping and praying their secrets stay hidden. Right?"

Alan stared back steadily, refusing to be bested by a man like this. "Then as far as I'm concerned, they can keep their secrets," he said coolly.

Jones bared stumpy teeth in a vicious grin. "Pillar of society then, aren't you, Mr Cawley? P'raps when you next see your pretty lady, you'll give her my compliments. 'Cos I reckon I bumped into her back in the war. I mean, a man don't forget a face like that. And p'raps if she asks where, tell her it was Catterick." He gave a hollow laugh. "Catterick, eh? I'm sure she'll appreciate that. I'll wish you good evening, Mr Cawley. I'm off back inside for another of these. Are you sure you won't join me?"

"Perfectly sure." Alan walked away, conscious of the man's scrutiny until he turned down Blackbird Lane. It had been a matchless day, and now in its quiet evening he found those anxieties which he'd tried hard to keep at bay beginning to grow and nag at him with every step.

For it must have been Eve whom Jones had recognised that Saturday evening at the Hall. If so, what might be the secret that she wished to keep hidden?

4

Thursday was early closing day in Durleyford, and with the shop door bolted and Miss Gray gone to her Mothers' Union meeting at the parish church, Alan used the time to catch up on work which had accumulated in the build-up to Piers Fullarton's visit. He wrapped and labelled the remaining parcels which he would take to the Post Office first thing the following morning and decided he ought to run along to the bank to cash a cheque before it too closed for business.

By then it was mid-afternoon, and as he made his way back up the High Street, Alan was glad to see the Corner House Café doing a roaring trade in afternoon teas. The café always remained open on Thursdays, as ladies heading for or returning from their various meetings liked to meet and converse over a late lunch or early tea.

Today was no exception, the two waitresses weaving back and forth between the little tables, and Alan noticed with some surprise Tony Ventnor occupying a seat near the window. As the girl Tania was one of the waitresses, he clearly didn't feel out of place among the twittering, gossiping clientèle in their summer frocks and hats. Indeed, he watched the girl at work, peering over the rim of his cup with a contented look on his face.

Alan paused, tapped on the glass, and Ventnor glanced round sharply, momentarily startled. He looked guilty too, and Alan grinned, knowing what had been on his friend's mind: it might so easily have been Madge looking in on him.

Tony's face broke into a grin: he'd been rumbled and would, as ever, shrug it off good-naturedly. He beckoned Alan inside, and Alan went willingly, because he wanted to share with Tony what was troubling him.

Ventnor was smartly turned out in blue herring-bone jacket, dark flannels and polished brogues, and Alan guessed he'd been meeting or was about to meet a client. But his hair and moustache had been newly trimmed and he smelt of expensive cologne, so Alan decided the client wasn't the only reason for the scrubbed appearance.

As Alan took his seat, his friend raised a hand and Tania came over. Tony looked her up and down appraisingly: she looked fresh and appealing in her dark blue uniform, apron and lace cap, her colour enhanced by a minute dab of rouge on each cheek. The girl seemed ill-at-ease under such scrutiny, as well she might; fidgeting slightly as she brought a pad and pencil from the pocket of her apron.

"Tea and a scone for Mr Cawley, my dear," Tony purred. "This is a busy afternoon for you."

"Yes, sir. Of course, sir." Alan sensed the tiniest hint of disdain in the 'sir', but on looking up he saw the girl frowning studiously as she jotted down the order. "Thank you," he said with a smile. She glanced down and briefly returned the smile before turning and walking away.

Ventnor watched her go. "Reminds me of a poem I came across not long ago," he sighed. "Something about when she moves, she moves more ways than one. How utterly and delightfully true. Ah, my dear old Al, don't you ever wish you were twenty years younger?"

Alan chuckled. "Sounds as if you're feeling your age, Tony. You know what Madge would say."

Ventnor's smile held an amused contempt. His gaze remained focused on the direction Tania had gone.

"Probably something along the lines of "don't forget to top up my G & T before you go out on the razzle, old thing." Which reminds me, I'm supposed to be meeting Madge when the Mothers' Union turns out at four. The wicked woman only goes there to put the wind up Mildred Paston and the self-righteous set. Blood will be spilled one day."

"A man can't be all bad if he dresses like a matinée idol solely to come into town to pick up his wife," Alan observed wryly.

"Oh, ha ha," Ventnor growled. "No, I was with a client this morning out Tewkesbury way. A goodly sale, I can tell you. The paymasters will be pleased, and so they jolly well should be. And damn it all, Al, if you've got to kick your heels waiting for your wife, you might as well wait in a place where the scenery is easy on the eye. Talking of which..."

Tania had returned with Alan's order. Although Ventnor's last dozen words had been spoken loudly enough for her to hear, she gave no indication that she'd done so, setting down the tray in front of Alan and off-loading the crockery.

Alan thanked her again. "Thank you, sir," she replied, turning away without acknowledging his companion. He grinned privately. Maybe he'd been right: Tony was getting a bit old for this sort of thing. But he wouldn't bait him any more: he rather wanted him on his side.

"Tony," he said, favouring the direct approach. "I'd like your advice, if you don't mind."

Ventnor looked up sharply from his wistful study of the girl's departing form. "Eh? What's that you say, old man?"

"Your advice," Alan repeated. "I'm curious about something that happened the other evening. Something which may actually turn out to be nothing at all."

"Oh, right." Tony gave him his full attention, as he bit distractedly into a scone. "Well, fire away."

"Thanks. Tony, Saturday's reception up at the Hall. About halfway through the evening, we fetched some food and sat down. There were Madge and yourself, Eve and I. Guilfoyle was there too, as I recall, chatting with James and Cicely. The bell rang, and Manners answered the door to a chap he admitted into the vestibule. He was a shabby-looking, middle-aged fellow in a blue suit that he might have been given on demob. Red-faced, balding, altogether down-at-heel. Manners came in and consulted Guilfoyle, who went out to meet the newcomer."

Ventnor nodded. "I remember Guilfoyle going out. But I didn't get a glimpse of this chap in the blue suit." He glanced across to where Tania was bending over a table to clear away crockery. "Dare say my mind was on other things. So what's the problem?"

"Manners had left the door ajar, and before Guilfoyle went out, the man looked through into the ballroom. He grinned, rather as if he'd recognised someone. Then Guilfoyle came and spoke with him, and he soon went on his way.

"This Monday afternoon, he was in the shop, thumbing through the stock. I got the impression he wanted to say something, but he didn't. Then last night, as I was walking home, he accosted me outside the Star. On each occasion he made veiled references to Eve, mentioned something about people around here with things to hide. But last night he told me he reckoned he'd bumped into her in the war, up at Catterick. He gave his name as Jones, although I don't for a moment buy that."

Ventnor frowned as he sipped his tea. Perhaps it was Alan's tortured imagination, but he seemed to hesitate before replying. "Catterick, you say? Well, that's off target for a start. Catterick's an Army base. As I recall her saying, Eve was in the WAAF before Special Operations Executive recruited her. And I believe she was stationed in Wiltshire, not up north."

Alan wasn't feeling any less anxious. "Hang on, I believe Jones was RAF, not Army. Or at least that's the tale he spun to Mr Guilfoyle."

His friend shrugged. "The RAF had rather a lot of people in it, old man. Guilfoyle, for a start. Me too. Then there's Carbury — and that chap Fullarton. I wouldn't read anything into it. Listen." He reached out and patted Alan's shoulder. "My opinion, for what it's worth, is that you're over-reacting. For myself, I'd say Jones found out where Guilfoyle lived and hauled himself up there to tap him for a few quid, using the old excuse that they'd known one another during the war. While he was up there, he happened to look through into the ballroom, spotted this amazingly attractive woman and hung around town in the forlorn hope of scraping up an acquaintance. I'd have said it's unlikely their paths would have crossed. Unless of course he happened to be in France and met her there. From your description of him, I wouldn't be in a hurry to put money on that."

Alan had never asked Eve much about herself, and neither of them had been keen to speak about the dark years of war. He supposed that anxiety had pushed him this far, and later he would feel cheap and underhand for having gone behind her back to find out things about which he hadn't the courage to ask her face to face.

But Tony seemed in a mood to talk. He often was; although here they were both at a loose end. Madge's meeting had a good half-hour to run, and the opportunity seemed too good to pass up.

"I –er, I'd gathered Eve was only in France for a few months?"

"About six, I think. But what months they were. She was right in the firing line, although for my part I'm rather glad she was. The first time I laid eyes on her, she pretty much saved my life, because I was on the verge of being hung, drawn and quartered without trial."

"So how did you meet?"

Tony Ventnor grinned broadly. He was in his element, obviously used to telling this story, and others besides. He'd had an eventful war, as his medals showed. Tony was always pretty full of himself, but Alan got the impression that he rarely exaggerated, rarely told the full story. Which was part of the reason he respected him.

Ventnor reached in a pocket and pulled out pipe, lighter and tobacco. Alan knew he was in for a long haul. He didn't care, as long as the end result meant that he could set his mind at rest.

"We'd set off in a Lancaster, a mission to take out some munitions factories across the German border. We took some flak as we reached the French coast. One of the engines on the starboard wing was damaged, but I didn't realise how badly until we got farther on. My first thought was to turn back, but I was pretty certain we'd never make it. I got the chaps to bale out, knowing by then that I was going to have to try to crash-land the old bus.

"We weren't far south of Rouen, which was infested with Jerry and one of the last places I wanted to put down. In the end I had no choice. I was flying low, an easy target. There was more firing, and damn me if they didn't get the other starboard engine. I scrambled clear, and the plane went down in a wood. I guessed they'd spend precious minutes picking through the wreckage once they got there, so I lit off over open countryside.

"So much for Lady Luck. I was so confident Jerry would be searching the woods for me that I blundered out on to a road and slap-bang into a patrol.

"I was taken to Rouen for interrogation and held there for a couple of weeks. I wasn't badly treated. Most of the time they tried the old soft-soap technique, but name, rank and number were all they got from me.

"They soon gave up, and I was bundled on to a train in company with a couple of hundred others. I think someone said we were bound for Ravensbrück, but we never got there. We couldn't have been more than an hour out of Rouen before the train got derailed. One of our chaps on his way back to Blighty had off-loaded a bomb not far in front of us. It tore up the track, and the engine and first two or three carriages ended in a heap.

"Everybody was thrown from their seats, and in the general confusion I managed to scramble out through the door and dive into the undergrowth. There followed a lot of yelling, lights and firing. A group of poor devils who made a break for it got mown down before my eyes. Dear God, I'll never forget that, for all the carnage I've seen.

"All I could do was lie low. There seemed to be soldiers everywhere. The prisoners who'd survived the derailment were herded into the remaining carriages, and they settled down to wait for another engine to arrive. I was out of there by the time it did, because dawn was breaking and I felt I had to make a move.

"I shuffled backwards through the undergrowth and made my way round the edge of a field into a copse. I had a view of the track from there, a quarter-mile or so off.

Another engine had arrived, and they hitched it up and headed back to Rouen.

"I was completely done up. I leaned back against the bole of a tree and went out like a light. I don't know how much later it must have been, but I awoke with a start. Someone was standing over me. The sun was in my eyes, and I couldn't see him properly, couldn't make out whether or not he was armed. I immediately supposed the worst. I hadn't endured much hardship in clink at Rouen, but I reckoned it wouldn't have been long in coming and was determined not to go back.

"I slowly hauled myself up into a crouching position, then launched myself at him. He may have had the advantage, and he was a biggish bloke. But surprise was on my side, and I ended up on top of him, my hands round his throat.

""I'm British, you idiot!"

"He just about managed to squeeze out the words, which was fortunate because I was within an ace of throttling him. I rolled off and got to my feet, and he looked up at me cautiously, wondering what was going to happen next.

""How do I know you're British?" I hissed.

"He identified himself as Flight Lieutenant John Emsley from RAF Syerston in Notts. He'd been shot down over the coast a week or so back. They'd all baled out, and he had no idea what had happened to his colleagues. Like me, he'd been imprisoned at Rouen and had been on the same train.

"Of course he had no papers on him, but neither had I. I told him who I was, but either or both of us could have been lying. He too had escaped from the wreckage, and from his account I guessed he'd been hiding in the undergrowth not far up the track from me.

"None of it meant anything, however, and I had no alternative but to take him on trust. Not that I felt there was any reason to doubt him. My opinion was that if he was in the enemy's camp, then he was a first-class actor. He was a big man, not far off thirty, sandy-haired with a trace of a northern accent and no sense of humour whatsoever. To look at him, you'd reckon him a bit of a lummox. Anyway, we agreed on a truce and got the hell out of there.

"I couldn't say what our plan was, or even that we had a plan. We reckoned we were somewhere in Normandy, and it was a good bet that Jerry was all around us.

"We had to avoid towns and villages and scavenge for food, which was nearly our undoing. We'd been lucky enough to happen upon farms from which we could filch a few eggs and even the occasional chicken. One time I managed to sneak into a kitchen and come away with bread, cheese and a bottle of very bad wine.

"Eventually we came across this farm, nicely isolated in a fold of ground. We carefully carried out a recce: the only inhabitants appeared to be an old man and a young girl. Emsley was all for marching boldly up to the door and asking if they'd give us a meal. My French was pretty fluent, and I could pass us off as displaced factory workers or some such. But caution had got us this far and, as I outranked him, I decided we'd do it the hard way, which had worked for us up to now. I'd spotted a hen-house round the back of the property: we'd try our luck there and maybe hole up for the night in one of the barns.

"By the time we'd reached the hen-house, the old man and girl had gone indoors. I told Emsley to keep watch while I crawled in and picked up some eggs. I wasn't in there more than two minutes, but on coming out the first thing I saw was Emsley, hands on head and a look of horror on his face. Two rough-looking customers stood nearby, with sten guns trained on us both.

"One of them barked at me to put down the eggs. I laid them down, keeping my arms well away from my sides as I straightened up, even though I wasn't armed. One of the men was short and wiry, little more than a boy, the other thickset and fierce, someone I was determined not to cross. He was rasping out some lurid names, the least of which, minus the epithets, was 'German spies'.

"The noise brought the girl and another man, tall, bearded and commanding, rushing out from the farmhouse.

"D'you know, Al, right at that moment I was in fear of my life, but I swear I fell in love with her on sight. She couldn't have been much more than – what? twenty, twenty-one – and looked so frail in an oversized shirt and dungarees. She wore her hair short in those days, and looked no more than a child, her face freckled and those big brown eyes so expressive and appealing. You felt you wanted to wrap her in cotton wool in case she'd break, but as I was to witness on numerous occasions, there was a vein of pure steel running through her. And this was to be the first of such occasions.

"She took charge immediately. "Fernon! Gaspard! Stop! These are British airmen – look at their clothes, their uniforms."

"The thickset man switched her a malevolent glance. "Wolves in sheep's clothing, my little Yvette," he growled. "They are spies. Can you not see?"

"The girl ignored him and turned to her companion, speaking in rapid French. He nodded and issued terse instructions to the little man, who turned and walked down to a gate some thirty yards away. From there he had a good view of the road which wound past the farm. His sharp eyes scoured the surroundings, before he turned and waved back at the girl. He laid the gun at his feet, lit up a cigarette and leaned on the gate post, puffing placidly away.

There was a barn behind us, and the girl indicated that we should go inside. She followed closely after with the two other men. Once there, she stood before us and started to fire questions in, to my amazement, perfect English, all the while keeping her voice low.

"I can't recall all the questions: about landmarks, London streets, names of towns, even ruddy Shakespeare. All quick-fire stuff, and both Emsley and I were rocked back on our heels – he more than I. We managed to answer some, though not all. I saw straight away that getting ten out of ten wasn't what bothered her. She wanted to hear us speak and at the same time watch our eye movements and facial expressions. Believe me, she watched us like a hawk.

"Finally she seemed satisfied and turned briskly towards the bearded man, addressing him in French. "I'm pretty sure they're genuine, Marius."

"Marius nodded, and even the ferocious man, Fernon, appeared impressed, his scowl changing into something related to a smile. Marius invited us inside, and the other two followed us in with their guns. I think that afterwards I appreciated that: they still weren't leaving anything to chance. But that was how they survived.

"As Yvette stood aside to let me pass, I thanked her and was rewarded with a tight smile. "If I am wrong, *m'sieu*, I give nothing for your chances." "You're not wrong," I said.

"They gave us a meal, those same eggs I'd been trying to steal. Then we were ordered to undress, and our clothes were taken away and burned. Of course, neither of us had washed for days, so we must have smelled pretty ripe. I'll never forget the luxury of wallowing in that tin bath. Mind you, old Fernon wasn't too careful about where he poured the hot water.

"They kitted us out in jackets, shirts and dungarees, and we were wheeled into a room, a stuffy old den, where Marius and Yvette awaited us. Fernon came in and closed the door behind him.

"Even now I can only marvel at her efficiency. On the outside she seemed a frail, helpless girl, but she was as dedicated and committed an operator as I've known. During the time Emsley and I had been stuffing our faces and getting cleaned up, she'd only radioed London and checked us out. She was determined to leave no stone unturned."

Ventnor set down his cup and knocked out his pipe in the ashtray. He checked his watch. It was almost four o'clock, and Alan knew he wouldn't want Madge to find him at the Corner House.

"Marius said he'd try to get us back to Blighty as soon as he could. His resistance cell had been very active in hampering Jerry, and from time to time they'd request a drop of arms and ammunition. Now and again they'd happen upon an escaped POW and get the plane to land and take him back. I'm wondering if this could be where your friend Jones hails from. I'm afraid there's nothing for it but to have a word with Eve." Ventnor pushed back his chair and got to his feet. "Anyway, old man, must dash. A truce will have been called and the blessed meeting over. Although, hang on a mo', you said Jones had called asking specifically for Guilfoyle. Why not speak first to the great man himself? He may be able to give you some background on the fellow."

Alan thanked Tony and watched as he strode into the street, having treated Tania to a cheery wave. He'd at least learned a little more about Eve and could understand why she hadn't talked much about the war years.

On his way back up the hill, he returned to the shop and put through a call to Durleyford Hall in the hope that Kelvin Guilfoyle would be able to spare him a few minutes. Manners answered and informed him that his master was up in London at his apartment and wouldn't return until the Friday evening. Alan thanked him and resolved to speak to Guilfoyle when he joined him for the pigeon shoot on Saturday morning.

5

Alan didn't take many Saturdays off as, along with market day, it could often be his busiest day of the week. But Guilfoyle had summoned them to the Hall for a ten o'clock start and had promised to provide a buffet lunch after the shoot, so he knew he'd be absent for most of the day.

He'd prepared Miss Gray for this but thought it only courteous to put in an appearance first thing. He knew that he really need not bother, for Ariadne was in her element. She hoped her employer would have "a truly lovely day"; although he hadn't said anything about the shoot and the merciless slaughter of many unsuspecting birds, as he knew she wouldn't approve. She waved him off from the shop doorway in good spirits, looking forward to stamping her librarian's order and method on the stock and running the shop in her own way.

It was another fine morning, and Alan enjoyed the short drive via country lanes up to Durleyford Hall. Judging by the crush of cars lined up in front of the stable block, he was the last to arrive, and he squeezed his creaky green Morris Minor in between the Ventnors' shooting brake and Colonel Prendergast's ageing Armstrong-Siddeley. He recognised Gerald Carbury's Jaguar and James Kedwell's Humber standing alongside Guilfoyle's magnificent Bentley.

Everyone had gathered on the terrace and, as he approached, Alan felt reassured that in his windcheater and stout hiking boots he didn't look too out of place among the shooting jackets, flat caps and wellingtons sported by the majority of the party. In fact, the only odd ones out were Madge Ventnor and Piers Fullarton.

Fullarton, as Alan recalled, had been staying at the Hall since the previous Wednesday. He looked fit and relaxed, and altogether bohemian in a baggy Shetland jumper and worn brown corduroys; while Madge was elegant in suede jacket and white slacks, puffing languidly at a cigarette in an ivory holder as she conversed easily with the poet.

Kelvin Guilfoyle was the first to spot Alan and strode up, offering his hand. "How good to see you, Cawley. I believe our little gathering's now complete."

"Great." Tony Ventnor had ambled up behind him, smirking mischievously. "Can't wait to get started. A bit out of practice these days. I dare say you've been reading up on the subject, Al. They do say there's a book for everything."

"And one day, Ventnor, you may even be driven to read one," Guilfoyle retorted. The men laughed, and their host moved off in search of Manners, who was setting up trestle tables at the far end of the terrace.

"So how's tricks, Al?" Ventnor clapped him amicably on the shoulder as he surveyed the gathering. "Gang's all here, by the look of things. Jane not with you this morning, Gerald?"

The estate agent turned from his conversation with Gussie Prendergast and the colonel. "Sadly, no. Touch of migraine. I recommended she lie in."

Alan didn't miss the informed wink which passed between the two men. He moved to where Madge stood with Fullarton, dragging Tony after him by an invisible thread.

Close up, Madge looked striking, and his immediate impression was that Fullarton was smitten. Madge was an eager gatherer of information as well as scalps and had dressed and made up in the knowledge that an unattached male would be present. It was one of the means she deployed to get back at her errant husband, and Alan didn't blame her.

Madge greeted Alan with a wicked smile and nodded towards the tables over which Manners, with much ceremony, was draping white cloths.

"Oh, no caterers today?"

Guilfoyle, who happened to be nearby speaking with James Kedwell, overheard the remark. "Oh, Manners is quite capable of rustling up some decent nosh, Madge."

Alan returned Madge's grin. The arrow had been intended for her husband and had in fact struck home. Embarrassment was a rare visitor to Tony's bronzed face, but he was uncomfortable and strove to deflect attention from himself by making a comment on the weather to Fullarton.

He was spared further unease by the abrupt arrival on the forecourt of a mud-spattered Land Rover, from which a wiry middle-aged man in waxed jacket and gaiters leapt nimbly out. Alan recognised him as Jeb Harris, the Hall's gamekeeper. Guilfoyle went forward to meet him, and the two of them fetched several shotguns from the rear of the vehicle.

The colonel and Ventnor had brought their own guns, and of the rest only James Kedwell and Alan needed Harris to show them how to reload. Neither had handled a firearm since the war and were glad of the instruction. Tony Ventnor stood at Alan's side smiling whimsically as they listened to Harris.

"That's called a shotgun, Al," he drawled. "You may not have been issued with those up in the Outer Hebrides. See that little catch there? Pull it, and the gun goes off 'bang!'"

"I'll try to remember which end is which, Tony," Alan returned drily, earning himself an encouraging pat on the shoulder from Guilfoyle. That pleased him and settled his nerves: he'd only come because he hadn't wanted to offend the MP, whose invitation had been kindly meant.

Harris offered a shotgun to Fullarton, who was standing nearby with Madge. He shook his head as he observed it with a mixture of fear and disdain. "Oh n-not for me, thanks. You'll understand if I sit this out, won't you, Gilly?"

"Of course, old chap. It's not obligatory."

"And I shan't take part in these barbaric practices, Kelvin," Madge asserted. "In fact, if he doesn't object, I'll remain here and keep Mr Fullarton company." She turned towards him with a winning smile. "You can tell me all about your work. The WI will be floored when I report back on my interview with one of England's leading poets. Come along, we'll park ourselves on the terrace."

She slipped an arm through his and wheeled him round. A look of pleasurable alarm registered on Fullarton's usually serious face. "Oh, I say."

"Madge," her husband scolded lightly. "The poor fellow's not to be eaten."

She glanced scornfully over her shoulder. "Oh, go and be savage, you irritating man."

Everyone laughed. "Manners will sort out drinks for you," Guilfoyle called after them. Alan wondered if he was the only one to sense the tension between husband and wife. Madge might be loud, flamboyant and too fond of the gin, but she was a remarkably handsome woman, and he wondered again quite what Tony was playing at in straying so far and often.

They followed Guilfoyle and Harris past the stables and down a path leading into some woodland. At the far edge of this, Harris had constructed a series of hides. Beyond them a field of stubble dipped down for a quarter of a mile before ending in more dense woodland. A pattern of decoys had been set out in the field, and a flock of pigeons had already gathered among them.

The hides, constructed from hurdles and draped with greenery, stood in a row about fifty yards apart. Gussie Prendergast and the colonel, with Gerald Carbury tagging tamely along, headed for the farthest one, Tony and Alan the middle and Guilfoyle and James Kedwell the other. Guilfoyle issued instructions that only one gun should be fired from each hide at any given time.

They settled and waited for more birds to gather. Then, at a signal from Harris, the firing began. Alan was rather pleased that he scored a hit with his second shot and quietly amused that Tony, for all his alleged prowess, had missed with his first three.

But his next shot soared wildly away to the heavens, for as he pulled the trigger a piercing scream rent the air and Ventnor, startled, cannoned into him, knocking him off balance. The remaining pigeons scattered, but the men paid no heed. Dropping his gun, Alan blundered out of the hide after Ventnor, who had recovered quickly and was off ahead of him. From behind them he heard Guilfoyle, Harris and Kedwell mashing through the undergrowth, as they all headed towards the farthest hide, from the direction of which came a second scream, not so shrill as the first.

They reached there to find Colonel Prendergast looking bemused and, deprived of a morning's shooting, a trifle annoyed, as with the gun resting in the crook of his arm, he surveyed the figures of his daughter and Gerald Carbury huddled in a clearing some twenty yards away.

Gussie's outstretched hand was pointing up at one of the trees. She was trembling and gasping hysterically, while Gerald, his arm about her, tried to comfort her and persuade her to turn away from the sight before them.

Alan stumbled to a halt beside Tony, and they were quickly joined by the others. Their gazes followed the direction of Gussie's hand to where a man's body, slightly obscured by the leaves, dangled from one of the lower branches of a huge oak tree.

The girl's scream had carried back to the house. They all turned as Madge, Fullarton and Manners came bustling down one of the paths.

"Oh, dear Lord -." Madge put a hand to her mouth and buried her face in Fullarton's bony shoulder.

Guilfoyle took charge. "We shouldn't stand around gawping. Carbury, Fullars, perhaps you'd escort the ladies back to the terrace? And Manners, old friend, you'd better get busy pouring drinks. We're all going to need one. Come along, chaps, let's get this poor fellow down."

The nimble Harris, brandishing a wicked-looking knife, shinned up the tree and severed the rope, while Tony, Alan and Guilfoyle gently lowered the body to the ground. "He's cold," the MP murmured. "Nothing at all we can do for him. Anybody recognise him? Looks like some sort of vagrant."

Alan had known right away who the man was, from his first sight of the scuffed shoes and blue trousers on the body hanging from the branch. As they laid the man out on the woodland floor and he saw the contorted face, protuberant eyes and the rope savagely biting into the fleshy neck, he was shocked and tried to feel sorry, but couldn't.

"He's been around this week, sir," Alan said. "He came into my shop on Monday and accosted me outside the Star the other evening. He called here at the Hall last Saturday evening. Don't you remember, Tony? He was the fellow I mentioned the other day. He told me his name was Jones."

"Ah." Ventnor nodded at the recollection. "So this is the chap. Can't say I got a good look at him last weekend."

"Of course." Guilfoyle stooped to get a closer look at the dead man's features. "Dammit, Cawley, you're right. He *did* call last Saturday. But Jones wasn't the name he gave Manners. Half a mo' and it'll come to me. Rennie – yes, that was it. Said he remembered me from the war, from RAF Northolt. Well, I had dealings with Northolt, but was never stationed there. For the life of me, I couldn't recall him to mind. I suspect it was just a ploy, and he was simply on the cadge. I got Manners to send him on his way with a fiver."

Colonel Prendergast had rumbled up in the meantime, looking indignant. "Dashed unsporting to top himself on your land, Guilfoyle," he exclaimed.

"Quite. Well, we'd best get back to the Hall and summon a doctor and the police. Harris, would you find something to cover the poor chap's face and stay here until they arrive? Good man. We'll get back to the ladies. My apologies, gentlemen: it's a poor return for the loss of a morning's sport. We must reconvene at another time."

They headed back to the Hall, stopping off to deposit the borrowed shotguns in Harris's Land Rover. Guilfoyle busied himself with the telephone, having first ordered Manners to serve drinks and lay out the buffet lunch.

Out on the terrace, everyone had taken refuge in alcohol. Gussie Prendergast was loudly holding forth on her first sight of the corpse and necking back gin as if it had gone out of fashion. They were all too polite to ask why she and Gerald Carbury had sought solitude in the clearing in the first place, having abandoned the colonel to blaze merrily away at the pigeons. Gerald was at Gussie's side now, tut-tutting and sympathising in the right places, a supportive arm at her waist.

Madge, glass in hand, sidled up to Alan, with Fullarton, looking pensive, not far behind her. "Tony tells me that you knew the poor man, Alan darling."

"I can hardly say I *knew* him, Madge." Alan explained that he'd bumped into the inebriated Jones/Rennie on two occasions that week and that on the first of those he suspected the man might have been contemplating a spot of shoplifting and only fell into conversation when he realised he'd been rumbled. He didn't want to say too much to Madge and hoped, given the strained relations between husband and wife, Tony wouldn't mention anything either.

Guilfoyle had joined them by this time, and Alan realised that he'd had no opportunity to raise the issue which was bothering him. Indeed, Jones/Rennie's demise had altogether pre-empted it, and he decided to keep the matter to himself for the time being. The MP seemed puzzled.

"Name Rennie doesn't mean anything to you, Fullars?" he asked. "When the fellow came up here last weekend, he told me he'd been stationed at Northolt. You were there early in the war, weren't you?"

"Certainly for a while," Fullarton replied. "But I don't recall him. I moved up to Leeming in '42 and got shot down in flames soon after that."

The police arrived shortly afterwards, Guilfoyle's status commanding a visit from the Chief Constable. Guilfoyle took them down to where the patient Harris was waiting with the corpse, and everyone else accepted the MP's cheery invitation to an early lunch. Alan observed wryly that, tragedy notwithstanding, no-one's appetite appeared diminished, and both wine and conversation flowed, the topics being anything other than concern for the late Rennie. He had been quickly forgotten by all but Alan Cawley.

Later, brief statements were taken from each member of the shooting party. The Chief Constable promised to make inquiries in Durleyford to find out where Rennie had been staying and what had been his business there. Alan felt that he wouldn't get far on the latter issue. There would have to be an inquest, probably some time during the week, but the police already seemed to have written off the man's death as suicide.

"Penny for 'em, old man," Tony Ventnor challenged him, as the gathering finally began to disperse.

Alan hesitated, his hand on the door handle of his car. Everyone else seemed otherwise engaged, saying their farewells to Guilfoyle and each other. Gerald, at his most solicitous, was ensuring that Gussie was comfortably installed in the passenger seat of her father's car, while Madge and Fullarton were deep in conversation. They seemed to have hit it off, and Alan wondered if Tony had noticed; or if he cared.

He'd confided in Tony so far and couldn't palm him off now. "I was thinking about Rennie."

Ventnor grinned sympathetically. "I rather thought you might have been. I dare say you were the only one."

"Nobody recognised him from anywhere. Or rather, no-one's owning up to it. So why did he come up to the Hall last Saturday? He must have had his eye on someone. Might it have been as a reminder that he was around and not likely to be going away?"

Ventnor nodded thoughtfully. "Good point. Then here's something else for you to ponder. Why did he come up to the Hall to top himself? Maybe a last shot at troubling someone's conscience?"

Alan shrugged. He wanted to let it rest there, because he had the uneasy feeling that Rennie hadn't committed suicide, and he wasn't ready to share that thought with anyone. He could, however, take one crumb of comfort from the fact that Eve couldn't have been involved in Rennie's death. She was seventy miles away in London, touring the capital with her students.

But he found himself fidgeting beneath Tony's languid scrutiny, as if his friend could somehow see inside his mind. "If it worries you, Al, perhaps you should speak to Eve. Let her set your mind at rest."

He grinned and patted Alan on the shoulder, as Madge finally broke away from Fullarton, their parting handshakes lingering perhaps a little too long, Madge's smile as she approached their shooting brake perhaps a little too contented for Tony's comfort.

But the Ventnors were more than capable of sorting out their own problems. Alan stirred himself so far as to say goodbye to Madge, got into his car and drove away.

It was a warm day, but he felt chilled. A storm was coming.

6

It was late afternoon when he met Eve off the London train. His first thought as they approached each other along the platform was that she looked tired, and he immediately felt guilty for having dragged her all that way for a stay of barely twenty-four hours. But he felt absolved by her smile as he relieved her of her overnight case, and they hugged one another fondly.

He'd picked up some lamb cutlets from the butcher's that afternoon and told her they'd eat at the cottage. Mrs Harkins, his regular char, would have been there for her Saturday clean, so the place would be looking spick and span; not, he thought, that it ever looked untidy. And she'd kindly offered to prepare any vegetables he'd left out.

Eve seemed content with that. He knew she'd have had a busy day and guessed she'd appreciate a quiet evening. He asked her how the tour had gone.

She smiled. "Hectic, to say the least. Jean-Paul and Colette were two of my students last term: a brother and sister from Belfort. They're returning home this evening, and I'd promised to show them some of the sights before they left. My, we've covered some miles."

"I was thinking how tired you looked."

"Hardly surprising when you include my dear mother in the equation. Last night was rather difficult to say the least. Our neighbour Mrs Parrish is looking in on her today and sorting out her meals. She's been a godsend."

"I'm sorry if I -?"

Eve laid a calming hand on his arm. "Sorry you asked me down all this way?" *Did she read minds as well?* he wondered. "Then don't be. I needed to get away. And not only that." Her hand lingered as she beamed up at him. "Your friendship means so much to me, Alan."

"Only friendship?" The words were out before he could prevent them, and he felt the colour rushing to his cheeks.

She patted his arm consolingly. "We still don't know one another that well."

"Not yet." Alan was astounding himself: what *had* got into him? He thought he'd better change the subject before his face quite literally caught fire. Eve pretended not to notice his discomfort, and he silently blessed her for that.

He told her he'd planned a relaxing day for Sunday. The weather was set to continue fair, and he suggested they motor down to Bibury and on to Cirencester, stopping off somewhere for a pub lunch and country ramble. Eve confessed she didn't know the area at all and was content to be led.

On the other matter, Alan resolved not to mention anything that evening. The rigours of the day had been more than enough for her. But before she returned to London, he knew he would have to broach the subject of Rennie. He wasn't looking forward to that but felt it a necessary evil.

They were in the car by now, driving slowly up the hill through the town, past his shop, past the Star where he'd had that last unnerving conversation with the dead man. There seemed an almost sinister calm about Durleyford. The shops were shut, and it was too early for the pubs to open: they didn't pass a living soul.

At the top of the hill, he turned into Blackbird Lane. Two hundred yards down it, just before the bumpy track narrowed into a bridleway, three cottages stood to the right. Alan's was the first of these, a plain two-up, two-down which he'd partly modernised with the money his parents had left him, enabling him to dispense with the outside lavatory.

The cottage was small, but he was immensely proud of it, particularly at this time of year: the slate roof gleaming in the afternoon sun, the window frames slick with a recent coat of paint and the Montana creeping up the walls and over the roof of the front porch.

He pulled the car up on the grass verge, hopped round and swung open the passenger door, offering a hand to help her out. A wicket gate close by led across his lawn – he called it a lawn, but it was little more than a square of grass which he kept closely mown – past the apple trees and vegetable patch to the side door of the house.

Eve was taking it all in: its smallness, its glorious ordinariness. He knew that she wasn't one to give herself airs, that she came from a poor background, and he sensed that she was impressed by what she saw.

Its seclusion and peace meant so much to him. He'd had his fill of London, lodging in Notting Hill and Islington over several years and criss-crossing the city to go to and from work in various bookshops. He felt as if he never wanted to trade it in. Although what she wanted would be the only thing likely to change his mind.

A lady's bicycle was parked beneath the kitchen window, and Alan was surprised to see it. "Mrs Harkins must still be here," he murmured, realising as he spoke that that was odd. Her husband was scorer for the town's cricket team and would be home for his supper within the next hour. According to his wife, he tended to be a little fractious if it wasn't awaiting him on his return.

Alan felt a bit annoyed. He'd mentioned in passing that Miss Ransom was coming back to the cottage for supper, and he wondered if Mrs Harkins, risking the sullen wrath of her husband, had decided to delay her departure so that she could report back to her knitting circle on 'Mr Cawley's young woman who'd come all the way down from London'. As the thought crossed his mind, he felt he was doing Mrs Harkins a disservice, for she was a kindly soul who fell outside the pale of the Durleyford gossip-mongers.

But there was no time for further speculation. Eve and he heard the noise at the same time and looked at one another in alarm: a thumping sound which came from behind the house, like someone beating a desperate fist on a wooden door.

He hurried round the back, hobbling slightly over the uneven surface, Eve at his heels. There was washing on the line and, as he ducked under it, he stumbled into a sheet which had been abandoned on the ground.

The noise came from inside his tool shed, the flimsy door shuddering under the assault. With a puzzled glance at Eve, he slipped the bar off the door and swung it open.

The dumpy figure of Mrs Harkins spilled out into his arms, her normally neat grey hair dishevelled, her face stained with tears and housecoat marked and rumpled from her imprisonment in the shed.

"Oh, Mr Cawley, it's you. I thought you was never coming. Oh, thank the Lord, thank the Lord."

"Mrs H., whatever's happened? Who did this?"

In the meantime Eve had grabbed hold of a garden chair and placed it so that Alan could deposit his stricken burden there.

"I was hanging out the washing, Mr Cawley. I never seen him. He stole up behind me, put a sheet over my head and bundled me in here and barred the door. It all happened so sudden and give me *such* perforations, it did."

The poor woman gave way to tears and Alan, in a dither, was relieved to find himself eased aside as Eve took over. She crouched beside Mrs Harkins and wound a comforting arm round her. "You'd better check to see if anything's missing, Alan. Let me take Mrs Harkins indoors and make her a good, strong cup of tea."

"Oh, bless you, my dear," Mrs Harkins warbled. "Thank you. You're so kind."

Alan led them back to the side door and held it open while Eve accompanied her charge through the tiny kitchen and into the cosy sitting-room, where she settled her in an armchair. Alan put the kettle on to boil before taking an apprehensive look round the cottage.

To his surprise and relief, nothing appeared to be missing. This being Alan, his prime concern was for his books. He owned a few first editions: Stevenson and Buchan, as well as some contemporary authors. But the bookshelves were intact, their contents tightly packed, and he could tell at a glance that everything was there. The little money he kept at home – three pounds ten shillings in notes – was in the bedside drawer where he'd left it.

He'd climbed the stairs cautiously, wondering if the intruder might be lurking there. He found no-one, nor indeed any trace of anyone other than himself having been there. Everything seemed to be as he'd left it.

And this made him suspicious and not a little uncomfortable.

Alan returned downstairs to be confronted by Eve and Mrs Harkins, who looked up expectantly from their armchairs.

"Well?" Eve asked.

"Nothing missing as far as I can make out."

"Then that's a relief."

The kettle began to sing, and Eve got to her feet. Her gaze lingered on his face, and he guessed she'd worked out that all wasn't well.

He pulled out a chair and joined them in a cup of tea. He offered to report the matter to the police, but Mrs Harkins, at least in some measure restored, dismissed the idea. She'd had a fright, but otherwise there'd been no harm done.

"It's these teddy boys, Mr Cawley, you mark my words. Why, there are even gangs of them in Durleyford."

Eve threw him an amused glance and reached out to pat the old lady's hand.

"Well, as long as you're all right, Mrs Harkins?"

"Oh, right as ninepence, dear. You and Mr Cawley have been so kind."

Despite Mrs Harkins' protests, Alan insisted on driving her back to her house in Lower Lane and promised to return her bicycle early the following morning.

"That's so good of you, Mr Cawley. I ought to get back and get busy in the kitchen. Harkins will be home before long, and he'll be absolutely *ravishing* for his supper."

Eve came to the door with them. "Shall I start cooking the cutlets, Alan?"

"That'd be good, Eve. Oh, and just as a precaution, lock the door after us, will you?"

"All right." The agreement was made with that tight smile of hers which he was coming to know so well. He'd wondered earlier if she read minds. Whether or not, she seemed to have his measure, and he was appeased rather than disconcerted by that. He started to explain where she'd find everything for preparing the meal.

"Don't worry. Leave it to me." She shooed him out and closed the door. As he walked over to the gate, shepherding Mrs Harkins in front of him, he was gratified to hear the click of the key being turned. He fought the urge to glance back, knew she'd be watching from the kitchen window and smiling mischievously.

She had the door open for him on his return. "Nothing adverse to report, Captain Cawley, sir," was her greeting as she mock-saluted him. He bent down and kissed her: no more than a peck, and she pecked him back. But she didn't linger, whisking past him to busy herself with the vegetables on his tiny range.

"Eve, that smells delicious."

"I do cook, you know."

"I can tell that."

He slipped off his jacket, rolled up his shirtsleeves and pitched in to help her. She'd found a couple of Oxo cubes and had made gravy. He found the aroma soothing and her nearness inspiring.

Before long they were sitting opposite one another at the kitchen table, sipping sweet cider and sampling the tender cutlets and a selection of home-grown vegetables. It seemed the right moment to broach the subject of his growing anxiety.

"Eve, I'd like you to stay here tonight. I've not booked Mrs Darvill's. Er, of course," he added hurriedly, "I will if you'd prefer me to."

The evening sunlight caught her face as she smiled back over the rim of her glass. There seemed something ethereal about her in that moment; something quite wonderful and out of his reach, an experience which took his breath away.

"Is this part of some evil plan, Mr Cawley?"

"Not at all, I promise. The spare room's made up. You can trust me, Eve."

She reached across and squeezed his hand. "Alan, I wouldn't be sitting here in the first place if I didn't feel I could trust you. But may I ask why you're so worried? Something's been eating away at you since you met me off the train."

"You're a perceptive woman, Eve."

"Hardly, my dear. You're a transparent man. And I mean that in the nicest way."

"Then, yes, you may ask. It's something I was going to bring up with you anyway, but I hadn't wanted to worry you tonight. However, in view of the incident regarding poor Mrs Harkins..."

He told her what had happened at the pigeon shoot that morning, then, working backwards, of his two encounters with Rennie during the course of the week.

"Eve, cast your mind back to this time last week, the reception up at the Hall. We fetched our food and sat at a table near the door. Madge, Tony, you and I, Guilfoyle and the Kedwells. This chap Rennie called then, asking for Guilfoyle. Manners admitted him and came through to speak to his master. I have the distinct impression from the look on his face that Rennie recognised someone in our vicinity."

Eve looked puzzled. "Then surely it was Mr Guilfoyle? After all, you say this man called asking for him."

Alan's mouth dropped open. He suddenly felt foolish, for he'd been so worried on Eve's account, particularly after Rennie's allusions to her, that that hadn't occurred to him at all.

"Well, I suppose it could," he admitted. "Although Guilfoyle is adamant he didn't know the man. The name doesn't ring any bells with you, does it?"

"I can't place him at all. Not that I got a good look at him. And the name means nothing to me. Alan, why is this man making you so anxious?"

He closed his hand over hers and sighed. "I didn't like or trust him," he said. "And I believe he was trying to wind me up. But he told me he remembered you from the war — from Catterick."

He could have sworn a shadow passed across her face. But it was there and gone in a moment.

"Catterick? But isn't that an army base? I was never stationed there, never even went there. I was a WAAF, stationed at Lyneham in Wiltshire, and when I was drafted into SOE, I underwent my training at a place in Scotland and then Wanborough Manor in Sussex. No, Alan. If he thought he remembered me, he was mistaken. I never knew him."

In the face of her forthright denial, he knew he had to leave it there. "That's fine, Eve. You've set my mind at rest." But his anxiety would remain.

It had been a long day, and they were both tired. He made coffee, turning the conversation to what they'd do the next day. He'd mentioned earlier that he'd planned a day out, and they sat and pored over an Ordnance Survey map as he pointed out the places he'd show her, and she listened with interest.

Then he escorted her upstairs to the spare room. "Cosier than Mrs Darvill's," she said approvingly. "I should sleep well after the miles I covered this morning."

He showed her the bathroom, and they said goodnight. She reached up and kissed him lightly. As she pulled away, he was sure she noticed the plea in his eyes.

"Goodnight, Alan. And thank you. I'm truly touched by your concern."

"Goodnight, Eve."

She closed the bedroom door, and he took the hint to return downstairs. He went round the house, locked and bolted the doors and ensured the windows were securely fastened before settling in an armchair by the redundant fireplace with a book.

He found his thoughts straying back to the incident with Mrs Harkins. Twenty-four hours ago, he'd have staked everything he had on her assailant being Rennie. But Rennie was out of it. So, had he had an accomplice?

Whoever it had been had clearly expected Eve to be at the cottage, had known she tended to come down at weekends. If he reckoned they were co-habiting, he clearly believed the relationship was farther advanced than it actually was!

At another time, the thought might have amused him. But not tonight. Giving up the unequal struggle with his book, Alan put out the lights and went upstairs.

7

Alan had always been an early riser, and the following morning proved no exception. He flung open his bedroom window to joyous birdsong and the heavenly fragrance of a crisp, sunlit morning. A light dew glistened on the grass, and the borders were ablaze with colour.

As he showered and dressed in flannels and check sports shirt, splashed some Old Spice on his face and prepared himself a quick breakfast of cereal and toast, his thoughts were of Eve and the day stretching ahead of them. Rennie was still there, but he pushed the image away, storing it on a dark shelf at the back of his mind. It would re-emerge later, for sure; but for the time being, he refused to contemplate it.

He prepared coffee, boiled egg and toast, set it all on a tray and bore it upstairs. His gentle tap on the door was rewarded with a bright "Come in!"; and he entered.

Eve was propped up on her pillow and gasped as she caught sight of the tray.

"My goodness, this is what I call service."

Alan set the tray on the bedside table, as she arranged herself into a more upright position, then passed it to her.

"Did you sleep well?" he asked.

"Like a log. Yesterday really took it out of me. But Colette and Jean-Paul fully enjoyed it, so it was all worthwhile."

"I'm glad you came down."

She beamed up at him. Her nightdress was one of the old-fashioned 'passion killers', but even so he was aware of her breasts, rounded and firm, beneath it. "So am I."

"Well, I'll leave you to eat in peace." In truth he was starting to feel a little hot under the collar. "The bathroom's free when you're ready. No hurry. Today doesn't have any kind of schedule. Oh, I'm just popping Mrs Harkins' bike back to her. I —er, I'll lock you in if you don't object?"

She laughed as she took the top off her egg. "I don't object. Why would I?"

He could hear her in the bathroom on his return, and before long Eve had joined him downstairs, looking fresh and pretty in blouse, slacks and sandals. She brought her tray into the kitchen. "Your breakfast was just what was needed. You'd make someone a good wife."

"I'd prefer to be someone's husband," he countered, and in the speechless seconds which followed sensed their mutual unease. He quickly grabbed the map from the sideboard and explained where they'd be heading that morning.

Their first stop was Bibury, busy on any Sunday of the year. He showed her round the bustling little village, its Saxon church, trout streams and the cottages in Arlington Row with their steeply pitched roofs, dating back to the seventeenth century. It was only just midday, but the hotel seemed pretty full, and he suggested they cut across country to Fairford.

For him, it was a well-trodden path: he'd driven, cycled, rambled around the area many times before, always thrilling, particularly on days such as this, to the sunlight filtering through the branches of the trees, the eager, babbling streams; a different aspect, mystery, delight, unveiled at each dip and turn of the bumpy lanes.

Eve seemed to read his thoughts. "It's all so unspoiled and peaceful," she said. "I can see why you opted out of London."

"London has a lot to recommend it," he replied. "Remember, I lived there for a number of years. But most of my boyhood was spent in rural areas, and I suppose I've always felt myself drawn back to them."

They settled on a pub just beyond Fairford. It had a large beer garden to the side, the trestle tables and benches filling up nicely for Sunday lunch-time. They were just passing through the wicket gate into the garden, when Eve pulled up sharply. "Alan – look. By the window at the far end."

He followed her gaze to the farthest table. Seated there were Tony Ventnor and the waitress from the Corner House, Tania Bredon.

Tony cut a debonair figure in a dark blazer, white corduroy trousers and red cravat. A briar pipe lay beside him on the table, smoking away redundantly. Had Alan called his name, he doubted he would have heard, for Tony was worlds away, utterly engrossed in the girl, as he leaned across the table staring into her eyes like an infatuated schoolboy, his two hands closed over one of hers.

Tania looked striking. She'd let her hair down, so that it brushed her shoulders, and its pale blonde hue was accentuated by her royal blue summer frock.

Back in Durleyford she'd seemed shy, almost embarrassed by the attentions of an older man. But here she seemed relaxed, smiling sweetly back at Tony, conversing freely. Alan couldn't help feeling too that she was alive to the appreciative male gazes cast in her direction, and that she was very much in command of the situation.

But, much as he liked Tony, he couldn't endorse what he saw. He found himself hurting for Madge, abandoned in the wilderness of Bayes Wood, once more betrayed.

"Eve, I think we'd best try elsewhere."

She nodded, and they withdrew to the car. As they drove away, she put his thoughts into words. "Madge puts up with a lot."

"I don't think she has much choice," he replied. "The house and money are Tony's."

Madge had never made any bones about being as poor as a church mouse, while Tony had inherited a fortune from his father, who'd been a merchant banker. And there had to be money to enable him to change jobs the way he did while living in a property the size of Bayes Wood.

So Tony held all the aces, and Madge the two options: put up with it or get out. Alan could see why she took solace in drink, and he knew whose side he was on in this instance.

They found a pub in Lechlade not far from the Thames. The seating outside was taken, but inside was dim and airy with gnarled oak settles and a flagged floor. Alan showed Eve to a seat, then went to the bar and ordered some lunch. He returned with a pint of mild, a half of shandy and the landlord's paper, which he'd noticed while waiting to be served. He'd asked if he could borrow it for a few minutes.

Eve raised a questioning eyebrow as he flicked through the paper. He showed her the item he'd been searching for. "I wondered if some enterprising reporter might have got in quickly," he said.

DEATH ON MP'S COUNTRY ESTATE

The body of Stanley Rennie, 48, of Wapping, London, was found on the estate of the Durleyford MP, Mr Kelvin Guilfoyle, at around ten-thirty on Saturday morning. Mr Guilfoyle was holding a pigeon-shoot with several friends when members of the party happened upon the body. It is believed that Mr Rennie, who was thought to be in financial difficulties, may have taken his own life...

Alan watched from across the table as Eve scanned the report. He saw no reaction and thought he should be relieved rather than disappointed.

She pushed the newspaper back to him and, as he reached for it, closed her hand over his. She was wearing her secret smile.

"Alan, I know you care for me, and I'm truly grateful. But I didn't know this Mr Rennie. Not in London, not while I was in the WAAF, nor when I was in France. In France I met many people, but I assure you he wasn't among them. Because not a day goes by when their faces aren't before me. Every last one of them."

He grasped and squeezed her hand. "Eve, all I ask is that you feel you can trust me. As my dear mother was forever reminding me: a trouble shared is a trouble halved. I know from what I've learned from Tony that you were very brave, and that your time in France wasn't for the faint-hearted. If ever you feel you need to talk, I'm ready to listen."

He believed that she was touched by his sincerity and concern, for she made no effort to pull away. "Thank you, Alan – and bless you. Ah, this looks like lunch, and worth the wait."

It was a timely opportunity to change the subject. She took it, and he allowed her to do so, but the roast beef, new potatoes and home-grown vegetables were an acceptable distraction. Between mouthfuls they lapsed into easy conversation. London and the area they were now in had the River Thames in common, and they discussed towns farther downstream which they'd visited over the years: Abingdon, Goring, Henley, Windsor, Richmond. Alan outlined a walk he'd planned to help them work off their lunch.

"No scrambling up mountains?"

He smiled, guessing she'd be more adept than he. "Not at all. A gentle ramble along the river bank for a couple of miles and back through the woods and across fields. We shan't get lost, I promise."

They left the car in the market square and set off. Once they'd struck off from the tow-path, there were less people around. He'd hoped for an opportunity for a heart-to-heart, and to his surprise it was Eve who set it in motion.

"All right, Alan. We'll talk about me, because I know I've told you very little. But first, what about you? How come a caring, handsome man like yourself isn't happily married with five children?"

He was caught on the back foot, he the would-be interrogator. But he'd known that it would have to come to this, particularly if their relationship was to progress beyond mere friendship.

Almost twenty years on now and it still hurt, a hammer blow to the heart, as he recalled those days when he'd cried until he ached, doubled over with emptiness and the searing pain of loss. He'd known this must come: but even so, even now, he couldn't have avoided being so unprepared.

He thought back to the VE Day celebrations in London: the noise, the booze, the endless partying. The ripping-out of sheer emotion: joy, relief, thankfulness that the long war at last was over. And he joined in all the congratulations, all the dancing, hugging, kissing, the general swirl of merriment.

Except that when it was over, alone in his darkened room having woken suddenly from drunken sleep, he was overwhelmed by a sense of utter hopelessness, a cavernous feeling in the pit of his stomach, a dull, persistent aching in his heart. And he sat on the edge of the bed, sat until the false, bright dawn, with his head in his hands.

She should be here with me...

He'd sunk lower and lower, day by day, into the mire of depression, desperate to escape it and yet knowing that there could be one true escape route; and this despite his upbringing, his unquestioning adherence to his parents' faith.

He'd bought the motorbike on his demob, ridden it down to London from where he'd been stationed in Scotland, thrilling to the sensation of slicing effortlessly through the crisp air, weaving down the A1, leaving the plodding motorists in his wake.

His exhilaration hadn't lasted long. Reality had soon pinned him by the tail, and now the bike, that symbol of his release from the war, promise of a fresh start, a new world, became the sword on which he would fall, the means of his obliteration.

It had started out as would any Sunday afternoon in the country. The villages and farms flashed by, faster then faster still. And it was cemented into his fevered brain what he was about to do.

He had chosen the spot. A wide bend to the right, slowing down, changing gear to negotiate its long curve. Beyond it the grass verge and a high stone wall, the altar on which he would make this final sacrifice. Dead ahead.

It went wrong. As the bike mounted the verge, it reared from under him. At frightening speed he was thrown clear, landing twisted and broken in a ditch, while his machine, of which he'd been so proud, smashed into the wall and lay pounded and irredeemable beneath a mound of stone.

Beneath all that stone, he raged silently and inwardly as he swam back to consciousness in his hospital bed. *I should be there, crushed and buried under stone. Not her. Not her...*

Finally he healed, his only souvenir a slight limp in his left leg, which he would bear for the remainder of his days, token of a wished-for oblivion, a constant reminder that his time had not yet come.

Eve had stopped in her tracks. She still clung to his hand, but her face was pale and shocked, as if she too had felt that blow. "You lost someone, didn't you? Oh, Alan, I'd no idea. Please, it it hurts too much to talk about it -?"

He shook his head, determined to be strong. "No, Eve, it's all right. I suppose it's just that I've never moved on, whereas so many others have. They've been right to do so.

"I don't speak about Dorothy often. I've fond memories of her, and we were very much in love, so those memories are full of pain. I was called up soon after the war began, and she desperately didn't want me to go. The ironic thing was that, even though I was in uniform, a soldier for practically the whole war, I never fired a shot in anger.

"And yet she, who was fearful of my going, was killed. She was a nurse. One night a bomb fell on the hospital where she worked. She went back in to help rescue some patients. A wall collapsed on top of her, and she was crushed to death.

"Dorothy was always so gentle and placid, so full of concern for *me*. I was overwhelmed with grief. I got through the war: I was determined to serve, because she'd died serving. She'd been brave, and it was down to me to honour that.

"But once the war was over, I found myself on the edge of all the euphoria. I had nothing to celebrate. I had a motorbike accident – no, not an accident. I'd planned to kill myself, bury myself beneath a wall, the way that Dorothy had died. It went wrong. I came out of it pretty much unscathed: just this confounded limp as a souvenir.

"While I was recovering, my parents were a great help to me. Dad was a Methodist minister, and the pair of them were steeped in faith, while I – well, I'm just a waverer. They reasoned with me that this life is a passageway to eternal life, where there'll be no tears, pain or mourning, and where Dorothy and I will meet and be together again one day."

"And did they convince you?"

The image of his father came to him, kindly if austere in his black suit and clerical collar. Alan had been aware of him on his slow return to consciousness, his father's eyes tightly shut and hands clasped, deep in prayer.

Those same hands, flecked with age, clinging to his own. "My dear son, you must finish the journey He has set before you. Your time has not yet come."

Percival Cawley's time had come within a few years, cut off by pneumonia in the harsh winter of 1954, his wife

Edith dying less than two years later. While Alan recovered, survived without his Dorothy, lived, worked, lived and worked.

"They convinced me that I must carry on, go wherever the path I'm treading leads."

"And of course you have your books." There was a lightness in her tone, teasing him in the gentlest of ways. "Do you need anything more?"

They'd reached a stile, and somehow her hand had slipped into his, how long ago he had no idea. He pulled her to a halt.

"Yes," he replied. "I know now that I do. A companion: someone to share the journey."

"Then, my dear Alan, you must make sure to choose a worthy companion."

She half-turned, intending to climb over the stile, but Alan held her back. The moment had surely come, for he couldn't guarantee another like it, an interlude so fitting. And surely she saw the yearning in his eyes, the pained twist of his mouth, his face hot with emotion?

"Eve, do I have to spell it out? I've fallen in love with you."

She stared back uncertainly. There was something in that look which shocked him, a bewilderment which he might almost have sworn was fear.

And then she seemed to relax, and her stern face broke into a smile. "Oh, you're such a *dear* man."

She brought her face up to meet his, and they kissed. Their lips touched briefly, lightly, and he so wanted it to be passionate, a sign of his longing. As she drew away, he tried to read something into her expression and failed. Yet he felt her kiss had had more of sympathy about it, of compassion as opposed to desire: a suggestion that she was unable – he hoped to God not unwilling – to reciprocate his feelings. And his words were left hanging in the air, finally to be whisked away on the afternoon breeze, chased away unanswered over the valleys, rivers and hills.

He helped her down from the stile, and as she joined him he was surprised once again. For her hand crept round his waist, tentatively as if for reassurance, and he gladly wrapped his arm around her as they walked on.

The silence had run into minutes before Eve spoke.

"I was born in France, in the countryside south of Alençon. My father, Hubert Ransom, was a British soldier serving in France in the Great War. He was wounded, got cut off from his regiment and stumbled into the farmhouse where my mother lived with her uncle and aunt. They hid him from the Boche, and she nursed him back to health.

"After the war, they married and settled in France. Papa's health was never good: his lungs had been poisoned by mustard gas.

"His father owned a public house in Bethnal Green. When he died, it passed to Papa. Our family was poor, and it seemed a heaven-sent opportunity to earn a living. By that time – it was the early 1930s, and I must have been seven or eight – Hitler's rise to power was beginning, and Papa felt we'd be safer in England. *Maman* had few close relatives: by this time her uncle and aunt were elderly and cared for by their daughter, who was hoping to take over the farm. She was happy to go for my sake. Thanks to Papa, she spoke good English, and I was already fluent in both languages.

"We took over the pub, adapted swiftly to the English way of life, and for a while things were good. But Papa's health deteriorated, and he died just before the last war.

Maman took over running the pub, and I helped where I could. But as the war intensified, my heart went out to the country of my birth. As soon as I turned nineteen, I enlisted in the WAAF.

" It was before that when I met Stewart. He was tall, romantic, dashing, with the most ridiculous little moustache. I was truly swept away by him. He wanted to marry me, and we so desperately wanted to be together. And yet there was danger all around us, and I had this deep sense of foreboding. He was a pilot, just twenty when he was killed in a mission over Belgium.

"I was heartbroken. My world caved in, but once I'd sobbed out my grief the war was still there and wouldn't go away. But I wasn't in the WAAF for long. Because of my French upbringing and fluency in the language, I was recruited by the Special Operations Executive, initially as a telegraphist.

"That wasn't enough for me. For Stewart's memory, for my suffering country, I had to give more. Poor Captain Hesketh-Wain. He was my superior, such a kind and caring man. I pestered the life out of him until he spoke to Colonel Buckmaster, and they finally agreed to send me out there.

"I think I surprised them all with my training, particularly the instructors. I'd always been athletic, but what they hadn't known was that from a very young girl I'd been taught to shoot and had become a crack shot.

"As fate would have it, one of the resistance groups needed a replacement wireless operator, and before long I was parachuted into France, to an area not far from Le Mans which I happened to know well. I was going home."

Alan had clung to her the more tightly when he learned about Stewart. Everyone had lost someone dear to them in the war. How had he supposed that she might have come through unscathed? And he could identify with the depth of her grief.

But for his own peace of mind, he knew he had to persist a little longer.

"Eve, I need to ask you something, and I'm sorry to keep forever bringing up the same old subject. But at the Hall last Saturday evening, when Rennie stared through into the ballroom, he seemed to recognise someone. Of course, I thought it was you, particularly after he asked about you in the shop the following week. After he'd left the Hall, you seemed preoccupied, and that's why I thought perhaps you'd recognised him from somewhere."

She smiled back patiently, she who had every right to be exasperated with him. He supposed the opening of their hearts to one another in the minutes before, the sharing of their sorrows, had brought them closer together, a sign of mutual trust.

"Let me set your mind at rest, Alan. I glimpsed that night – what? – a look, an expression, and it plunged me back into the past, to when I served in France. It wasn't even proper recognition: just the briefest snatch of a face in a sea of faces, there and gone in an instant. But I know it couldn't have been him. I expect that was what made you wonder about Rennie."

"But if it wasn't Rennie, who could it have been?"

8

ve didn't answer his question, instead relinquishing his hand and walking the few yards to the next stile. For a moment Alan was confused, interpreting it as rejection. But then she turned and beckoned, and he stumbled forward to join her.

She leaned on the stile, looking down across the river to the rolling countryside beyond, alive and fragrant with the sounds and scents of summer.

"It's so peaceful, isn't it? So unspoiled. Did we win the war, Alan? Did we swear we'd never let anything like it happen again, ever? Because, do you know, it's still with us. Our generation will be forever haunted by it, our children and maybe even theirs tainted by it."

He couldn't argue with that. "We came through the war, Eve, and all of us who did suffered in some way. It's down to us to build a better future, knowing the horror of what's gone before."

"Oh, I agree. But to paraphrase our good Lord's words: *'the war you have with you always.'"*

She sat down on the stile, shifted along to make a space for him, and when he joined her took hold of his hand and gazed reflectively ahead. She sighed, and Alan, realising that she was about to answer his question, waited patiently for her to speak.

"On that long, lonely parachute jump, I wondered if I'd been hasty in pestering poor Captain Hesketh-Wain so much. Was this *really* what I wanted: a life on the edge of danger, continually on my guard, never knowing what the next day might bring, or even if there would be a next day? But it was no time for second thoughts. As I hit the ground, I knew there was no going back. It wasn't a question of being pitched in at the deep end. I'd jumped in – willingly, impetuously. I'd wanted to serve my country; and here I was, about to serve.

"The resistance group I'd joined had for a long time been a thorn in the side of the occupying forces. We didn't know when D-Day would be, just that it was imminent and we had to be ready for it. The Germans knew that too and were sending troops and munitions to the coast. Marius, our leader, was committed to doubling the group's efforts to hamper movements and disable factories.

"Our base was a farm some miles north of Maillerons. The group's wireless operator, George Bazeley, whom I'd met during my training, had been wounded and flown back home. I was sent in as his replacement.

"They hadn't wanted me to go: Colonel Buckmaster, the Head of F section, felt I was too inexperienced, but Captain Hesketh-Wain argued my case, and besides they could see I wouldn't take no for an answer. My cover was good: I knew the area from when I was young and spoke fluent French. I went in as the old farmer's, Gaston's, niece, who'd worked in a Paris department store. And again, I knew Paris well from several visits before the war.

"Soon after I got there, we acquired two British airmen. They'd escaped the previous week from a derailed train while on their way to a prison camp. We caught them trying to steal eggs from Gaston's hen-house. One was Tony Ventnor, the other a Flight Lieutenant John Emsley. Fréderic, a British officer who was SOE co-ordinator for the groups in the Maillerons circuit, was keen to get them back to England with the minimum delay.

"I contacted London and arranged a date and time for a Lysander to pick them up from a field we'd occasionally used between Maillerons and Noiret.

"That was where it all started to go wrong..."

* * *

She was quicker than both of them, much lighter on her feet. She paused occasionally, reassured to hear them behind her, lumbering through the undergrowth.

Finally she came in sight of the farm, nestling in its hollow. Gaston had left a lamp burning, to guide them home.

She entered the kitchen and, propping her sten gun against the sink, filled the kettle from the jug and put it on the stove. Gaston's voice leaked through from upstairs. "It is you, *chérie*?"

"Yes, uncle, I'm back."

"Is all well?"

"No, uncle. All's not well."

The kettle was wheezing away, and the old man had come down to the kitchen in his night-shirt, shaking his head and trundling out Hail Marys by the score, when they came blundering in.

They were wild-eyed, scared, scratched by thorns and branches and gasping for breath. The big man, Emsley, collapsed on to the nearest chair, while the other, Ventnor, dithered near the stove, for once lost for words.

"Christ," Emsley blurted out, "I thought we were done for."

Yvette struck the table, making them all start. "In *French*, Jean-Paul. Always in *French*," she hissed. "How do we know someone's not at the door listening now? If you can't speak the language, keep your trap shut."

"Sorry, Yvette." The apology was slow and grudging, but at least in French.

"They knew." Ventnor had recovered breath and composure. "How did they know?"

She didn't reply right away, trying in her garbled mind to answer the same question. "That's what we have to find out. But not you, Antoine. You must go home with Armand, always assuming he makes it back."

As if on cue, the clatter of heavy feet sounded in the cobbled yard, the latch clicked and two men spilled into the room: Armand and little Gaspard.

Gaston had busied himself making coffee, black and bitter, and handed it round in battered tin mugs.

The two new arrivals made to speak, but Yvette held up a hand. "Say nothing, I beg you. We're all asking the same question. Marius and Fernon – they were with you?"

"They brought up the rear," Gaspard piped up. "Julien was with them, and they made a diversion so that we could get away." He grinned. "Most of the Boche blundered after them. I bet they've led them a merry dance."

Yvette nodded, wishing she shared the little man's confidence. In his eyes, Marius could do no wrong, not far short of invincible. He admired Fernon too, listened enthralled to the stories of his exploits in the Great War. Tremendous deeds, overcooked with daring. She wondered how many of them might be true.

They went on waiting. Old Gaston nodded off in the corner. Armand made more coffee for those who wanted it. Yvette raised her eyes to the carriage clock on the mantelpiece, unnerved by its slow, mournful tick.

When finally she heard footsteps, she leapt from her seat, and the others looked up startled. As the door crashed open, she cursed herself for her slow reaction, moving too late towards her sten gun by the sink. *Alert, Yvette*, her instructors had drummed into her. *Alert always.*

But it was, as she'd hoped and prayed, Marius who came into the room, tall, imposing, dark-clad. Fernon followed moments later, his beret askew, his ugly, whiskered mouth drooping open in a fight for breath. He slammed the door behind him, leaned back heavily against it.

"Where's Julien?" she asked.

Marius' black eyes flashed towards her. "He didn't make it."

She gasped, looked to Fernon for confirmation. He poured out a torrent of abuse, aimed at the enemy. Confirmation enough. She turned back to Marius. He flung himself into a seat, leaned forward with both hands on the table. Gaston served him coffee, but he didn't notice it, his baleful gaze sweeping the room and resting on each face in turn.

"We were trapped," he said bluntly. "The plane didn't land. It was warning enough for us when it turned round and headed off. There were Boche everywhere. We led them off through the forest, towards Noiret, because the roads would have been no good. Julien got hit in the leg. I wanted to carry him, but he swore at us to keep going. He hunkered down behind a tree and must have held them off for five minutes or more. As soon as the firing stopped, we knew they'd got him. He'd done us proud, bought us time to get through the woods. We knew the ground too well, no way they might have caught up with us after that." He laughed mirthlessly. "The bastards are probably still farting around in the woods. Let's hope they lose themselves there forever."

"Might they have captured him?" It was the English airman, Ventnor, the one who fancied he looked like Clark Gable with his sleek little moustache, dashing good looks and — as he at least believed — irresistible charm. Three times since he'd been with them, his hand had covertly explored some area of her body, and Yvette knew that neither time had been an accident. Three times she'd dashed the offending hand away.

Marius turned on him sharply. "Not Julien," he growled. "He would never let them take him, and believe me, my friend, I *know*. He has died a hero — died for France."

Yvette let her mind linger for a moment on an image of Julien. A small man, feisty, fiercely loyal. There: her mourning done. She'd been with them little more than five months, and yet she knew that, for Marius, the subject was now closed. She was relieved when Ventnor didn't pursue it further.

Fernon had finally stopped wheezing and lumbered over to the table. Gaston had placed a bottle of cognac there, and the old soldier snatched it up and took a long pull. He thumped the bottle down and glared at the gathering.

"We were set up," he snarled. "Some bastard betrayed us." He started to curse again, but a movement from Marius silenced him.

"We need to take time to examine what went wrong," he said. "But for now, Armand, Gaspard, Antoine, get back to the village. Leave your weapons here, and for God's sake get off the road quickly if you run into a patrol. We've lost one man too many tonight. Jean-Paul, get off to bed. You look bushed."

They rose wearily and filed out, mumbling their goodnights. Gaston closed and barred the door behind them, turned and indicated the stairs. Marius nodded, and the old man returned to his bed.

Fernon guzzled from the bottle again, before turning on the other two with a face of thunder.

"Someone sold us out," he growled. "And I'm wondering if one of our brave Englishmen might not be what he seems."

He looked directly at Yvette, because he thought she had something going with Ventnor. She disliked Fernon, always had. He was a lecherous old man, forever undressing her with his eyes.

She avoided his gaze and turned to Marius. "Fréderic met with both men last week, *patron,* and has since been in touch with London.. Although regarding Ventnor, there was no case to answer. He has an admirable war record, and Fréderic knows him personally."

Marius nodded. "And Emsley?"

"Everything about his story checked out. Where they flew from, where they were shot down, the names of the crew. Fréderic felt, as do I, that he's genuine."

"But?" The resistance leader had caught the note of doubt in her voice.

She was reluctant to answer. Because it was nothing really: just that she couldn't warm to Emsley. He was big, gangling, aloof, slow of speech. None of that made him a traitor.

"Nothing we can pin down." She chose her words carefully, strove to redress the balance, because she knew she was being unfair. "I'll say again: he checks out. There's something about him I'm not sure of – probably just my prejudice."

"Fréderic?" It would be the clincher. Fréderic and Marius were men cast in the same mould: daredevils, utterly loyal to their cause, and they respected and trusted one another.

"The same." She muttered the words grudgingly.

"Then that is enough for me." Fernon had been listening avidly and now broke in. "We should get rid of Emsley."

"Not so fast, *mon vieux*." Marius was calm and reasonable. "The only conclusion we can draw is that we must be on our guard. Has our friend had any contact with Bosquet?"

"Bosquet? Pah! That little rat."

Fernon again, but Marius had asked the question of Yvette. Bosquet lived in Calombes, the nearby village, and worked in the bar, but made weekly visits to Maillerons, ostensibly to see his mother. He'd fed the group reliable information in the past but tended to be a mite too interested in what was going on, an inveterate gatherer of facts, and Marius suspected he might be in the pay of the Germans. Everyone had been instructed to let slip to Bosquet as little as possible.

As Gaston's niece, Yvette was able to travel freely between the village, Maillerons and Noiret, passing messages to and from Fréderic and Marius. She'd taken Jean-Paul with her on her errands to Calombes a couple of times. He was supposed to be her cousin, who was a bit wrong in the head. It explained his halting French.

"Bosquet sat with us in the café last week," she admitted.

"As he would," Fernon sneered. "Being another of your many admirers."

"They may have been alone for a few minutes," she replied defensively. "Father Bernard happened to look in, and I went to the door to chat with him. Marie also, from the *patisserie*. But remember too that Antoine goes there with Armand, often for their lunch-time *pastis*. And there are other layabouts there."

Fernon growled his unwillingness to contemplate this, and she was glad she'd touched on a sore point: his younger brother, Gérard, was one of the layabouts. His mind was fixed on Emsley. But Marius was ahead of him.

"Bosquet may well have got to either of them," he said. "And that's always supposing Bosquet's our man. But if either Antoine or Jean-Paul is leaking information, here's an idea which may help us flush out the guilty one."

Yvette listened. In the months she'd been with the group, she had seen why everyone looked up to Marius. He was a big man physically, and anyone would think twice about arguing with him. But he was a born leader, travelling the sub-circuit as an itinerant farm worker, gathering and disseminating information, evaluating, planning and putting those plans into action. Even grumpy old Fernon admired him. He was listening now, nodding his head here and there in approval.

Because that night's mission had been aborted, Marius knew, as did Yvette, that London would leave a decent interval before making a second attempt to pick up the two airmen. However, Ventnor and Emsley weren't to know that.

Marius suggested that they pick two locations some distance away, places they hadn't used previously and were never likely to use again. Ventnor would be told that the plane would land at location A on a certain night;

Emsley would be told location B. Both men would be sworn to secrecy.

Yvette and Armand would ensure that the two men were given the opportunity to speak to Bosquet over the next few days. Then, on the evening in question, Marius would inform them that London had called off the mission. However, he and Gaspard, Armand and Fernon would visit the locations at the appointed time. If there was German activity at either one, they would know who the leak was, and their suspicions of Bosquet would be confirmed.

"Bravo, *patron*!" Fernon exploded, and was immediately shushed to silence. There was fire in the old soldier's eyes. "We shall root out our traitor and get back to the main task of driving out the accursed Boche."

Marius didn't share his elation. His face might have been carved from stone, and his voice was stern.

"No-one else must know. Not one word, do you hear? Even Armand will not be given the full details. Remember we lost a good man tonight. If we have been betrayed – and nothing is certain yet, old Fernon – then we must rid ourselves of the traitor. This, to my mind, is the best and surest way."

9

Two days later, Yvette took Emsley with her into Calombes. She felt awkward with him. His understanding of French was limited, his pronunciation slow and halting, and she felt he was a liability. She'd become known in the village: Gaston's niece who'd worked in a Paris department store and had returned to keep house for her ageing uncle. It was good cover, enabling her to travel around at will and liaise with Fréderic and, through him, the other groups in his circuit.

She was grateful for Marius' trust, although she understood that George Bazeley had put in a good word for her. Marius had entrusted Emsley to her: her brief was to keep a close eye on him and, as a general rule, not leave him alone for too long.

Today that rule would be broken. She was to leave him in the bar while she went about her errands. If he was the traitor, he would have ample time to pass on information about the rendezvous. However, she dreaded that he might be tricked into giving away something which would compromise their whole operation. It was a risk; but they took risks every day.

They'd issued both airmen with forged papers, mainly so that they didn't have to keep them holed up at the farmhouse for what had now become several weeks. Emsley was Jean-Paul, and most of the time Yvette did the talking for him. Ventnor – Antoine – was a different story. He was a decent mechanic and fitted in nicely as Armand's garage hand. Added to that, his impeccable French – he'd lived in Paris as a boy — and sublime self-confidence ensured that he blended in with the community.

As they walked, Yvette took the opportunity to explain to Jean-Paul that London would try again on Friday night and described the location to him. She warned him to tell no-one. He took it on board with his usual sullen air. She had to admit that he played his part well, but wondered just how hard he had to try. He was a big man, quite handsome in a way, but naturally slow-witted. Was it just that he was out of his depth, a stranger, prisoner almost, in a foreign land and missing his family?

She could sympathise with him up to a point, although she couldn't say she liked him. He was quite graceless and a poor companion. But she feared for him too.

Their first stop in the village was the bar, and the ritual fending-off of the obsequious Bosquet. As a relative newcomer to the area, young and pretty into the bargain, she'd been prepared for being the centre of attention, although the majority of men who came on to her filled her with revulsion. How different it had been with Stewart, in those few brief months! How her heart had overflowed with love for him, his hopes and dreams for them both, his kindness, tenderness. But Stewart was gone, and what she was doing now wasn't only for France, but for him and the memory of their matchless time together. Above all, she strove to focus on playing her part.

Bosquet brought her coffee and a beer for Jean-Paul. He was a dapper little man in a white apron which reached his toes. His hair was slick with pomade, his weedy moustache reminded her of a wriggling caterpillar and he smelt of garlic. As he bent over to set her cup before her, his hand contrived to massage her shoulder.

Suppressing a shudder, Yvette began to converse with him in rapid French. She had a few errands to run. Would Monsieur Bosquet be so kind as to keep an eye on her dear cousin, and – please – nothing stronger for him than beer? She'd settle up for the drinks on her return in twenty minutes or so. Naturally Monsieur Bosquet was only too delighted and begged her to address him as Emile. He was always at her service.

She masked her disgust by gulping down her coffee. Sweetly smiling at Bosquet, she turned to Jean-Paul and explained carefully that she would be back in a short while. The kind Monsieur Bosquet would attend to him. Understanding what was required of him, Jean-Paul nodded vigorously and grinned back idiotically. Yvette picked up her shopping basket and went out, alert to the barman's simpering gaze chasing after her.

She crossed the square to the church, lit a candle for Julien and knelt at the altar rail for a few moments in prayer. She'd wanted to speak with Father Bernard, for the little priest, well aware of her situation, always lifted her with words of encouragement. However, he was occupied in the confessional, so she slipped out, picked up a few provisions from the grocer's and called in at the garage.

The merry clinking of spanners suggested that Armand and his garage hand had enough work to keep them busy. Deep in the cavernous building, skipping round the oily puddles on the pitted floor, Yvette found them attempting to breathe new life into an ancient Citroen van.

Ventnor's smile was a flash of white in a grimy face. His overalls were filthy, and Yvette was relieved that they prevented him – Armand too, for that matter – from giving her the customary greeting. It always went on a little too long, and they pressed against her a little too intimately for her liking.

"Armand – Antoine – good news."

"*Bon.*" Armand craned his neck to ensure no-one was hovering around the entrance and ushered her into his cramped and cluttered office. Antoine followed, and Armand signalled to him to close the door.

"London will try again." Yvette kept her voice low. "There's a field beyond the woods to the north of Vertran."

"I know where you mean," Armand affirmed. He'd been born and bred in the region, and there was very little about it he didn't know.

"Be there by ten on Friday night. And keep it to yourselves. No-one else must know."

"You'll accompany us, *chérie*?" Antoine, with his winning smile. "I will show you London."

Little did he know that she was probably better acquainted with London than he was. She smiled tightly. "My work is here, *m'sieu.*"

"*Dommage.*"

"Perhaps. And remember. Not a word."

"You won't mind if we celebrate with a *pastis* at lunch-time?" Armand knew his instructions: Marius had been in touch with him. He was to give Antoine the opportunity of passing the details on.

She smiled, relenting. "Just the one." *They all knew it would be three or four.*

"You'll join us?" Antoine was nothing if not persistent.

"Alas, I must take my poor cousin back to the farm. Enjoy your drink, boys. And, please, discretion at all times."

"We shall do everything you say, my pretty Yvette," replied Antoine, with a mocking tug of the forelock.

She turned and walked away. The trap was set. There'd been something underhand about it, and she'd not liked that. Although this was, after all, war. Life and death. And if one of the two airmen fell into the trap, then it was all justified.

Yvette returned to the bar to collect Jean-Paul. It was approaching midday, and trade was picking up. He sat at the table where she'd left him, and he had company: Bosquet, Fernon's brother Gérard, whom she loathed, and a couple of other layabouts.

Jean-Paul was the worse for wear. They'd got him on to *pastis*, and several empty glasses littered the table. He was spluttering gamely away in French, but she knew that could fall flat at any moment. Time to move on, and all the better if it had been ten minutes earlier.

His new-found friends pleaded for him to stay. *"Il est tres amusant, ce cousin."* But Yvette was adamant, and Jean-Paul didn't put up a fight. She settled the bill with Bosquet, turned and walked out to the usual chorus of sly wolf-whistles and mumbled suggestions. Jean-Paul lumbered after her.

He could tell she was angry and swore he hadn't drunk that much, although one or two of them had been eagerly plying him with drinks. He said that Bosquet had remonstrated with them, but they'd overridden him. And he hadn't said anything in English, he'd swear to that.

Yvette relented. "It's not your fault. Mine, rather, for leaving you at the mercy of those good-for-nothings."

Back at the farm, she gave Marius her report, glad that Fernon wasn't hanging around. Gérard could do no wrong in his eyes, but she didn't trust him.

Marius took it on board grimly. He didn't say as much, but she could tell that he suspected Jean-Paul of being the leak, wittingly or otherwise.

Two nights later, a few hours before the plane was supposed to land, Marius sent Yvette to Calombes to inform Antoine that the mission had been aborted. London's excuse was that the plane was needed elsewhere: in other words, something hush-hush. Antoine was clearly crestfallen. He made some joke about having more time to win her round, but she could tell he wanted to go home, to take up the fight again. But then, she'd never felt that had been in question: his war record was impressive.

She told Marius of his disappointment. He responded with a vague nod. "And Jean-Paul?" She'd just returned from breaking the news to him.

"The same. But he's a strange one. I can't make him out. We'll have to see what tonight brings."

Later that evening, Marius took little Gaspard with him and set off for the location they'd described to Jean-Paul: a field beyond Noiret, ten kilometres away. Armand and Fernon headed for Vertran, Antoine's location. It was after midnight when the latter two returned, looking disgruntled.

"Two hours in wet bracken," Fernon grumbled. "I'm chilled to the marrow. Enough to freeze your balls off out there. Where's that bottle? I need something to warm me up."

It was getting on for an hour later when Marius and Gaspard showed up. Marius' face was pale, his eyes cold and hard. "The place was infested with Boche," he snarled. "We counted three troop carriers and a couple of armoured cars. They were ready for us."

Fernon's fist came down heavily on the long-suffering table. "Bring him here!" he thundered. "I will kill him!"

"No, *mon vieux*." Marius was stern and commanding. "You will go home now. Armand, Gaspard – you too."

"But he has betrayed us all!"

"Then he will be dealt with. No more argument. Go!"

For a moment it seemed the old soldier would make an issue of it, but Armand and Gaspard hustled him out through the door. They heard him swearing liberally as he was escorted away.

"Find Gaston," Marius ordered. "Tell him to roust out Emsley and send him in here."

Yvette hurried away, found Gaston dozing in an armchair, shook him awake and delivered the message. Not long after she'd rejoined Marius in the kitchen, Emsley shambled in, rubbing sleep from his eyes.

Marius pointed him to a seat at the table, then remained standing, which immediately placed the Englishman at a disadvantage. Yvette moved across to guard the door.

Sensing the atmosphere in the room, Emsley looked from one to the other in alarm.

"Who are you?" Marius' harsh voice slit the uneasy silence.

Emsley looked confused, his eyes wild with panic. "Wh-what do you mean?"

"Your name's not Emsley, is it?"

"Not -?" Emsley's face turned crimson, and he swore strongly in English. "You bastards. You've been checking up on me. Well, damn the lot of you, I'm telling you I'm exactly who I say I am: Flight Lieutenant John Emsley, based at RAF Syerston in Nottinghamshire. Get on your blasted wireless and check it out again."

Marius passed over that and, once Emsley had finished ranting, let silence set in. When he spoke again, there was a distinct edge to his voice.

"What did you tell Bosquet the other day?"

"Bosquet? The barman? Nothing I shouldn't have. Your girl here told me to say nothing. I kept to that."

"All right, then if not Bosquet, how about one of the others? You had three or four of them round you."

"They were only trying to be friendly, damn you." Emsley was quivering with agitation. "And I've not had much in the way of friendship from you or your people."

"We sheltered you, *m'sieu*. And we are, sadly, not in the business of friendship. We are at war."

"I demand to be sent back to England. I want to return to my base. My family."

"Until you give us your real name, you're going nowhere."

"We'll see about that, chum."

In a flash, Emsley was off his seat and at the door. He grabbed Yvette by the shoulders and flung her aside. The suddenness of the assault knocked her off balance, but as she fell she instinctively threw out a hand and snatched at his ankle. He kicked out savagely, catching her in the rib-cage, but she'd done enough to stall him. Marius had caught him up, whirled him round and swung a fist.

The blow struck the Englishman on the ear, but the force of it was enough to send him staggering back against the dresser. He stumbled, tugging at a drawer in an effort to stay on his feet. Marius strode forward and pitched him back in his seat.

He remained there sullenly, head bowed, one hand massaging his sore ear, as he regained his breath. Marius kept a close eye on him as he helped Yvette to her feet.

Emsley threw them a peevish glance. "All right," he said at last. "I'm not John Emsley, but neither am I a German spy, because I guess that's what you're driving at. My name's Brennan, Corporal Ronald Brennan. I'm from where I said: RAF Syerston. Emsley was our co-pilot. We got shot down over the Normandy coast, and I was the only survivor. I assumed his identity, because I thought that as an officer I'd get better treatment if I got caught. Also I might get a better chance to escape, make my way back to England." He grinned ruefully. "Some hopes of that, eh? Well, that's it. There's nothing more to add, because that's the truth."

Marius hadn't lost his sternness, and Yvette was looking pained from where Emsley/Brennan's boot had smacked into her ribs. He looked at each of them, his face darkening as he interpreted their expressions as doubt.

"Damn it, neither of you believe me, do you?"

"What about last night's rendezvous?" Marius asked tersely.

"What d'you mean, what about it? It got called off, didn't it? Hopes raised and then dashed again. You're getting good at that."

"It was never on," Yvette said quietly.

Her words stopped Emsley in his tracks. His anger fell away. Without it, he seemed unsure of himself, stripped of any lingering self-confidence he might have possessed.

"Never *on*? Then what are you saying? That the whole thing was a hoax?"

Marius leaned forward on to the table and explained about the two false rendezvous at Vertran and Noiret. Someone had leaked information which had got back to the Germans. He told Emsley that the field beyond Noiret had been crawling with enemy troops.

"And you, my friend, were the only one to whom we gave details of that location."

Emsley was silent, thinking furiously. He stared at Marius in disbelief, his eyes out on stalks. Yvette, watching him, guessed that he simply couldn't get his head round the idea.

"But what about Ventnor?" he finally spluttered. "Why me? Why not him? He was supposed to be escaping with me. He knew about it too."

"We gave each of you a different location," Yvette pointed out. Seeing his confusion, she was touched with compassion, tried to let him down lightly. "What happened? Might you just have let something slip in an unguarded moment to Bosquet or any of his cronies?"

"I said nothing." His voice sounded hollow. He stared back at them sightlessly. "You told me not to. I said nothing."

Silence again, and then he seemed to jerk into life, his gaze raking the room. She thought he was about to make another bolt for freedom and stepped back to bar his way. As she did so, she noticed the drawer he'd yanked open as he'd steadied himself after Marius had hit him.

Emsley had spotted it too. And the revolver in the drawer.

He'd leapt for it before she could get halfway there. Marius was helpless, for the table was between them. Emsley snatched up the gun, waved it at each of them in turn. "Keep back," he growled. "You — Yvette — open the door slowly. I want to know — is the van in the yard?"

She darted a glance at Marius, at the knife in his belt. For an uneasy moment, she thought he was going to reach for it. His face was inscrutable. She shook her head almost imperceptibly: a warning.

"Well?" Emsley's voice was shrill with desperation. "Answer me!"

She pulled open the door. "It's there."

"Give me the keys."

"They're in the ignition." She spoke without thinking: too quickly for his liking. He was trembling, pushed to the edge of reason.

He brandished the gun menacingly. "If they're not, bitch, then the first bullet's for you."

"They're there." She tried to keep her voice level. Because she knew they weren't. A quick glance at Marius, and she understood that they were on the same wavelength.

"Out you go, girl. Slowly. Marius, follow her. No false moves, or you'll regret it."

He waved Marius round the far side of the table, hung back while they passed through the doorway.

Too far back. As Marius drew level with the door, his hand shot out and dragged it shut. As it closed up, a bullet crashed into it, but he'd known the wood was too thick for it to pass through.

Just as the door reopened and Emsley emerged, Marius drew his knife. At any other time, the end would have been swift. Yvette had seen him use the knife before, his aim deadly.

Not this time. As he turned sharply, he slipped on the wet cobbles and the knife fell to the ground.

"Merde!"

Yvette reacted swiftly. Emsley's attention was fixed on Marius as he raised the gun purposefully.

She raced forward and flung herself at him, dislodging the gun from his grasp to send it skittering away over the cobbles. Moving quickly for such an ungainly man, Emsley swooped for the knife, beat Marius to it and, as the Frenchman stumbled back, lifted it to strike.

Locating the gun, Yvette whisked it up and fired twice. The bullets thudded into Emsley's back, jolting him forward, pitching the knife from his fist. He staggered back a pace, half-turned towards her.

· There was a curious expression on his face. Like so many other gruesome trophies of the war, this was one which would haunt her forever down the years, never relinquishing its grip on her.

He looked directly at her, astonished, helpless. *Innocent too?* But how could she have known? How could she have acted differently in the circumstances?

Emsley coughed, looked away, took another step and collapsed face down on the cobbles, blood oozing from his wounds.

Yvette dropped the gun. She felt her head spin, and then the world turned black.

The next she knew, she was seated at the kitchen table and they were gathered round her: Gaston, Fernon, Armand, Gaspard, Marius. Fernon was dosing her up with cognac and smiling: something almost unheard of. "You did well," he grunted. "Dear God, you did well."

"Is he -? Is he -?" she spluttered,

Marius was beside her, his strong, comforting arm around her. "My brave Yvette," he said solemnly. "You saved my life. I shall never forget it."

She burst into tears. Again he sought to console her. "He was a traitor," he said. "Never forget that. He doesn't deserve your sympathy."

* * *

"And there you have it, Alan," Eve Ransom said, as they sat together on a Cotswold stile on a cloudless August day seventeen years later. "We buried him in the woods behind the farm and went back to fighting the war. If someone's out to get me, it could well be because of that. And nothing at all to do with Rennie, unless someone was paying him to track me down."

"But the other night at the Hall," Alan Cawley persisted. "The likeness you saw -?"

Eve shook her head. "Maybe it was no more than a trick of the light. It was there and gone in a moment: an expression, a look which brought back a memory. Because it couldn't have been him. I *know*, I above everyone else."

"Couldn't have been who?"

"Emsley."

10

S he switched him a rueful smile and got to her feet. He stood aside as she climbed the stile, then scrambled over after her.

"Alan." Once again her hand found his. "We're wasting a beautiful afternoon talking about what's long past. This is the present, and we're *living* in it. Let's try to be content with that."

She was saying that enough was enough, and all he could do was go along with her. They returned to Lechlade and the car and made their way back across country to Durleyford, Alan picking out an alternative route so that she could savour more of the picturesque little villages, the quiet lanes and peaceful countryside.

All the way back to the car, her hand had remained in his. For reassurance? It was clear Eve hadn't wanted to talk further. Perhaps she'd confided more than she'd intended. But he was certain that her need, whatever it was, hadn't gone away. If the subject should be raised again, he would provide the listening ear; and in the meantime remain alert.

They drove back to his cottage. It seemed bathed in peace, as did everything in that beautiful swathe of England on a warm August Sunday afternoon. Everything but their unquiet minds.

He served tea on the lawn, Eve with him in the kitchen, helping to prepare sandwiches and cut cake, while he brewed tea. Previously, while she'd been upstairs freshening up, he'd looked out, from the depths of his wardrobe, his Uncle Tom's old service revolver, a relic from the First World War, and stowed it behind some tins in the pantry.

He'd looked after it down the years. Tom had particularly wanted him to have it, and it was all he had left to remember his uncle by. Tom had been his mother's elder brother, and the young Alan had always looked forward to his visits to the Manse. They'd promised football, tennis, cricket, a bit of rowing, even a little shooting – although his parents had never learned about that. They'd have been scandalised, as they would have been about Alan having kept the gun, more than a decade after Tom's death.

He smiled fondly at the thought. They'd been good, gentle, faithful people. He hoped he'd repaid them in part by being a fairly dutiful son. He knew his father had been disappointed that Alan hadn't followed him into the ministry. Percival Cawley had hidden that disappointment well. "Follow where He leads, my son. But always – *follow.*"

Was he following now? Shy Alan Cawley, a man who'd never tried to make waves, tried to stay on good terms with all people. Never cheated, never lied – well, rarely. He couldn't be sure.

And Eve, where was she leading him? He hauled his thoughts back to the present, as they carried their tea out across the lawn to the weathered oak table and chairs he'd inherited with the cottage.

They'd just settled down when an awful rumbling noise disturbed them. The sky was clear blue, so there was no way it could be thunder. As it continued, Alan realised that a powerful car was making its way up the track to the cottage.

He set down his cup and rose from his seat so that he could peer over the hedge. The car slowed to a halt on the grass verge beyond it: a maroon, open-top Bentley, probably pre-war but in spanking condition. Alan grinned. He didn't need to see him to guess the identity of the driver.

Kelvin Guilfoyle appeared at the wicket gate in blue shirt, mauve cravat, beige flannels and brown brogues. He was wearing a flat cap which he doffed as he caught sight of Eve.

"Miss Ransom, this is a pleasant surprise."

Alan met him at the gate and shook hands. "We're not long back," he said. "Come and join us."

"I'll fetch an extra cup," Eve smiled, shaking hands with their guest before disappearing into the kitchen.

Alan showed Guilfoyle to a seat, offered him a sandwich as Eve returned with a cup and saucer and poured more tea.

"You're both very hospitable to an unannounced guest," the MP declared. "Particularly one who comes with a profound apology for what happened at the Hall yesterday. I take it Cawley will have informed you, Miss Ransom?"

"Yes, he has. I'm sorry that it should have happened at all, let alone where it did. It must have been most distressing."

"Especially for Miss Prendergast. She was first to spot the poor fellow." Guilfoyle looked doleful. "The PM's not too chuffed either. A communication has been sent to me by his Private Secretary, although Lord only knows how I was meant to prevent the wretched man from ending it all, or from choosing that particular spot."

"Did you know the dead man, Mr Guilfoyle?"

Alan perked up at Eve's question. He'd sensed a keen edge to it, suggesting that she was unable to brush Rennie aside, whether she'd known him or not.

Guilfoyle gazed back thoughtfully. "I can't say that I did, my dear. Although he seemed to think he knew me. At first he reckoned he'd been in my squadron. Manners, who has a voluminous memory for names and faces, quickly squashed that. Then Rennie changed tack and wondered if we'd been at the same school. I almost laughed in his face: after all, it was Harrow, and he didn't seem quite public school, don't you know? No, I'd conclude that Rennie was simply an ex-serviceman down on his luck – it may well be he'd had a drink with myself and my crew at some stage – and he was trying to scrape up an acquaintance in order to get his hands on a bit of cash."

Guilfoyle frowned as he sipped his tea. "There is something odd, though. Harris tells me he can't account for one of the guns we used at the shoot. Whether or not in all the kerfuffle over Rennie someone simply left it lying around, I don't know. But Harris can't find it anywhere. It's probably got nothing to do with anything, least of all with poor Rennie. Inquest's set for Wednesday, by the way, down at the Memorial Hall. Can't say there can be any other verdict than suicide whilst balance of mind disturbed."

"Has anything been found out about Rennie?" Alan asked. "For instance, where he was from, if there was family?"

"No family," Guilfoyle replied. "And the fellow owed money here and there. Apparently he was a private detective somewhere in the East End. Of the shadier variety, I don't doubt. The police have been to his office. What files he kept were mainly grubby divorce cases. No mention of anything to do with Durleyford or any indication of what might have brought him here."

As the MP had been speaking, Alan had switched a covert glance at Eve. She looked pale, but if she'd been at all shocked had collected herself well. He was sure the same question was running through both their minds: had Rennie for some reason been checking up on her?

Guilfoyle smoothly changed the subject and asked Eve what she thought about Durleyford and the Cotswolds. She gave him an account of their day, and he weighed in with his own impressions.

"It's a beautiful part of the world," he proclaimed. "Why, even old Fullars has been waxing lyrical about it. A couple more weeks down here, and we'll turn him into a pastoral poet yet."

As he prepared to take his leave, Guilfoyle asked Eve if she was remaining in Durleyford for long?

"Sadly, no. I'm returning to London tonight."

"Well, I have to drive up to town early tomorrow morning. May I offer you a lift? I intend starting at seven, so you'll be at your work-place in good time." He nodded towards the Bentley. "The old girl rattles along at a fair rate of knots, I can guarantee."

"Thank you. That would be very kind."

"I'll call by at seven, then. I wish you a pleasant evening, Miss Ransom, Cawley."

They waved him off down the track.

"I didn't like to refuse," Eve said, when he'd gone. "I'd better telephone Mrs Parrish and ask her to look in on *Maman,* I'll call back there before work in the morning to make sure all's well. We've only summer students at the moment, and I'm not due to start before ten."

They sat, talked and read in the garden until the sun began to sink behind the distant hills, then went inside and shared a light supper. She kissed him as she made her way upstairs and thanked him for a wonderful day. He settled in an armchair with a book, until he was sure she was asleep. Then, checking the bolts on the doors, he went up to bed.

* * *

The Bentley thundered up the track promptly at seven the next morning, and Eve and Alan were at the cottage's front door. Guilfoyle, immaculately suited, hopped out with a cheerful "Good morning!" and placed Eve's suitcase on the back seat.

Like the gentleman he was, he politely turned away as the couple said their farewells.

They kissed again, but, Alan felt, not without tenderness on her part. "Be careful, Eve," he whispered, as they drew apart.

He wondered if she might counter it by telling him not to be ridiculous, but she seemed to have been struck by his warning. She smiled back uncertainly. "I will."

"And phone me."

"Yes. In the middle of the week."

"Before then. Particularly if-." He lowered his voice still further, not because he thought Guilfoyle might be listening in. "If anything crops up relating to Emsley."

But by now the old confidence was back, with a resolute shake of the head. "I don't know what got into me that evening. Because of course it wasn't him, couldn't have been." She took a pace forward, hugged him, scarcely breathing the words. "It couldn't have been more than an expression, some trait that reminded me of him. Because I *killed* him, remember."

As he held open the passenger door, Alan caught a glimpse of her as she must have been during those turbulent months in France: the doughty resistance fighter, steeled to face whatever might come. And as he waved them off down the bumpy track, he felt more drawn to her than ever before, more protective; because he knew that, though brave, she was vulnerable too.

After a leisurely but lonely breakfast, he walked into town and opened up the shop. It was a Monday morning, traditionally quiet, and he and Miss Gray were able to get the shop straight and the weekend orders sent off to publishers, in between identifying some obscure theological work for Reverend Paston, talking hunting memoirs with the voluble Colonel Prendergast – "Oh yes, Gussie's quite recovered, thank you. Spirited gal. Nasty business though, what? Dashed awkward of the fellow to have topped himself on Guilfoyle's estate"; and the latest blood-and-thunder with the sparrow-like and unnervingly bloodthirsty Miss Timmins.

With lunch-time approaching, Alan gathered up the orders and took them along to the post office. He had to pass the Corner House Café on the way and couldn't help noticing Tony Ventnor seated at a table near the window. He was staring up soulfully at Tania Bredon, who was setting out coffee and a sandwich in front of him. He clasped her hand and mumbled something, probably amorous if Alan knew Tony, and there didn't seem to be a lot of resistance on her part.

Alan liked Tony, valued his friendship; but he liked Madge too and felt for her at that moment. As he passed, Ventnor happened to look up and recognised Alan. He relinquished the girl's hand, raised his own in greeting and smiled guiltily, while Tania stared out at him almost with indignation, as if she thought he'd been spying on them. Alan returned the greeting and moved on quickly, wondering if all three hadn't been discomforted by the encounter.

Having concluded his business at the post office, he called in at the Coach & Horses for a spot of lunch and a half of mild. Here another surprise awaited him.

"With you in a moment, Mr Cawley," Badger grinned, as he bustled past with a tray. He was heading for the little snug, and Alan stepped across and opened the door for him. Over Badger's shoulder, he glimpsed the couple the landlord was serving: Madge Ventnor and Piers Fullarton.

Madge clocked him right away and seemed amused, probably by the look of astonishment on his face. "Alan, hi! Do come and join us."

He dithered in the doorway, but Badger settled the matter for him. "The usual, is it, Mr Cawley? I'll bring it along in two shakes."

That meant five minutes, because the affable landlord would have to prepare the sandwich, and Alan was left with no choice but to arrange his features in a welcoming smile and blunder into the snug.

"You know Piers, of course."

"Yes, how d'you do, Mr Fullarton?"

Fullarton rose to shake hands, his unease on a par with Alan's, who felt kinship with him. "Oh, Piers, please."

"And this is Alan, so now we're all on first-name terms," Madge enthused. "And Alan, darling, do take a seat and try not to look so *puzzled*. Piers has been staying with Kelvin, as you well know, and being a perfect gentleman he's gallantly asked this grouchy old fish-wife out to lunch."

Alan recovered his senses. "I'd certainly not describe you as a fish-wife, Madge."

She looked striking, if not stunning, and he thought that as a girl she must have been quite pretty. She hadn't ladled on the make-up as heavily as usual. Her face was still rouged and red-lipped, but there was too a vibrancy about her, and she looked most presentable in a pastel green two-piece and matching hat, crisp white blouse and black patent leather court shoes.

"And I can tell you," Fullarton put in eagerly, "that she's the direct opposite of grouchy. As I may have mentioned, Alan, I'd like to get away from London. I've a hankering for the Dorset coast, but Madge is trying to tempt me with one or two likely properties in the Cotswold area."

"Alan knows the Cotswolds well," Madge said. "He's bound to bear out my recommendations, aren't you, darling?"

Alan's beer and sandwich arrived, and he spent a pleasant half-hour discussing with them the merits of various parts of the Cotswolds. He was glad for Madge. There was about her something carefree, almost girlish, and he could tell that Fullarton was taken with her.

The poet was his usual hesitant, likeable self, smartened up somewhat for the occasion, but still looking pleasantly rumpled. Madge flirted with him, and he flirted back, delighting in her attention. As soon as he decently could, Alan excused himself, settled up with Badger and headed back to the shop.

He hadn't been there long when Miss Gray came scuttling back from her own lunch break in a state bordering on alarm.

"Why, Mr Cawley, I happened to pass the Corner House on my way back, when whom should I see but Mr *Ventnor* of all people in the doorway to the café with that young woman who works there! My goodness, what will his poor wife think? Such wickedness and debauchery. I really don't know what the world's coming to."

Alan could only tut-tut and shake his head as was required of him, although he was sure the fair Ariadne was equally disapproving of his friendship with Eve Ransom. Even so, he was glad that the afternoon was slack enough for him to send her home half-an-hour early, because no sooner had she gone than the *ping* of the shop doorbell heralded a visitor in the shape of Tony Ventnor. Alan could tell straight away that he was a little the worse for wear.

"Aft'noon, Al. You busy?"

"Nothing that can't wait, Tony. Something the matter?"

Ventnor lolled against the display table, upsetting several copies of *Collins' Nature Guides*, which Ariadne Gray had painstakingly arranged earlier in the day. But Tony was oblivious to the damage.

"I saw her earlier this afternoon, Al."

"Who, Tony?"

"Madge, of course. My beloved spouse. And do you know what? She was walking down the High Street with that ruddy poet fellow."

"Fullarton? Yes, I met them in the Coach & Horses. They were having lunch there."

"But what was she *doing* with him?"

Ventnor's outrage was almost laughable. However, he certainly wasn't finding it funny, and Alan felt obliged to keep a straight face.

"He's thinking of moving to the Cotswolds," he explained. "Someone, presumably Mr Guilfoyle, suggested that as Madge knew the area well she might be able to give him some guidance."

"Well, as long as that's all she's bloody giving him."

Alan felt he had to make the point. "Tony, in all honesty, can you complain?"

Ventnor looked indignant. "Oh, taking sides, are we?"

"Not at all. But there you were this morning with Miss Bredon, and there was Madge at lunch-time with Fullarton. Honours even, I'd suggest."

Ventnor scratched his head and looked blank, making Alan wonder how many he'd had. "Well, yes," he finally conceded. "I s'pose you've got a point. Anyway, must make tracks. Got a call to make out at Stow."

"A call? Are you in a fit state to drive?"

Tony grinned, that mercurial, schoolboyish grin, which so many people, particularly women, found disarming. "Very self-righteous, aren't we, Mr Cawley? Thanks, but I know my limit. Dare say I'll take a few more on board if I know my next client. And don't worry, my fine, upstanding old pal. I'll put up at the Unicorn in Stow for the night. If you see my wife, tell her she'll be sleeping alone. Oh, but of course she may not be." He laughed and shook his head. "Ruddy poet, indeed. No good him comparing Madge to a summer's day. Unless he's short-sighted, of course. Blind, even."

"Drive carefully."

"You bet." Ventnor left the support of the display table and walked with reasonable steadiness to the door. "Oh, and Al?"

"Yes?"

"Catch!"

Alan had seen him whip a book from Ariadne's now jumbled display and knew what was coming. It was a typical Ventnor ploy.

He plucked the book neatly out of the air and glanced at the spine. *"Hymn Writers of the Cotswolds.* What redeeming tastes you have, Mr Ventnor."

"And how nimbly you field, young Cawley. My, you couldn't have caught it better if it had been the lovely Eve. Now *there's* a project for a summer's evening."

"Good *day*, Tony."

"Cheers, Al." Again the grin, and Ventnor was gone. But if Alan had thought that was to be his last contact with the Ventnor clan that day, he'd have been mistaken.

11

M aking his way down the lane late that afternoon, Alan glimpsed a movement in his garden. Did his eyes deceive him, or was that someone fair-haired wearing something blue? His heart beat faster, and he quickened his pace.

For it could only be Eve, dressed in the blue cardigan she'd worn on her last but one visit to Durleyford. What she was doing there concerned him, but any anxiety was quickly set at nought by the overwhelming fact that she was there.

The side door was open, and he could see her in the kitchen. He pushed open the wicket gate and crossed the lawn with as much speed as he could manage.

"Eve? This is a marvellous surprise. What brings you back so soon?" The words had tumbled from his lips before he'd reached the door.

"Why, your irresistible self, my darling Alan."

The voice was a long way from being Eve's, and as he appeared in the doorway his face must have been a picture.

"My goodness! Madge!"

"My, but you're quick."

"What are you doing here? Is everything -?"

Madge finished making a pot of tea and turned towards him with a smile. "Well, the truth is I was out for a bit of a stroll and happened along the lane. Your priceless Mrs Harkins recognised me and let me stay, assuring me you wouldn't be long, not on a Monday, and that you wouldn't mind if she left me to it. Seems I passed muster as a respectable married woman, although it's twisted logic if you ask me. Come along, Alan dear, don't look so retarded. I've made tea, it's a lovely afternoon, so let's take it out into the garden. Did I notice some shortbread biscuits in the pantry?"

Alan brought the biscuits out to the garden table and sat opposite Madge while she poured the tea. She'd obviously been home, as she'd changed from her lunch-time clothes into the blue cardigan, striped slacks and low-heeled white sandals.

Alan fixed her with a stern stare. "Now, Madge, this is all very pleasant, but to what do I *really* owe this pleasure? And where's Mr Fullarton?"

Madge lounged back in her seat and bit into a biscuit. "Oh, he's halfway to Dorset by now, I should think. He's viewing a couple of properties near the coast in the morning." She giggled. "Such a dear man. I think he wanted me to go with him but was too much of a gentleman to ask."

"And would you have gone?"

"Why the hell not? I'm past caring about Tony. Oh, but separate bedrooms, darling, of course. Wouldn't want people to get the wrong impression now, would we?" She grinned wickedly. "Just fancy. Old prim-knickers Paston and her cronies would have a field day. Enough gossip for them to choke on. I can see the headline in the *Advertiser* now: 'Sin Swamps Deadly Durleyford'. Piers and I. You and Eve. Tony and anything in a bloody skirt."

She set down her cup with some force. He expected anger and guessed she'd called because she wanted him as a sounding-board. But when she gazed up at him, he felt she looked lost, helpless, and he could see the beginnings of tears in her eyes.

"No, Alan. As you clearly understand, I'm kidding myself. Because I'm not past caring. Darling -?" She took up her cup again and ruefully examined the dregs. "I'm sorry, but might you have anything stronger?"

He nodded, smiling. "Wait there."

He went to the pantry and found a half-bottle of gin, took it and a glass out to where she sat smiling up at him gratefully.

"Look what I've found. Half a mo', and I might be able to rustle up some tonic water."

"To hell with the tonic water." Madge wrested the bottle from him, splashed some into the glass and necked it back. "Oh, that's got a kick. Just what I needed." She poured another drop, this time more sedately, reached across the table and patted his hand. "Thanks, Alan. You're a good friend."

He took her hand, hoping she wouldn't misinterpret the gesture and glad there was the table between them.

"Madge, Tony came into the shop this afternoon. He seemed quite distraught."

Her eyes flashed: the old antagonism was back. "And you're expecting *me* to sympathise? I've lost count of the times when *I've* been distraught. Alan, you're an honest chap. Give me the truth, please. Is he rogering that little tart from the café?"

He gave her the truth as he saw it. "I honestly don't know, Madge. He's been evasive, for sure. But I get the impression it's not gone beyond infatuation – he's over twenty years older than her."

Alan neglected to mention that he and Eve had stumbled upon the couple at a country pub the previous day. Tony might have made all the running, as he usually did. But something told him that Tony wasn't totally at ease in the girl's company. It was the age-old story of an older man pursuing a young woman. He sensed a certain artfulness about Tania Bredon; suspected that she was gaining the upper hand.

"I should walk out on him, shouldn't I?" Madge was determined not to be easily appeased. "He's done this to me once too often."

"Madge, this isn't any of my business. But if you're looking for company, why look further than Piers Fullarton? I felt today that I'd not seen you so relaxed in a long while."

"Oh, Piers is the perfect gentleman. Too much so for my liking. Sometimes that's not enough for a woman."

She was staring at him earnestly, smiling dangerously. She set down her empty glass with purpose, got to her feet and came round the table.

Alan became alarmed. He knew right away what she was thinking and was trapped between Madge on one side and an apple tree on the other. Without a by-your-leave, she squeezed between his chair and the table and pitched down unceremoniously on his lap. The force of her landing was such that he had to brace himself to prevent them from toppling over.

Madge thrust her face close to his. "I'm presuming Eve's safely in London, and I've no idea where Tony is. Oh, my sweet, gentle, utterly irresistible Alan, I'm so badly in need of comforting."

He tried, as apologetically as he could, to draw back from her but was firmly wedged in his place. "Madge, this isn't a good idea. It can't go any farther."

"Oh? Can't it?"

She had the advantage of him and took it. Her mouth bore down greedily upon his, and he felt the weight of both her and her passion. Neither was inconsiderable, but above all and most forgettably, he was forced to endure the pungent taste of neat gin, never his favourite drink, particularly at second-hand. It seemed for a moment as if she was about to suck the life out of him.

At last Madge drew back, her face alight with a wicked red smile. "S'pose I'd better let you come up for air."

"Madge, really. I must insist. This can't -?"

She overrode him gleefully. "You're hardly in a position to dictate what can't or mustn't be done. Now, my darling recalcitrant Alan, give me one more good reason why we shouldn't -?"

Madge was interrupted by a sound like a cork popping, and a split-second later her glass, on the table beside them, exploded. Madge screamed, collapsed forward on to him, and in the next instant the chair had tipped over and the pair of them were sent sprawling into the long grass of the tiny orchard. To make things worse, Alan landed squarely on top of her.

Despite shock and her sudden dishevelment, Madge was smiling mischievously. "Why, *Mister* Cawley. Talk about fast!"

Alan didn't wait around. Madge was gripping both his arms, but he wrestled free, hauled himself up and blundered across to the kitchen, rapping out an order to her to stay where she was.

He yanked open the pantry door and fished out Uncle Tom's revolver. Someone had taken a pot-shot at them, and he knew the gunman had to have been standing in the copse across the track from his wicket gate.

Amazed at the speed with which he was moving, Alan loped across the lawn and tore open the gate, aware of Madge resting on her elbows and watching him with something uncomfortably like awe.

He crossed the track and caught a glint of metal in the late sunshine. It was from deep in the copse, and he wondered if he'd acted rashly, if the gunman might fire again. But his reason told him that he hadn't been the target in the first place and, brandishing the revolver, he plunged into the copse.

From some distance ahead, Alan heard the sound of a body crashing through the undergrowth. He put on a spurt in an effort to get a glimpse of the figure, but it proved to be his undoing. His trailing foot snagged on a tree root, he tripped and the revolver flew from his grasp to land in a cluster of bracken. By the time he'd picked himself up and retrieved it, the sound of the gunman's escape had faded. From far off, an engine kicked into life, a motor scooter possibly, and the noise of it died away down the track. Alan dusted himself off and went back to Madge.

She had made it to a seat and was surveying the scattered ruins of her glass. Her hand was bleeding where a sliver had struck it, and she looked shaken. Alan helped her to her feet and led her into the kitchen. He sat her down at the table and, without her noticing, restored the revolver to the pantry.

Behind the dollops of rouge, Madge was pale. "Who the hell was that?" she demanded. "Alan, we could – could have been -?"

He tried to pass it off lightly. "Probably some lad with an air rifle," he said, knowing full well it had been nothing of the sort. "They get out this way sometimes."

"I'd tan his bloody hide if I was his mother."

He grinned. The same old Madge had resurfaced. He poured her another gin and sat beside her to wash and dress her cut.

"You'd make a good mother," Madge commented, her eyes twinkling. "And, I should guess, an even better lover. I must ask Eve's opinion."

Alan smiled back, relieved to feel in control of the situation. "I'd better drive you back home. Tony'll be worrying about you."

"Of course. And pigs are flying all over Durleyford."

First ensuring that he'd removed all traces of Madge's lipstick from his face, Alan drove her back to Bayes Wood, the rambling property two miles out of town which Tony had inherited from his parents. He'd neglected it too, as was his wont, and it was far too large for he and Madge, but the Ventnors had ever liked to keep up appearances.

Alan was surprised to find Tony at home. Glass in hand, he appeared at the door a little unsteady, his eyes widening at the sight of them together. "Client's down with flu'," he announced affably. "So back early. Abandoned by wife – took to bottle. Hell's bells, what's a chap supposed to do?" He looked from Alan to a slightly pale Madge and the bandage round her hand. "What's this, old girl? Tried slashing your wrists? You should have said. I'd have helped you."

"She was out for a ramble, tripped in some woodland and cut her hand," Alan explained effortlessly, he and Madge having previously agreed on their story. "She was within spitting distance of my place and very sensibly called in to have me dress the cut."

Tony was listening and watching him intently, and Alan felt uncomfortable for he recognised suspicion in his eyes, although it was there and gone in a moment. "Here, old thing, take my arm."

"Oh, don't fuss." Madge pulled back from him. "It's no more than a scratch. And what I'm dying for is a drink."

"Then let me get it."

"No, I'll do it myself. Alan dear, you'll join us, won't you?"

"Er, no. Thanks, Madge. I'd better be getting back."

"Awaiting Eve's phone call, I don't doubt," Ventnor said with a wink. "And spend the rest of the evening whispering sweet nothings to each other down the line."

"Just a bit of paperwork to catch up with, actually," Alan lied unconvincingly.

"Alan – thanks for everything." Madge was back to her old mischievous self. "Truly a friend in need." She reached up and brushed his cheek with her lips.

Again he noticed the flash of suspicion in her husband's eyes. "Yes, thanks, old man. So good of you."

He could feel the colour rushing to his face, grinned back uneasily and took his leave. As he got in the car, he turned to wave. Madge had gone inside, but Ventnor was still at the door. He waved back and stood watching as Alan drove away.

He was back home frying some bubble-and-squeak for his supper when the phone rang. Wondering if Tony Ventnor's prophecy might be about to come true, he picked up the receiver to find that the caller was Kelvin Guilfoyle.

"Ah, Cawley. I tried phoning earlier, but you must have been out. Listen, this may mean nothing, but I thought I'd better pass it on. I dropped Eve at her college this morning, and it was only as I was driving off that I noticed this fellow. Big, lumbering, bearded chap in a greatcoat. He seemed, well, out of place, and it was as if he'd been waiting for her. She didn't seem awfully pleased to see him, and, well, as I say, I guess it's nothing -?"

"Thanks, Mr Guilfoyle. I have a feeling Eve's mentioned this man before. He works at the college – maintenance, I think. Always on the cadge, but I'm pretty sure he's harmless. Thanks all the same for letting me know."

They concluded the conversation with a few more pleasantries. Alan felt he'd placated Guilfoyle, but for himself, he was disturbed. He smiled mirthlessly at the thought that he was turning into a consummate liar, having dreamed up the maintenance man issue on the spot. But alarm bells were ringing.

He went outside. The light was fading, but he searched copiously in the long grass where he and Madge had had their spill. After about ten minutes, he found what he was looking for and took it inside for a closer examination.

He'd learned a bit about guns from his army days. In his hand was a spent shell. And he was fairly certain that it had come from a similar shotgun to those used on Guilfoyle's estate that Saturday past.

One of those guns had gone missing.

He thought back to earlier that afternoon when he'd returned home and glimpsed Madge in his garden, wearing a cardigan similar to one of Eve's. He'd mistaken Madge for Eve.

Had the gunman done the same?

12

A lan reached the shop early next morning and fussed around inside, waiting for Ariadne Gray to arrive. Often she'd be in the doorway waiting for him to open up: today, of course, she wasn't. He glanced at his watch for the umpteenth time and shifted some books around needlessly.

It still wanted two minutes to nine when she walked in. "Good morning, Mr Cawley. You're bright and early."

"Good morning, Ariadne. Er, I have to go up to London, I'm afraid. Would you mind awfully looking after the shop?" He pulled the spare keys from his jacket pocket.

"Why, of course." Miss Gray carefully deposited her mackintosh and handbag in the tiny office. "It sounds like urgent business – almost a matter of life and death?"

He wished he could have avoided his agitation showing. But the moment she'd arrived, she must have guessed something was in the wind by the way he was prowling around the shop.

The lilting tone of her last sentence had begged to be told more, but he was careful not to fall into that trap.

"Do you know, I believe it might be."

"Oh, my goodness!" Ariadne's hand sped to her lips, and her eyes widened.

Alan tried to disarm her with a smile. "But, as you've guessed, it's pretty urgent anyway, and I'd better get a move on if I'm going to catch the nine-fifteen. I probably shan't be back till late. Thanks again, Ariadne. I really do appreciate it."

He was halfway out of the door by then, chased by a simpering little laugh. "A pleasure, Mr Cawley. And good luck."

He caught the train all right but missed his connection at Reading and so didn't reach London until midday. As he made his way across the city by tube, it occurred to him that it couldn't be far off Eve's lunch hour and that she'd told him she usually ate at a little café called the Bay Tree, just off the north end of Regent Street.

Alan left the tube at Oxford Circus. It was one of the busiest parts of London, and he was glad of the crowd to minimise any chance of his being spotted. By now it was half-past twelve and, locating the Bay Tree tucked into its side street, he crossed the road and stole a cautious glance through the window. He saw Eve straight away, sitting alone at a table to the side of the counter, a plate of sandwiches and glass of milk before her.

She didn't seem far off the end of her meal and, relieved that she didn't look up, he scurried back across Regent Street to take refuge in a shop doorway some fifty yards down. Ten minutes later, Eve came into view, walking briskly. She crossed to his side of the street and continued up it for a short distance before turning off into a cul-de-sac.

Alan recognised its name: she'd mentioned it before, and from what she'd said he understood Parkway College to be at its far end. He followed at a distance, but the avenue offered plenty of cover, lined on both sides with plane trees in wrought-iron cages. He spotted the college in the corner of the cul-de-sac, a tall, white Regency building set back from the road. Alan paused as he watched Eve turn through the gateway and walk down the gravelled path to the front door.

He watched her go inside and checked his watch. She was due to finish at four-thirty, and that gave him more than three hours to kill. There was no sign of the bearded man Guilfoyle had mentioned. Not that Alan had expected to see him, but that wasn't to say he'd not be waiting when Eve left work.

He returned to Regent Street and found a milk bar where he had coffee and a sandwich. He tried to work out her route home and guessed she'd take the Central Line from Oxford Circus and get off either at Bethnal Green or Mile End.

The afternoon dragged by. He walked back along Oxford Street and through Hyde Park before returning to the milk bar for two more coffees in trendy transparent cups. Four or five young men in leather jackets were huddled round the juke box, swishing combs through their Brylcreemed locks and nodding along to the beat. The disc of the day appeared to be Del Shannon's *Runaway*. The words seemed strangely apposite; and Alan felt increasingly out of place.

He felt grubby too. Here he sat furtively, a supposedly respectable bookshop proprietor on the cusp of middle age, lurking at a steamy window for a view of the woman he professed to love, so that he could follow after her like some down-at-heel private eye and find out if she was meeting up with another man.

What was he worried about? Guilfoyle had been fairly certain that she'd not been pleased to see the man. Perhaps he was a past lover. But if Alan had thought that, he'd have left the matter well alone. What was really motivating him was that he sensed danger all around Eve. He was concerned that she wasn't totally alert to it, and that this man might be part of it.

So he was there to protect her, was he? Then he was treading a thin line. Because if she caught him tailing her, slapped his face and told him she never wanted to see him again, he could have no cause for complaint.

By four o'clock he'd had enough, left his post and wandered down the avenue towards the college. He took up position diagonally across from the entrance, concealed himself behind a tree and watched as half-a-dozen laughing students, gabbling away in French, spilled out through the doorway and made their way up the avenue. He wondered if they were going to the milk bar and decided they were welcome to it.

After five minutes, Eve came out. There was a man with her, and they were talking animatedly. He wore a beard, but was short, well-groomed and dressed in a light-coloured windcheater. Alan decided he must be a colleague, and this was borne out when the two of them, on reaching the top of the avenue, waved cheerful goodbyes and parted in different directions.

Eve turned down Regent Street, and Alan, guessing she was heading for the Underground, hurried after to keep her in view. She'd helped him by wearing a mauve headscarf, and he maintained a distance of some twenty yards between them.

The rush hour had begun, and he had to push his way through the dense crowd to keep up. He saw her bright head disappear down the steps at Oxford Circus and knew he had to catch the same train. He wasn't sure where she'd get off, and he'd never asked her address, although he presumed she'd be heading home.

He found himself a long way back in the queue at the ticket office, gambled on Mile End and scrambled on to the escalator bearing a press of humanity down towards the

Central Line. As he stepped on, he was rewarded by the sight of Eve's scarf as she left the escalator at the bottom.

A train was in when he reached there. It was packed, and he barely managed to squeeze on before the doors swished shut, almost trapping the tails of his jacket. As soon as he'd steadied himself against the lurching of the train, he looked around for Eve. As luck would have it, he glimpsed her right away in the next carriage, where a man was gallantly offering her his seat. She took it, her head bobbing in thanks, while the man stood up awkwardly and, for his pains, had his bowler hat knocked over his eyes by a stray elbow.

The crowd hadn't thinned out much by the time they pulled in to Bethnal Green, and he peered through into the next carriage, caught a snatch of mauve and realised she wasn't getting up.

There was more of an exodus at the next stop, Mile End, and this was where Eve got off. Alan, by dint of being so close to the doors, was among the first out on to the platform. As she alighted, she was little more than five yards away. Fortunately she didn't look round, and he hung back deliberately to lengthen the distance between them.

It was as well that he did. She was halfway up the long flight of stairs to the street and Alan at the bottom when she came to an abrupt halt. Alan stopped too, and as he looked past her he saw why.

At the top of the stairs a man was waiting. He looked huge, his size reinforced by the enormous greatcoat draped round his shoulders on an August afternoon. He had an unruly mop of dark hair, a full black beard and wore baggy blue dungarees and workman's boots.

Michael Limmer

Eve continued her climb. Alan wondered for a moment if she might try to duck past the man, but she paused for a few moments alongside him, muttered a few words and walked off. He turned and loped along beside her.

Alan hurried up in pursuit and, once he reached street level, saw them walking away down Mile End Road. Eve moved briskly along, her companion speaking with some urgency; but when she replied it was only briefly. Clearly she didn't want his company.

They turned off down a side street, stopping at its far end. Alan stayed back, lurking in the shadow of the terraced houses. He saw Eve snap open her handbag and pull out two notes. The man muttered something, probably his thanks. As she moved away he made to follow, but she turned sharply and pointed him off in the opposite direction, waiting while he slunk away.

The man continued on his way down the next street, while Eve headed off down a cul-de-sac. A tall tenement building stood at its far end, a weathered board on a scrubby piece of grass in front identifying it as Meadowside Court. From the mouth of the cul-de-sac, Alan watched Eve enter the building and guessed it must be where she lived with her mother. He made a mental note of the street he was in, for he intended coming back. But first he thought he'd find out where the bearded man was going.

The man was still in sight, and Alan hurried along, cutting the distance between them to some fifty yards. The streets grew narrower, the surroundings less salubrious. Eventually they came upon a row of shops: a grocer's, laundrette, cobbler's and café.

The man disappeared into the café. Once Alan arrived there he loitered outside, pretending to study the flyblown menu. His quarry was at the counter, talking to the woman behind it. He seemed to have difficulty making himself understood, but finally both nodded, he handed over one of the notes and she gave him some change. He went and sat in a gloomy corner at the back of the room.

Deciding he couldn't hang around indefinitely, Alan went in and ordered a mug of tea and a bun. The café was thinly populated, and he took a seat over by the window, where he had a good view of the man without appearing obtrusive. His bun was stale and tasteless and the tea, which had slopped over the rim of the chipped white mug, was stewed. He sipped primly, chewed doggedly, feeling as out of place there as he had in the milk bar earlier that afternoon.

He watched as a slatternly girl took the man tea and a plate of sausage, egg and chips. The man nodded and tucked in, his head bent low over his plate. He ate ravenously, then swilled back his tea in one mighty gulp. He scraped back his chair and lumbered past the counter and out into the street.

Alan gave him a good thirty seconds before going off in pursuit. He spotted the man some way off to his left, moving with deceptive speed, and hurried after him as quickly as his leg allowed. At the end of the street, the bearded man took a sharp left, quickening his pace. When Alan reached the corner, he found himself in a wider thoroughfare, and although there was little traffic and few people about, his quarry was nowhere in sight.

Alan wandered along for a couple of minutes and came upon a narrow alley, its opening concealed between two tall buildings. He started down it, then paused as he heard the sound of running footsteps which grew ever more distant.

Further pursuit was hopeless, and Alan guessed that the man had rumbled him. He turned back, walking slowly as he considered his options, and finally decided to return to Eve's apartment and explain himself. He was feeling hungry, having only consumed the forgettable stale bun since lunch-time. But he guessed that all that would be on the menu for him would be humble pie, or maybe worse.

Meadowside Court belied its name, an ugly red-brick Victorian tenement, four storeys high and without a lift. A furred square of card on the doorpost informed him that 'Ransom' occupied Number Twelve on the third floor, and he trawled up the wide flights of stairs, noting a gloom about the building, a weariness and shabbiness, almost as if it had given up the ghost. He wondered why someone as lively and attractive as Eve should be living there, but he supposed it was out of duty to her mother. Also they had no choice: she'd mentioned that they had very little money.

He longed to take her away from it all. Durleyford seemed like a Utopia by comparison, and his ramshackle little cottage a palace.

He hesitated before pressing the bell outside Number Twelve. It croaked back at him, and he waited uncomfortably. He heard light footsteps, and then the door swung back and he was face to face with Eve.

He opened his mouth to speak, but she beat him to it,

"Alan! What are you doing here?"

Something like shock had passed across her face at the sight of him. He tried not to show his discomfort, so his voice must have sounded stern.

"Eve, we need to talk."

She stared at him incredulously. Now she was the one lost for words, while a querulous voice piped up from inside the apartment. "Who is it, girl? Who's there?"

Eve quickly collected herself. "I shan't be a minute, *Maman*."

She stepped forward, forcing Alan out on to the landing, and closed the door up behind her.

"What's this about, Alan?"

"Eve, the man you were with, the man who met you at the station. Please – who is he?"

"Who -?" She stared up at him in disbelief, although in the next moment her face clouded with anger, her body stiffened and she held her small fists bunched at her sides.

Alan had never seen her like this, combative, aggressive, furious, the fighter she must have been, that in all probability she still was. He backed away a pace, wishing he could hide the guilt which, despite his best efforts, must have shown all too plainly on his face.

"Why are you spying on me, Alan? *Why*?" She hissed the words, and he prepared himself for the worst, knowing only too well that his own folly had brought it about.

But then her features somewhat relaxed. She continued to stare at him, but her fury had passed. She shook her head slowly, and a grim smile played upon her lips.

"Oh, Alan, what am I to do with you? The man you saw me with is called Sam Perkins, an old friend of my mother's. He used to help out when she ran the pub. He's out of work now, and I give him a little money from time to time. Although to be truthful, he's getting to be a nuisance. And now, Alan, it's your turn. Perhaps you'd be good enough to explain why you're in London and following me around?"

She was calmer now, and he was glad of that. But he felt cheap, as he'd felt all day, because he'd been spying on her like a jealous schoolboy, and he was ashamed. And he couldn't rid himself of the conviction that the situation was growing increasingly serious. Surprising himself, he answered bluntly.

"Two reasons, Eve. Firstly because I care about you. I care damnably. Secondly, because I'm convinced you're in danger."

The querulous voice struck up again, shrill and demanding. "Eve! What are you doing out there? Who are you with? Eve! Answer me!"

"One moment, *Maman*!" Eve raised her voice as she called back through the half-open door, her anger simmering. "I'm coming," she added more reasonably. "Be patient."

She turned back to Alan and he tensed, suspecting that she wasn't done with him. She wasn't, and he was almost floored by her reaction. For she smiled ruefully, reached up and kissed him, and as they drew apart he found himself fighting for breath. It had been an altogether more welcome assault than the one to which Madge had subjected him the previous day.

"Well, I must say that's made the journey worthwhile."

"You'd better come in." She took him by the hand. "You can meet my dear mother – and on your own head be it. We'll talk later, once she's in bed. And I'll give you some tea. I dare say you've been so busy being gallant that you've not had time to eat properly."

He smiled his gratitude and allowed himself to be led into a large, dim room made dimmer by the cumbersome ancient furnishings: sofa and armchairs in brown, the wallpaper slightly yellowing, a grandfather clock, sideboard, dining table and chairs all in dark wood. But the room was tidy and cosy enough for all that. Two doors led off to what he presumed were bedrooms, while over to the right through an open doorway was a tiled kitchen from which a big pot on a range gave out a delicious aroma of stew.

Before him in one of the armchairs sat an elderly lady in a woollen skirt which reached her ankles and a white shawl. She was small and frail, appeared half-consumed by the chair. Her white hair caressed her shoulders, and a bony hand hovered over the empty fireplace beside her, seeking warmth. There was an expression on her face which might have been a smile but probably wasn't, and her eyes, ice-blue and gimlet-sharp, studied Alan voraciously as Eve pulled him farther into the room.

"*Maman,* this is Alan Cawley, my — friend from Durleyford. I've mentioned him before."

Alan beamed, lifted by Eve's hesitation over the word 'friend'. It told him she considered him to be more than that.

But his ordeal was about to begin.

"Ah, Alan Crawley, yes. Sit down, young man. There, across from me in that chair, so that I can see your face. Come along, I won't bite."

"You can never be too sure," Eve murmured.

The old lady's hearing was as sharp as her scrutiny. "What's that? Stop mumbling, girl, and get on with the tea. I'm hungry, sat waiting around here all day." She fixed Alan with a stare as he lowered himself into the armchair she'd indicated. "Mmm, yes, I suppose you *look* honest enough. Tell me, what do you do for a living? Eve must have mentioned it."

"I own a bookshop."

"Books, eh? Seems an honest enough occupation. And it's about time she settled down. I dare say your intentions are honourable. Not like some of those others over the years..."

"*Maman,* please -."

"Wolves in sheep's clothing. That man who came to console you. Huh! *Console,* indeed. If I hadn't been there that day, the good Lord alone knows what might have happened."

"*Maman!*" Eve's voice was shrill with anger. "*Tais-toi! Ah, mon Dieu! Ce n'importe plus!*" She turned to Alan, her face flushed with embarrassment. "Pay no attention to her. It's something that happened years ago, during the war in fact." She glanced at her mother. The old lady was shaking her head and tut-tutting away, seeming to gaze at the non-existent fire but in reality staring far beyond it, back down the long tunnel of the years.

Eve sighed, took Alan by the hand and led him through to the kitchen, where she stirred the stew, diced vegetables and chunks of meat in a creamy broth.

"Poor *Maman.* She thinks every man I meet has seduction at heart. And she forgets I'm hardly a girl any more. Do you know, Tony and Madge came here once. They were taken aback by the crimes she accused them of: he was going to answer for his sins, and she was no better than a prostitute. Well, Madge had gone overboard on the warpaint that day! Still, at least they were able to see the funny side of it. Although I don't know if Mr Guilfoyle will speak to me again. She shouted at him from the window to keep away from me. She knew what his game was." Eve laughed. "Come along, enough of this. If you'll hand me some plates from the cupboard to your left, I'll serve you up a meal which, I'm afraid, comes with yet one more helping of *Maman*."

13

Stella Ransom had been right when she'd said she was hungry. No sooner had Eve installed her at the table and set her plate before her than she attacked her food with gusto, not bothering to wait for the others.

But it seemed to mellow her mood. "She's a good girl, my little Evie, even though I'm such an old grouch."

"It's not your fault that you can't get out, *Maman*."

"But I do so *worry* about her, Mr Crawley. An attractive woman alone in London. It's not *right*, you know. There's so much evil around. Hopefully once I'm gone, she'll be able to move away from here and settle down."

"Oh, *Maman*. Please don't talk like that."

For the rest of the meal, the old lady concentrated on eating, while Eve and Alan talked among themselves. Eve knew this part of London well, having lived there close on thirty years, while Alan didn't know it at all, and he listened with interest as she spoke of Bethnal Green's history of market gardening and weaving, which had now died out; and how Stepney had grown out of a medieval village built around St Dunstan's church. Both districts had suffered badly in the Blitz: Bethnal Green had lost upward of three thousand houses, whereas a third of Stepney's housing had been destroyed. However, a new beginning was beckoning and much rebuilding had gone on, replacing the former slum dwellings. Eve didn't say as much, but Alan read the message: some good was coming out of the horror of war.

Once they'd finished, Eve helped her mother across to her chair, then took Alan into the kitchen and brewed some tea. On their return, Stella seemed lost in thought and barely acknowledged the cup her daughter placed before her.

"Ah, it's a wicked world, Mr Crawley. Poor Peggy. She was a wild young thing, and I was so often impatient with her. I was thinking of her just then."

Eve reached across and patted her mother's hand. "As you do so often, my dear. But that was long ago, during the war. And the war's over now."

Stella nodded and focused her weary gaze on Alan. Her smile was broad and genuine, and he was rather taken aback.

"Look after my little Eve, won't you, Mr Crawley?"

"Come along, *Maman*." Eve took hold of the old lady's arm. "It's time for bed. You're starting to ramble and before long you'll nod off in that chair and then scold me for waking you up."

"Oh, all right." Stella struggled to her feet. "I can manage, girl, I can manage. Don't *fuss*."

Eve took a while settling her mother. By the time she returned, Alan had taken it upon himself to make more tea and set a steaming cup before her.

She smiled her thanks as she sat down across from him in the armchair Stella had vacated. She shook her head fondly as she cast a glance back at the bedroom door she had just pulled shut. "As you can see, Alan, my mother's quite a handful. She's beginning to lose the thread, I'm afraid. But she will keep wittering on about the past as if it were yesterday. And it's the war. Always the war."

"Who was Peggy?" Alan asked. "Some relation?"

"A barmaid at the pub. I knew her briefly. Poor *Maman*. She had the knack of choosing the most unsuitable people."

"Like Sam Perkins?"

"Sam?" Eve stared at him blankly, before it dawned on her that he was referring to the bearded man who'd met her at Mile End station. "Oh, Sam. Well, no, he was one of her better choices, I'd say. It's only been in the past few years that he's fallen on hard times."

Alan could tell that Sam was a subject she didn't want to discuss, so he changed tack.

"Eve, you mentioned Mr Guilfoyle earlier. He was here?"

She laughed, genuinely amused. Any tension there might have been had evaporated. "Why, yes. Yesterday morning I had to pick up some paperwork for college. He stopped off here while I ran in to collect it. Then he took me all the way back to Regent Street, despite having collared both barrels from *Maman*, who for some reason saw him as the embodiment of evil. Quite the opposite in my opinion: he's the perfect gentleman."

"And does that mean I'm not?"

"Alan, I do believe you're jealous."

"Well, I'm trying not to hate him. I'd find that rather hard to do."

"Anyway, the poor man got more than he bargained for here. I bet he wishes he'd never got out of the car for a cigarette. But he took it in good part. I told him she was mad." They both laughed, and Eve reached over and took his hand. "And yes, Alan *Crawley*, you are a perfect gentleman, even if you do have a habit of spying on defenceless women."

"Because I care."

"I know. And I'm grateful." Her expression grew serious. "So now, my dear, at last and without risk of interruption, you can tell me what brings you here. And how, pray, am I in *danger*?"

Alan settled back in his chair and gave her an account of the incident at the cottage the previous evening.

"And he even has the brass neck to admit it! An assignation with Madge Ventnor. Tea and sympathy, perhaps? She's an attractive woman."

He squeezed her hand. "There are better-looking women. And besides, I didn't think you'd placed me in the category of Great Seducer."

"I hadn't and don't. So there."

"Thanks." Alan continued with his story. He mentioned that Madge was concerned over Tony's dalliance with Tania Bredon.

"The point I'm trying to make is that Madge was wearing a blue cardigan similar to one of yours. As I came down the lane, I glimpsed her from the back and mistook her for you.

"Fortunately the shot missed us both. I think I succeeded in convincing Madge that it was some youth larking around with an air rifle. But once she'd gone, I hunted around and found the spent cartridge. It came from a shotgun similar to those we used at the pigeon shoot. And if you recall, Guilfoyle told us one had gone missing."

Alan looked her squarely in the eyes, his face grim. "Eve, I think you were the intended victim. I ask again: who wants you dead?"

She pulled her hand away and, with gaze cast down, sat in silence for a while. Finally she appeared to reach a decision, got up and walked over to the sideboard. When she returned, she was carrying two glasses of brandy. She handed him one, then resumed her seat and stared into her glass as silence set in again, following the long, echoing passageway back down the years.

* * *

The train for Maillerons was running late, and so crowded that Yvette was lucky to get on it. She would have much preferred to remain standing wedged in the corridor as it puffed and heaved its way out of Calombes station.

But the young German captain, resplendent in neatly-pressed uniform and highly-polished jackboots, was eager to impress a pretty girl. He insisted loudly that she take his seat and stood over her for the rest of the grinding journey, spewing out compliments in garbled French. The rest of the carriage, a mixture of village women and elderly men, remained sullenly unimpressed, and Yvette equally so.

She hoped he might let her go her way once they reached Maillerons. But the captain decided it was his destination too, and as it was almost lunch-time might the pretty *Fräulein* care to join him at the Hotel Des Roches? It was couched as a question, but she knew she had no choice. She tried to excuse herself: she was meeting her elderly uncle, and he would be anxious if she were late. The captain shrugged and smiled winningly: he was sure her uncle would understand.

Already she was late for her meeting with Fréderic: he would be glancing at his watch and worrying. The captain ushered her to a table and snapped his fingers self-importantly. A waiter scurried over, and they were quickly served drinks, champagne for them both, while the captain perused the menu. He ordered for her as well, continuing to chat up and leer at her in between times.

Yvette tried to appear relaxed. They were a long way from the door, so there was no point in trying to make a run for it. As soon as the captain poured himself a second glass, she pleaded a need for the ladies' room. He nodded his gracious permission, stood, bowed and clicked his heels. She took care to leave her shopping basket beside her chair to reassure him that she'd be back. After all, there was nothing in it. But she took her handbag with her.

The window in the ladies' room was high up and narrow. Neither proved an obstacle to Yvette. She dropped softly into the alley at the side of the hotel and made her way to the comparative safety of the main street. She hoped fervently that the gallant captain would choke on his lunch. Perhaps he'd eat hers as well and make a complete job of it.

It was a kilometre or so to Fréderic's lodging. Yvette walked briskly through the maze of side streets and turned into the avenue where he lived, expecting to see him at the gate, gazing anxiously about for some sign of her. Time was always of the essence for Fréderic: always the enemy, as it was for them all.

But he wasn't there. Halfway down the avenue, a crowd had gathered around one of the houses, and across the road were parked two German staff cars.

Her heart sank. She didn't need to go any nearer to identify the house or know why they were there. *Alert, Yvette: there is always danger.* She crept forward to the fringes of the crowd.

Two German soldiers guarded the doorway, guns at the ready to keep the onlookers at a distance and discourage any rescue attempt. She watched horrified as a Gestapo officer came striding out, impatiently shooing people aside to make a pathway to the cars.

Two men followed behind, both immense and forbidding in full-length leather coats, hats pulled down over their eyes. They towered over the man who walked between them, wiry and clean-shaven in a thick woollen jumper and beret, who, despite what the future might hold, carried himself with an air almost of nonchalance:

Fréderic. And yet Yvette, who'd known him for only a few months, knew he'd be keyed up inside, always planning ahead, seeking an opportunity to escape and quietly resolved to tell them nothing.

Behind him, two more soldiers escorted an elderly couple, the man proud, upright, his arm around the woman's shoulder as she stumbled along, weeping.

Fréderic paused at the car, waiting as one of his escorts clambered in ahead of him. He looked round casually, and Yvette knew he'd seen her. His mouth twitched in the parody of a smile, but his eyes stared right through her.

She watched dumb-struck as the other man bundled him into the back seat and the old couple were loaded into the car behind. Then both vehicles pulled away, horns blaring imperiously, scattering people to the safety of the pavements.

Yvette turned and hurried back to the station, praying with every step that she would not encounter the gallant captain. She clutched the crucifix round her neck and thanked God for her uneventful arrival there, as well as the timely warning that Fréderic had been taken; and she prayed too that he would be delivered safely out of the hands of his inquisitors.

She returned to the farm, where she rousted old Gaston from the hen-house. "Fetch Marius immediately. Fernon and Armand too. Something terrible has happened. Now. Quickly. *Go!*"

She rushed inside and barred the door. As she climbed the stairs, she heard the farmer's ancient van sputter into life and rattle off down the track.

Yvette pulled open the trap door above her bed and scrambled up into the loft. Crouching in a corner there, she brought out her wireless set and made contact with London.

She was back downstairs, seated at the kitchen table by the time they arrived. She didn't bother with greetings, just pointed them to seats. They obeyed, faces pinched and tense. She nodded to Gaston, and he returned to the farmyard to keep watch, closing up the door behind him.

"Frédéric has been arrested."

"Mon Dieu!" The exclamation came from Armand, while Fernon swore savagely and thumped the table.

Marius remained silent. He was watching Yvette closely, understanding what she was about to say. Did he fear it too, then, just as she did? Yes, she was sure that was the case. But, as he himself would say, this was war, they were caught up in the middle of it and had to do what was practical.

"I've radioed London," Yvette went on. "Frédéric was in touch with them late last night. He feared that the circuit had been infiltrated and intended passing the message on to me today." Her gaze locked with that of Marius. Did he look downcast? It was always so difficult to know what he was thinking. Not like herself: fighting to hold back tears, vowing that she would *not* weaken in front of them, above all Fernon.

"I've been called back to England. They're sending a plane tomorrow night. The usual time at the new rendezvous the four of us agreed upon, behind the woods above Calombes. Antoine is to travel with me. Until then we are urged to exercise extreme caution."

She felt her resolve crumbling, turned it into rage. She kicked back her chair, upending it, and beat her fists on the table. All three men leapt up in alarm.

"But no! Damn them all! Antoine will go alone. I'm staying here. I won't go back, *won't*, d'you hear? This is where I belong."

Marius was by her side, as Armand righted the chair. They lowered her gently on to it, and she felt the pressure of Marius' strong hands on her shoulders.

"You must go, *petite*." His words were softly spoken, but she was alert to his command. "London orders it. So too do I."

She wriggled in his grip, prepared to rant and rave, but was forestalled by, of all people, grumpy, lecherous old Fernon. He stood before her, and she saw in him what she'd never noticed before, something noble and honest, and his simple words went not only to her heart, but revived her sense of duty.

"When I knew they would send us a young girl, I thought, Pah! she will be no good, she will fly into tears at the smallest upset. But you, little Yvette, are the best and bravest of us all. Go back and continue to fight. You have so much to give."

She gave way to her tears. She stood and embraced the rough old soldier, saw what she suspected might be a tear even in his bloodshot eyes. She embraced Marius and Armand too, and as Marius sat them down around the table, she was enlivened by the old spark of daring in his demeanour, the mark of the fighter who would never give in, who would never give less than his all for his compatriots and country.

"Tomorrow night," he said crisply. "*Mes amis,* we must make a plan so that the plane will get safely away. Now, tell me what you think of this. There is a bridge over the Loire near Meniers which bears the main railway line to the coast. Tomorrow, ten minutes before the plane is due to land, we shall sabotage it and create such a diversion that every Boche pig in the vicinity will be sent there."

"I know the bridge," Armand said, frowning. "We've tried before, but it's been well guarded. And there is besides a German garrison at Meniers. *Patron,* do you not think -?"

Marius held up a hand and grinned. "And ten kilometres further north, there is a bridge at Marronvert. What if, *mon ami,* our friend Bosquet were to learn that *this* was the bridge we intended to attack?"

Armand caught on. "Perhaps I should pass on that information this evening, *patron.* After one's fourth or fifth *pastis,* the tongue can find itself a little loose."

Fernon laughed croakily. "And with his big ears, friend Bosquet will no doubt hear and, dutiful soul that he is, pass the message on. We can also be sure," he growled, "that the next night I will pay a visit to the bar after it has closed and slit the slimy bastard's throat."

Marius smiled grimly. "Have no fear, *mon vieux.* The Gestapo will surely reward him: let's leave him to their tender mercies. Armand, you will make sure Antoine is ready to leave tomorrow night. The mission will exhaust our cache of explosives, but in any case, with Fréderic captured, we must find ourselves another base. It is time we allowed old Gaston to see out his days on his farm in peace."

14

Yvette scarcely slept that night, and the day which followed dragged by listlessly. Waiting, waiting: could they do nothing except wait? And all the time she was hoping fervently – praying – that London would contact her with the news that the mission had been aborted. But the news never came.

The night was warm and clear. She'd shed tears again, such hateful tears, as she'd said her goodbyes to Marius, Fernon and the rest. "Go with God, my dear girl," old Gaston had croaked as she'd hugged him farewell. He'd driven them in his rickety van to the top of a lane north of Calombes, she and Ventnor. Here they met two of Marius' band: Pierre, who would take up position at the far edge of the field and signal for the plane to land, and Anselme, who'd keep watch on the road. Both men and Yvette carried sten guns.

She wondered where Marius and the others must be now: they were on her mind the whole time, pushing away thoughts and fears for her own safety. They'd be lurking in the undergrowth near the railway line, checking on guard positions, quietly and ruthlessly homing in on their target. She glanced at her watch. The plane was scheduled to land in the next half-hour. Another twenty minutes, and she'd hear the first barrage of explosives from the bridge ten kilometres away.

Yvette waited with Ventnor in the cover of some trees on the edge of the field, listening for the distant throb of the plane's engine. He was smoking a cigarette, offered her the packet.

She waved it away. "I don't know how you manage to stay so calm."

"Calm?" He laughed drily, blowing smoke rings and watching them fritter away into the gloom. "Don't you believe it. I'm a bag of nerves. Can't wait to be on that plane. Dear God, what wouldn't I give to be on it now, and then to touch down and feel the delicious thump of my feet on blessed old English turf. No, Yvette. If anyone's brave, my dear, it's you. They've all remarked on it. How long were you with them to win over so many stubborn Gallic hearts?"

"Just about six months."

"It might have been six years. You undertake everything with the efficiency of a woman twice your age."

"You're very kind, *m'sieu.*"

"Not at all – *mademoiselle.*"

Ventnor smoked in silence for a few minutes, then flung the remains of the cigarette to the ground and mashed it beneath his foot. He turned towards her and spoke. There was a catch in his voice, and in the dimness she saw him standing there awkwardly and with an uncertainty she'd never imagined possible.

"Yvette?"

"Yes?"

"When we're back in England, might we -? I mean, can we stay in touch?"

"I expect to return to France almost immediately, *m'sieu.* And your Air Force will no doubt have much need of you. The war is far from over."

"Oh, Yvette – if that is your name. By the way, what *is* your real name?"

"I am known as Yvette, *m'sieu -*."

"Oh, *m'sieu. m'sieu.* Damn it all, girl. Why must you be so detached, always so confoundedly *on duty*?"

She made to answer, but he forestalled her by stepping boldly forward and crushing her in a violent embrace. She fought with increasing desperation to free herself but was powerless, detesting the brutal, whiskery touch of him, his breath reeking of cigarettes and cognac, his manhood hard and urgent against her stomach.

The plane saved her. They heard it at the same moment, saw the muted flash of Pierre's lamp from the distant edge of the field. Ventnor's grip relaxed, and Yvette burst free, furious as she swung back her arm to smash it into his insolent face. He caught her effortlessly by the wrist. He was grinning hugely; and she hated him.

Only then did she come to her senses, snatching a glance at her watch. *The plane was on time.* And yet Marius had promised to set off the first batch of explosives ten minutes before it was due. There could have been a number of explanations as to why he hadn't done so.

But she *knew*. She flinched as the cold stab of fear pierced her heart: fear for them all but above everything, perhaps, fear for him, he who'd been so good to her.

In the next moment, those debilitating fears were borne out. They heard, from several kilometres away, the deadly, rapid chatter of machine-gun fire.

"Oh, dear God..."

There was a noise behind them in the undergrowth, and Yvette wheeled round, sten gun at the ready. Anselme appeared, looking distraught.

"Yvette – you must see – in the village."

They hurried after him to the other side of the trees. Down on the road, heading out of Calombes towards them, they saw three sets of lights, heard the hungry grumbling of engines. Troop carriers. Far beyond the village, the machine guns continued to fire.

"Yvette, the plane's touching down." Ventnor's voice was harsh and grating in its urgency. "We must go."

He grabbed her arm and dragged her back to the field. By now the plane was taxiing across the turf, following Pierre's directions.

With a gigantic effort, she wriggled free. "No. You must go. I shall stay. Anselme, fetch Pierre."

"But Yvette -?" Anselme's young face was a mask of indecision.

She backed towards him, her gun levelled at Ventnor's chest. "I am staying here to fight. This is where I belong." *In my country, with my compatriots, my children...*

"You stupid bitch." Ventnor's face was dark with rage. "They've been ambushed, betrayed − can't you get that into your thick head? You're finished here. Marius told − ordered − you to go. It's all up with him, and you can't let him down now. You must fight on − but not here, not now."

He signalled to Anselme behind her. She might have known the young man wouldn't heed it, too confused to budge. It was a blind. She dropped her guard, and Ventnor moved with unbelievable speed, knocking the gun from her grasp and in the same moment hoisting her up over his shoulder.

Pierre was running towards them, frantically waving his arms. "*M'sieu* − Yvette − the plane − you must hurry!"

"Anselme, Pierre − get out while you can," Ventnor barked. The two men turned and ran towards the far end of the field. Already they could hear the troop carriers thundering towards them through the lanes below.

Halfway to the plane, Yvette, kicking and lashing out with her little fists, caught Ventnor such a blow on the side of the head that he stumbled and dropped her. As she scrambled madly to her feet, she saw the door of the plane slide open. She began to run away from it, blinded by tears, her heart close to bursting.

But Ventnor was behind her. He grabbed her shoulder and swung her round. Turning, she slung a fist at his face, caught off balance as it met empty air.

Something boomed out of the darkness towards her, clattered her jaw. She scarcely had time for the pain to register as she found herself collapsing into an onrushing darkness. Before it became complete, she had a sense of strong arms lifting her.

* * *

Alan watched as Eve sipped her brandy. Her thoughts were years away, and she was staring at a point far beyond him.

"The next I knew we were airborne, heading back across the channel. My jaw was throbbing from where he'd hit me. But now he held me tightly, protectively. He told me we'd had a narrow squeak – his exact words. The troops had reached the screen of trees and had started firing at the plane as it took to the air. The only consolation was that Anselme and Pierre got away."

"And Marius, Fernon and the others?" Alan asked.

"I asked that question. Tony simply shook his head. My God, I was angry, although how he could have prevented it I just don't know. But he was there with me, surviving, and I blamed him. I pummelled him with my fists, screamed at him. He apologised until he was close to tears himself. I'd wanted – even then I'd wanted – for him to let me go, let me sacrifice myself because I belonged with them.

"But what Tony did was right. He saved my life, something I was too twisted up to appreciate at the time. And do you know, strangely, I don't think I've ever properly forgiven him.

"At the time, I certainly didn't thank him. When we landed, I just walked away. He called after me, but I didn't look back; would have caught up with me, I think, but Captain Hesketh-Wain was there to meet me and took me down to Wanborough Manor. There they debriefed me, and all I could say – say? no – *demand* was that I should be sent back to France without delay. Oh, Alan, I screamed at that poor, patient man until I was blue in the face, and then cursed myself – oh, my language was foul – when I broke down in tears again. His secretary bore me away and poured gallons of sweet tea into me, until finally I calmed down, apologised to them all and collapsed into a deep, troubled sleep. I did return to France, but only when the war was over."

"But you stayed in touch with Tony Ventnor?"

"No – I certainly didn't." She spoke with asperity, stung by the suggestion, then shook her head and smiled wanly. "I didn't see him again for years. He kept trying to make contact, but I didn't want to have anything to do with him. Tony's reputation went before him. And there was something which he'd conveniently forgotten to mention when he asked if we could 'stay in touch'. He was already married.

"Of course, it was inevitable that we'd run into one another again, although it wasn't until quite recently. He must have learned from someone that I was back in London, because I got the impression he'd been scouring the city for me. Fortunately on this occasion Madge was with him. I liked her right away, but I think she believes

Tony and I have a history. If I told her we haven't, I doubt if she'd believe me. But it was through Madge that I met you. I'm grateful for that." She reached across and squeezed his hand.

He allowed a diplomatic pause before asking his question. "So what happened to Marius' group?"

She sighed. "It was wiped out that evening at the bridge. Marius, Fernon, Armand, little Gaspard. The others, some of whom were no more than boys. They all died. When I went back after the war, there were so few faces I recognised in the village. I found only distrust and sadness."

"Then what you're saying is that Emsley -?"

"Was innocent. Yes. Someone else betrayed us."

"Bosquet?"

"Almost certainly Bosquet passed the message on. He was shot at the end of the war along with many other collaborators. However, I've always suspected he wasn't alone, because the whole of Fréderic's circuit was compromised. Having said that, it had to be someone close to us who passed on the information in the first place. Maybe it was nothing more than a slip of the tongue: I doubt if we'll ever know. But the damage was done."

Alan was struggling to get to grips with all that she'd said. "Then why does someone want *you* dead? Who's left?"

"People from Calombes. One or two from the group who didn't accompany Marius to the bridge. Old Gaston's long dead. But Anselme survived, as did Fernon's brother, Gérard. I didn't like him, nor he me. Rumour may have got around that I betrayed them, simply because I was one of the few left. I went back to the village after the war and met with animosity, mainly because I'd got out alive.

London may have recalled me, but some people would have seen it as running away. But I can assure you, Alan: I loved them. I would never have betrayed them."

He was immediately touched by the simple honesty of her words. She seemed glad of the comfort he offered: surely she knew that he would stand by her, come what may?

"Eve, I think we should go to the police with this. I firmly believe that you're in danger."

She shook her head, and in her face, her whole attitude, he glimpsed courage, sensed that vein of steel. She'd been a plucky fighter; and old habits died hard.

"No, my dear. The police can do nothing with our suppositions. If I'm in danger, there's one sure way to bring our friend into the open. This is no time for hiding away: the sacrificial goat must be tethered in plain sight. Tomorrow I'll arrange a replacement at the college and get leave of absence for a few days. Go home now. I'll meet you at the shop tomorrow afternoon – that is, if you don't mind putting up with me for a while?"

"And what do you think will be my answer to that?"

He pulled her towards him, and they kissed. As her body pressed into his, he realised with satisfaction that this was their most intimate contact so far. There was no way she could mistake his yearning for her, and Alan wondered afterwards where it might have led had they not been interrupted by the plaintive cry of "Eve! Eve! Where are you, girl? Come quickly."

Alan released her: she looked so tired, and he shared her disappointment.

Eve smiled dolefully. "Reality beckons. A safe journey, dear Alan. Until tomorrow."

"Darling Eve, I -?"

"Tomorrow." She took his hand and led him to the door, opened it, stood on tiptoe and planted a kiss on his forehead, waved him goodbye.

As she closed the door, her mother had started to call out for her again.

15

In the excitement of his mercy dash to London, Alan had forgotten about the inquest on Rennie, scheduled for ten o'clock the following morning at the Memorial Hall. It took Ariadne Gray to remind him of it, and he hurried down the street to arrive just as proceedings began.

Everyone from the ill-fated shooting party was present with the addition of Jane Carbury, now liberated from her migraine and in attendance purely to chaperon Gerald, whose plans had most likely involved sitting beside and providing a consoling shoulder for Gussie Prendergast.

Gussie, statuesque in a tasteful grey two-piece, her jet-black hair newly permed, gave evidence in a clear, resolute voice. She had gone into the glade for a cigarette, seen the body and called Mr Carbury over. The coroner sympathised with her over the shock she'd suffered, and Gussie smiled bravely, no doubt tugging at a number of male heart-strings, before resuming her seat. The look Jane Carbury directed at her could well have resulted in a second inquest.

Kelvin Guilfoyle was also called. A commanding figure in the witness box, he informed the court that Rennie had visited Durleyford Hall the previous week, claiming firstly that he'd served under Guilfoyle during the war and secondly that he'd attended the same school as the MP. Guilfoyle assured the court that Rennie had been mistaken on both counts. His own feeling was that the man had been down on his luck and had called simply to cadge money. Wanting the man gone, as he'd had guests present at the time, he'd sent him away with a five-pound note. "Most generous, Mr Guilfoyle," the coroner drooled.

The local police inspector bore out what the MP had said. Stanley Rennie had had a succession of jobs, mainly in the East End of London, and had been sacked on at least two occasions for dishonesty. The past year had seen him set up as a private detective in a dingy office in Wapping. From an examination of his records, the business had been far from successful. Added to that, Rennie owed money to a number of local traders.

The coroner soon drew the proceedings to a close, recording a verdict of 'suicide whilst of unsound mind'.

"The only conclusion he could have drawn," Guilfoyle said, as he shared a drink at the Coach & Horses with Alan, Tony, Madge and the Prendergasts after the inquest.

But Alan wondered if it should have been that straightforward. He hadn't been called to give evidence himself, because there'd been nothing he could add beyond what had already been said. Rennie was dead, yet Alan didn't think that Rennie had finished with them. He accepted that Eve hadn't known him. But the man had seemed to know about her. He wondered if Rennie had been silenced; and if so, by whom? It could only have been the anonymous person who spelt danger for Eve.

On his return to the shop, Miss Gray remarked that Alan seemed preoccupied. "No doubt because of the inquest? It must all have been quite distressing?"

If she wanted chapter and verse, Alan thought, she'd have to make do with the report in the *Durleyford Advertiser* at the end of the week. He smiled privately, about to conjure up a juicier carrot for her to gnaw on.

"One of those things that has to be endured, Ariadne," he replied easily. "No, my friend Miss Ransom is coming down for a few days. She's been having rather a difficult time with her elderly mother. I'm just hoping that she's managed to get away on time."

"Ah!" Ariadne's face burst into a sweet smile. "Well, I do hope the break will do her good."

Alan bent his head to his paperwork. He knew exactly what was going through her mind. Word had the habit of spreading like plague in a small community such as Durleyford, and he was sure that Ariadne's sandwich lunch in the churchyard would also embrace the passing-on of this precious information to other votaries of local gossip.

But, as they'd agreed, Eve wasn't coming to Durleyford to hide away. She would be set out in plain sight, and because of that word had to travel far and wide.

They'd also agreed that she'd come straight from the station to the shop, before going back to the cottage at the end of the day. He was greatly relieved when she showed up mid-afternoon, complete with suitcase and looking as glad to see him as he was to see her.

He took the case and greeted her with a kiss. As luck would have it, Mrs Paston, the vicar's wife, was in the shop at the time, issuing Ariadne with a directive about the church flowers for that weekend. She looked unimpressed, staring the long distance down her nose at them, while Miss Gray tried to pacify her with an apologetic smile that seemed to say we all know they're sinners, dear, and beyond the reach of grace anyway.

That morning, his preoccupation notwithstanding, Alan had suggested that Ariadne might like a few days' leave. A holiday was overdue, and earlier in the week she'd been dropping subtle hints about visiting her sister in Sidmouth while it was still high summer.

Here was a heaven-sent opportunity. Miss Ransom would be willing to carry out a few light duties in the shop in Miss Gray's absence. Ariadne jumped at the chance; perhaps more so at the tasty titbit that Eve and Alan would be *alone* in the shop over the next few days. What was the world coming to? And in *Durleyford* of all places?

By the end of the afternoon, the fair Ariadne had been safely dispatched, and Eve and Alan started to put out the word that Miss Ransom would be staying in Durleyford for the next four days.

"My poor mother's getting so confused, and I fear it's getting me down. She can't get the last war out of her head – something which happened during the Blitz. Our neighbour Mrs Parrish has been very kind. She lives on the same floor and is more than happy to keep popping in and out. I'm really grateful to her for the chance of this break."

Over the rest of the afternoon and the following morning, the Ventnors, Carburys, Kedwells and Prendergasts were apprised of the news. So too was Mrs Paston, and that was the trump card. Alan was sure she'd inform the world, and wondered about the state of the nation's soul if only she would relay the Christian message with equal zeal.

"You dirty old devil, Cawley." Tony Ventnor nudged him slyly in the ribs. "Promise to let me know if you need a hand."

"Seriously though," Eve confided to Alan that evening, as they ate a simple but leisurely supper in the kitchen. "She's beginning to get me down. Can't get the war out of her head, particularly about Peggy, the barmaid who disappeared. From what little I know about the girl, she probably ran off with a soldier. But my mother is convinced that someone – the soldier, I should imagine – did away with her. She feels guilty because the girl was unreliable, and she was on the point of giving her notice. My opinion is that Peggy simply made off. Apparently she always had a lot of money, and I wonder if it was come by honestly."

During the next two days, Alan found himself firmly back on cloud nine. He felt good having Eve beside him throughout the day, and she adapted effortlessly to the demands of the little shop. There was about her, as he'd remarked before, almost an ethereal quality, and she brought into his humdrum world a freshness, a newness, a vision of how his life could and should be. She brightened the surroundings with her colourful summer frocks, her ready smiles, eagerness to carry out the most mundane tasks and her willingness to listen and help.

But these things didn't blind him to the element of danger, and Eve, he could tell, was ever alert to it. While he remained tense, watchful, checking round the cottage when they arrived back from work, shooting the bolts on the doors before retiring for the night.

Their new togetherness caused the Durleyford tongues to go into overdrive, and Mrs Paston and her ilk had a field day. "They're not married, you know." "Living together in that cottage all the way down that lane, as if no-one can tell what they're up to." "Sent poor Ariadne Gray away so that they could cavort around in the shop. *Such* wickedness." "I'm surprised at Mr Cawley. A minister's son, too. Methodist, though."

Alan chuckled at the thought of the inoffensive Reverend Paston being summoned to rail against the wages of sin in Sunday's sermon. What a pity he and Eve wouldn't be there to hear it.

Sadly there was no foundation to the gossip. Alone in a cottage for several nights with a beautiful woman; but, as

Eve had complimented him before, a gentleman to the last. Alan, shy and awkward in women's company, was never likely to be reckoned an Errol Flynn, nor even a Gerald Carbury.

If he broached the subject – and no matter how tentatively he might do so, she always seemed to know where he was heading – Eve would smile back sympathetically and ask him to be patient with her.

And they would kiss goodnight, longingly on his part. He would leave the matter there and remain downstairs, his mind unfocused on his book, knowing that there was something she couldn't bring herself to share. And because of it, she was unable to commit herself to him.

* * *

Friday morning was busy in the shop, despite or possibly because of the alleged sinful state of the proprietor and his attractive assistant. Eve was becoming well versed in the intricacies of *British Books In Print*, and both sales and orders showed a healthy increase on previous weeks. One of the heaviest purchasers was Gerald Carbury, paying his third visit to the shop in as many days. Alan wondered if the charms of Gussie Prendergast were beginning to wane; although, as seemed likely, Jane had effectively clipped her husband's wings in that direction. Whatever the reason, it was good for business.

Lunch, as on the previous day, consisted of coffee and a sandwich in the office, with the shop door bolted. And in so far as he could, Alan kept a careful eye on customer comings and goings when the shop was open.

The last two evenings he'd cooked them a meal to make up for the frugal nature of the lunch. But on the Friday afternoon, Eve insisted that she would provide and prepare dinner and, as things had quietened down in the shop, set out to walk to the butcher's at the bottom of the High Street.

About ten minutes later, the unmistakable roar of Kelvin Guilfoyle's Bentley drawing up outside the shop announced the MP's arrival. He bounded in, looking smart in a brown hounds' tooth jacket, flannels and cap.

"Afternoon, Cawley." He glanced round the shop. "Miss Ransom out to lunch?"

"Just popped down to the butcher's."

"Ah, well. Give her my regards. This is just a flying visit to invite you both up to the Hall for dinner tomorrow evening. We'll be pretty informal. Mrs Foster's agreed to cook, and young Miss Bredon will serve. I've given Manners the weekend off, by the way. Some elderly aunt's in distress. Although, come to think of it, Manners *is* an elderly aunt. Fullars is back tomorrow, so there'll be we four, the Ventnors, Kedwells and the Pomfret sisters. I'd like us to try some of the Pomerol I discovered in the cellar last weekend. Old Ponsonby must have forgotten about it when he sold me the Hall."

Alan found himself stifling a grin. Guilfoyle was extremely personable but embarrassingly naïve. Not only was he inviting the potential triangle of Tony, Madge and Fullarton, but bringing the winsome Tania Bredon into the mix. He thought of the warning printed on the paper casing of fireworks: *light blue touch-paper and stand well back.*

It wasn't as if this was the first such gaffe. The other week his dinner guests had included Colonel Prendergast and daughters, and Jane and Gerald Carbury. The gossip over that potential conflagration was only just now subsiding.

Even so, Alan accepted gladly for them both.

"I take it Miss Ransom's well?" Guilfoyle inquired.

"Oh yes. Miss Gray's visiting her sister, so Eve's helping out in the shop for a few days. She needs a little time away from home."

"Ah, Mrs Paston mentioned it this morning." He grinned. "At length, as you can imagine. Nearly made old Manners miss his train. What was it? Eve's poor mother confused about something which happened in the war? Well, small wonder. It was a hell of a time for all who lived through it, eh, old man?"

For some reason, an image of Dorothy flashed across Alan's mind, and the old pain returned, fleeting but violent, like a jab in the gut. Guilfoyle was alert to it, and concern showed plainly on his face. He patted Alan gently on the shoulder.

"We all lost someone, didn't we. Cawley? A very dear elder brother in my case. Impossible to forget these things, eh?"

Alan smiled bravely, lifted by the other man's compassion. He was struck by Guilfoyle's goodness: he was a human being first, a politician second. A rare breed.

Guilfoyle glanced at his watch. "Well, I'll hang around to wish Eve good afternoon. Might as well have a browse while I'm here. Any decent biographies arrived this week?"

Before Alan could answer the roar of an engine and manic clashing of gears sounded from outside the shop.

Guilfoyle flung down the book he'd been holding. "My godfathers! That's my ruddy car!" He sprang towards the door, with Alan close behind, and reached the pavement just as the Bentley drew away from the kerb. Guilfoyle leapt for the running-board. He got one foot on it, but the car was picking up speed down the hill, and he tumbled to the ground. Alan blundered past him. He had no hope of catching the car but was trying to get a glimpse of the driver.

All he saw was a figure hunched over the steering wheel, a light raincoat around his shoulders and a black trilby rammed down over his head.

But what he saw beyond the car struck terror into him. The Bentley had begun to hurtle down the High Street and, not twenty-five yards away, walking up the hill with a brown-paper parcel under her arm, came Eve.

This was the moment he'd feared above all. He screamed at the top of his voice: "Eve! Eve, *look out!*"

She looked up to see the huge car bearing down upon her, lurching as it mounted the pavement. From where he stood helplessly, Alan saw her eyes widen in horror, but for a split-second only. Thankfully her reaction was swift and decisive. She flung herself into a doorway, her body thudding into the door, while the parcel slipped from beneath her arm.

And then the Bentley had sped past, gathering yet more speed as it thundered down the hill before turning left at the crossroads at the bottom to disappear from view.

Guilfoyle started to run towards her, then spotted Sergeant Batts emerging from the police house down the street and heading towards him. "Batts!" he called. "Over here, quickly!"

Alan might have been unable to move freely because of his injured leg, but he took advantage of Guilfoyle's pause to burst past him and reach Eve first.

She was cowering by the door, her body pressed tightly against it. She was crossing herself and thanking God for her deliverance. Her eyes were wide and frightened and, as he got to her, she fell into his arms, gasping for breath, gasping out *his* name.

"Eve, my darling, are you all right?"

"I think so." Her mouth twisted in the parody of a smile. "Your warning – just in time. I was miles away. And Alan –." She was looking up at him now, steely resolve in place of her fear. "You were right. I should never have doubted you. There *is* danger."

"Did you get a look at him?" he asked.

She shook her head. "It all happened too quickly. But the car, wasn't it -?"

"Mine, I'm afraid." Guilfoyle had joined them, having issued the scurrying Batts with a catalogue of instructions. "Damned mountebank! I was only in the shop a couple of minutes, and he was into my car and away. Oh, Eve, I'm most awfully sorry. He must have missed you by a whisker. It's my stupid fault for leaving the keys in the ignition. Rank carelessness. I won't make the same mistake again."

People had begun to gather round inquisitively. Mrs Paston – but the woman was everywhere! – Tania Bredon and Mrs Dale from the Corner House, James and Teddy Kedwell, Gerald Carbury and Tom Badger. Alan noticed the Ventnors' old shooting-brake as it pulled up across the road. Madge had got out and was asking one of the bystanders what had happened.

"Let's get you back to the shop," Alan suggested. "We'll lock ourselves in and brew a good, strong cup of tea."

Eve smiled faintly. "Dear Alan. You're so – British."

He laughed in spite of himself. "Eve, my darling. You should know by now that tea is a panacea for every ill."

He threw his arm around her and started to walk her back up the hill. She leaned against him, grateful for his support, while Guilfoyle brought up the rear, stern and angry, and the crowd parted obediently to let them through.

"I'm sorry about the steaks," Eve said.

She indicated the brown paper parcel on the edge of the pavement. It had burst open, and the meat bore the signs of a tyre-mark, while blood had spattered over the kerb. Alan realised that it could so easily have been hers, and he drew her closer to him.

The crowd trailed after them back to the shop, but the determined efforts of Guilfoyle and Sergeant Batts soon dispersed them. Madge Ventnor managed to squeeze past them for long enough to assure herself that Eve was unhurt.

"I'm so glad you're all right, dear. Tony will be shocked when he hears about this."

Sergeant Batts returned to the police station. A patrol car had been sent out to locate the Bentley, and he promised to report back on progress.

Guilfoyle stayed for a cup of tea with Eve and Alan, then went off only to return with a brown-paper parcel containing two fresh steaks. "The least I could do."

Batts arrived too, with good news. The patrol car had discovered the Bentley, abandoned but undamaged, down a track off Forest Lane, a mile or so out of Durleyford. Before long, an eager young constable brought the car back to its grateful owner.

"The work of some young hooligan, I dare say, sir," Batts surmised. "He's well away by now. I've noted the description given by your good self and Mr Cawley. It's not much to go on, I have to admit, but it may lead somewhere."

Before long, Guilfoyle took his leave, full of apology. He looked forward to their company the next evening. "And try to put today's awful episode behind us, eh?"

"He'll try again, of course he will," Eve said, as they walked back to the cottage, having closed up the shop for the afternoon. "I was caught off guard. I should have been ready." *Alert, Yvette:* the warning snapped back at her from down the years. *Always alert.*

To Alan, she seemed fully recovered: resolute, spiky. As she'd pulled her powder compact from her handbag before they left the shop, he'd noticed the tiny black automatic nestling inside.

"Next time, Alan, I shall be ready."

16

The following day, Saturday, saw things return to normal in the shop. One or two people dropped in to commiserate with Eve over what could have been a very nasty accident. Mrs Paston wasn't among them, and Alan believed that was just as well, because she probably saw it as a judgement and would have taken great delight in saying so. As out of touch as he felt with his faith, Alan could picture his father shaking his wise old head and saying that God didn't operate that way.

They closed for lunch earlier than usual, as Eve needed to visit the outfitter's to purchase a suitable frock for the evening invitation to the Hall. Alan made sure to accompany her, standing guard inside the door, where he had a good view of the street, while Eve went into the far reaches of the shop with the proprietor, Mrs Lacey.

Her purchases made, they called in to the Corner House for a quick bite to eat before returning to the shop and a quiet afternoon.

That evening, Eve quite took his breath away. She'd refused to show him her new frock until she had it on. It was predominantly white with an intricate pattern of aquamarine twirls around the waist and hem. She'd pinned up her hair and wore a pale blue necklace at her throat and a white shawl to wrap around her bare shoulders.

"Eve – you look utterly ravishing."

She laughed as she reached the foot of the stairs, thrusting out her hands to repel his advance. "And you look as though you're about to smudge my lipstick."

"I hope to do so later if I'm to be denied the opportunity now."

"We shall see. And by the way, you look very handsome. I shall be proud to enter Durleyford Hall with such a smart gentleman on my arm."

He wondered if she could feel half as proud as he did then. He was looking forward to the evening but at the same time longed for it to be over; for them to return here, mellowed by good food and fine wine. And for him to advance his case once more, asking for her trust, her confidence and above all her love.

They were in good spirits during the drive up to the Hall, the conversation light, both anticipating an entertaining evening. Alan was glad the Kedwells would be there, as Eve seemed to hit it off with Cicely, and he'd always got on well with James, just as he enjoyed the company of Fullarton and Guilfoyle. He guessed that the Ventnors might be the only flies in the ointment.

As they rounded the wide gravel sweep to park over to the far side of the house, Alan took note of the other cars there. He recognised Guilfoyle's Bentley, a low-slung sports car, a Triumph, which he supposed must belong to Fullarton, the Ventnors' shooting-brake and James Kedwell's gleaming Humber.

Remembering the missing rifle and conscious that her assailant might not be above taking a pot-shot at Eve, Alan kept close beside her as they walked across to the house, shielding her with his frame.

Kelvin Guilfoyle was waiting on the steps and greeted them genially. "I feel I should announce you," he laughed. "This manservant business suits me. Manners may find himself down at the Labour Exchange when he gets back."

He closed the huge oak door and ushered them through to the drawing room where the guests had gathered. Piers Fullarton was holding an audience with the Kedwells and the Misses Pomfrets, the two sisters clinging awestruck to his every word; while Madge lolled in a nearby armchair, looking sultry and studiously ignoring her husband.

Tony Ventnor sat alone and a little distance away, pretending to take an interest in the portraits of Guilfoyle ancestry, which were ranged around the walls.

This, for Alan, was something unprecedented, for Tony was always in the thick of things, the life and soul of every gathering. He had the air of someone altogether excluded from the company, seemed lacklustre and subdued.

Alan, with Eve on his arm, made his way over, and Tony perked up a little at the sight of them. Being Tony, the first thing he did was to hug Eve closely and compliment her on her appearance. Then he became voluble. It had been a lovely afternoon, and he'd been to a race meeting at Stratford. He launched into a tale of bets lost and won, and past horses which had badly let him down.

The arrival of Tania Bredon perked him up still further, as she entered with a tray of sherry glasses and brought them round. She looked demure in her dark uniform and lace cap, served them with a brief smile and walked away. Tony's gaze went after her, a trifle forlornly, Alan felt; and then with a garbled excuse the rest of him followed. Alan looked towards Madge: there was an un-Madge-like air of helplessness about her, as she watched her husband trail after the girl. Fullarton was alert to it too, came over and laid a consoling hand on her shoulder. With a wan smile, she placed her hand over his.

As they approached, she eyed Eve with obvious disfavour. Madge was made up to the hilt, bejewelled and glistening in a silver evening gown, contrasting oddly with the simplicity of Eve's attire, worn with such grace and accentuating her natural beauty.

"You should be grateful that your man prefers the older woman, my dear," she remarked acidly.

Alan tensed, wondering how Eve would take this. But to his amazement, her attention seemed to have been elsewhere. She'd been gazing distractedly in the direction Tony Ventnor had gone and was suddenly holding tightly to Alan's hand. Then she released it and turned to face Madge.

As he'd expected, Eve wasn't likely to buckle under Madge's spiteful comment. She smiled sweetly. "He knows where to draw the line, certainly," she replied and moved off to enter into conversation with Cicely Kedwell.

"Sorry, Alan," Madge whispered. Her face was lined with misery.

He smiled back. "No damage done"; and felt gratified by the relief on hers and Fullarton's faces.

Alan talked with Fullarton for a while, mainly about poetry, while Madge listened politely. She said very little, but Alan was pleased to see her approach Eve before they went in to dinner and offer an apology for her vicious remark. "Not quite myself this evening," he heard her say; and was impressed too by Eve's gracious acceptance.

Dinner passed off well, with Mrs Foster's cooking to its usual high standard. Prawn cocktail, sole Véronique, saddle of lamb and lemon soufflé came and went, and for the most part empty plates were borne away after each course. Tania Bredon served and cleared away with brisk efficiency, and Alan noticed that Tony, despite redoubling his efforts, seemed to cut no ice with her.

Somehow the girl seemed preoccupied. Whenever someone addressed her, she responded politely but distantly. Alan, watching her, got the impression that Tania was tired of her chores and of the evening. She simply wanted to be away from there and, by association, away from Tony Ventnor.

He wondered if he was the only one taking note of these things, for around him the conversation was flowing. Alan was seated between Madge and the elder Miss Pomfret, and their talk revolved around books, particularly the classics; and London, where all three had been born and brought up. Guilfoyle seemed most attentive to Eve, who sat on his left, and as always conversed easily with Madge to his right.

James Kedwell was to Eve's left and beside him the younger Miss Pomfret. Tony Ventnor, ever the dinner party wit, raised several tinkling laughs from her, but Alan felt his heart wasn't in it, for his forlorn gaze would latch on to Tania whenever she happened to be in the room. Cicely Kedwell and Fullarton sat to Tony's left, the poet greatly animated as he talked about his own and his contemporaries' work. Cicely was chairwoman of the town's Poetry Circle, so he was assured of an appreciative audience.

At the end of the meal, Guilfoyle strode out to the kitchen and led in Mrs Foster and Tania, who were applauded generously for their efforts. Then the men stood, as the ladies withdrew to the drawing-room, and sat to more conversation as a particularly fine port was passed round.

Before long, however, it was time to leave; the Kedwells first, taking the Misses Pomfrets with them. Alan suspected that for some reason Madge had been waiting for them to go. Once they'd departed, he found out what it was; and for the first time that evening it struck him that the Ventnors had arrived separately.

Tony had wandered off, ostensibly to the lavatory, although Alan felt he was probably seeking out Tania Bredon. He guessed the girl was bent on avoiding him, but Tony had never been good at taking 'no' for an answer. Mrs Foster had long gone, her husband having called to pick her up in his van: it was likely they'd taken Tania with them.

However, Madge made use of the opportunity to take her leave, and Fullarton went with her. "Be in touch," she murmured, as she hugged Alan on her way out. Fullarton shook hands with them, looking a trifle disconcerted as he escorted Madge to his car.

Poor Guilfoyle, however, looked most perplexed of all. Alan tried to cover it by thanking him for the evening, and Eve, alive to the situation, added her thanks, but any further awkwardness was averted as Tony Ventnor blundered back on to the scene.

As was his wont, Tony had been drinking steadily all evening. By this time, Alan remembered from past occasions, he would normally be as drunk as a lord. But this evening there was something different about him. He'd seemed detached all evening, but now he seemed – yes, that was the word – cold. On the outside he appeared the same old affable, mocking Tony. But his eyes were like stones.

He thanked Guilfoyle effusively for his hospitality, although Alan detected a hint of sarcasm which seemed lost on their host; hugged Eve briefly and pumped Alan's arm up and down until he thought it might drop off. He tried to read the message behind those eyes, but saw nothing there nor in his friend's idiotic grin.

"Wonderful evening, wonderful," Tony enthused. Then he turned, fell down the steps and only just prevented himself from falling flat on the gravel, before staggering away into the darkness.

Eve and Alan took leave of their host less flamboyantly, but they hadn't gone five yards when Eve remarked that she was missing her shawl. "I must have left it in the drawing-room."

"Go ahead and wait in the car," Alan said. "I'll fetch it."

Guilfoyle was still on the steps, ready to wave them off. "Forgotten something, Cawley?"

"Eve's shawl. She thinks it may be in the drawing-room."

"Right-o. Let me get it. Be two shakes."

Alan wandered into the hallway, and Guilfoyle was quickly back, flourishing a white shawl.

"That's it. Thank you once again."

"My pleasure. Here, let me walk over with you and say goodnight to -."

They halted abruptly at the top of the steps, frozen in horror at what they saw, unable for a moment to believe what was happening.

The lights from the hallway behind them picked out Alan's Morris Minor across the courtyard. The car was rocking violently on its axles, and Alan made out Eve's white frock in the passenger seat.

Both men hurtled towards the car. As they approached, they saw that Eve was tilted back in her seat, struggling for all she was worth, while behind her a dark figure loomed, arms locked round her throat.

Driven by panic and despite his game leg, Alan made it there first. He yanked open the passenger door and chopped viciously at the offending arms, bringing a squeal of pain from Eve's assailant. The grip slackened, and he tore at the arms until finally he'd freed her.

And then he saw the knife.

In a fair contest, he guessed Eve might have had the strength to wrestle free. But the blade of a carving knife had been thrust through the back of the seat, and she'd had to concentrate all her efforts on arching her back to prevent herself from falling on the point of the knife.

The danger remained, and Alan's next act was to pull Eve forward by the shoulders and drag her from the car.

By this time Guilfoyle was round to the other side, had swung open the driver's door and pushed forward the seat. His voice, though calm, resonated with authority.

"Come out of there this minute. Slowly, and without the knife. Come on, let me see your hands. Do as I say. I'm armed and shan't hesitate to shoot."

Alan knew for a fact that his host had no gun, but the command in his voice was convincing enough. The assailant blundered out of the car and fell at Guilfoyle's feet. Unable to see who it was from where he stood, Alan gathered up Eve, dusted her down and asked if she was all right. She nodded, and he planted a kiss on her forehead. She clung to him as they stumbled round to join Guilfoyle.

Kneeling at his feet, hair ruffled and uniform awry, Tania Bredon glared up at Eve, her eyes blazing.

"You murdering bitch! You deserved to die! Oh, why couldn't I have killed you when I had the chance! Just one clean thrust – that's all it would have taken. Oh, *hell!*"

Eve and Guilfoyle were staring in horror at the girl's angry, twisted features, and only Alan was distracted by the sound of a car door creaking open. He glanced across and glimpsed the white, terrified face of Tony Ventnor as he climbed stealthily into his car. Beyond it, something he'd missed on arrival, stood a motor scooter, parked against the barn wall.

He recalled the afternoon at the cottage, when someone had taken a pot-shot at Madge before escaping on a motor scooter. So that had been Tania, believing she'd been firing at Eve. But how had she obtained the gun? She hadn't been at the Hall on the morning of the shoot.

He didn't have to ponder long over that. If, as seemed likely, the gun in question was the one which had disappeared from the Hall, might it not have been obtained for her by Tony Ventnor?

Guilfoyle helped the girl to her feet. Her stockings had been torn when she'd tumbled to the gravel, and one knee was bleeding. "Let's go inside," Guilfoyle said. He took her by the arm and marched her across the courtyard, up the steps and into the long, echoing ballroom. Here he switched on a light and lowered her into a seat.

Alan followed, helping Eve along. She seemed to be in a state of shock, and he alone heard the throaty growl of the shooting-brake as Tony brought it to life and drove slowly away.

As soon as they were gathered together, Guilfoyle nodded towards the despondent figure of Tania Bredon. "Keep an eye on her, Cawley. I'm going to telephone for the police."

Eve came to life. "No, Mr Guilfoyle. Not the police."

Tania had been sitting slumped in her chair, her gaze on the floor. At the sound of Eve's voice she suddenly resurfaced, her face aflame.

"Why not? It's about time the whole world knew the story, knew you for the cold-blooded murdering bitch you are!"

Guilfoyle resumed control. "That's enough, Miss Bredon. You've come very close to committing cold-blooded murder yourself tonight. We demand an explanation."

The girl's answer was to stare dumbly at Guilfoyle for several seconds, then bury her face in her hands and burst into tears. The MP stood over her, arms folded, and gazed up at the ceiling in exasperation.

Eve slowly unravelled herself from Alan. At the sound of her quiet, reasoning voice, the girl stopped crying but didn't uncover her face.

"Perhaps I should explain," Eve said. She turned to Alan. "You recall a fortnight ago, here at the reception? In that sea of faces, just for the briefest moment, I glimpsed an expression which reminded me of someone I'd known a long time ago. I caught that same expression again tonight, and this time I saw the face clearly, recognised the likeness." She looked down at Tania. "Corporal Brennan was your father, wasn't he? The man I knew as John Emsley?"

Tania snatched her hands away from her face. She was red-eyed, her features blotched and scowling. "Yes. And thanks to you, the father I barely knew. I was five years old when the war ended, hoping and praying that my daddy would come home. And now, finally, I've learned the truth – that you killed him."

"How do you know that?"

"It's enough that I know. You murdered him in cold blood – I know that too. Are you going to deny it?"

"I admit I killed him. But not in cold blood. We had reason – good reason – to believe that he'd passed on information to the Germans which would jeopardise our resistance sub-circuit. We confronted him with this, and he snatched up a gun and attempted to escape. In the struggle which followed, he was about to kill a colleague of mine – an unarmed man. I had no choice but to do what I did."

The girl stared at her in wide-eyed disbelief. "Then you were wrong. My father was no traitor – he wouldn't have passed information to the Germans – he hated them. You're just – damn you, you're making all of this up to get yourself off the hook!"

Eve shook her head sadly, tears in her eyes. "He was so distraught, he didn't deny it. Everything pointed to him, and his actions confirmed our suspicions. We fought – and it was inevitable that someone would die. But you're right – he wasn't a traitor. It was only after his death we learned that it wasn't him. But we were at war, suspicion and betrayal all around us. I'm sorry for what I did. Please believe me when I say that it's something which has always haunted me and always will. An act of war – but not an act carried out in cold blood."

A long silence set in. The girl seemed, if anything, to slump further in her seat, staring blankly at the floor.

"Tania." Eve called her name, but still she didn't look up. "I don't know how you found out about this, but there's something you need to know. There were three of us in the room that night: your father, myself and my colleague who was killed by the Germans a few days later. Please believe me, it's the truth: *no-one else was there.*"

By degrees the girl dragged her gaze up from the floor and turned in her seat towards the other woman. She looked bemused, stared at Eve long and hard, as if unable to take in what she'd just said.

"But – what do you mean?" she stammered at last. "He said – said he'd seen you -? That he was there too..."

"No, my dear." Eve was adamant. "I swear by the Almighty God. Just we three. No-one else. *No-one.*"

She got to her feet and took a step towards the girl. Alan tensed, suddenly fearful that Tania might have another weapon or might renew her assault. But Guilfoyle had been monitoring the situation and motioned for him to remain where he was.

"I'm sorry, Tania," Eve said again. "There's nothing else that I can say. Yes, I killed him. But it happened the way I told you. I'm sorry."

The girl's gaze had locked with Eve's. For several moments they stared at each other, both hesitant, uncertain, anxious. Then Tania rose slowly to her feet. Eve stretched out her arms, and Tania stuttered forward and collapsed into them, sobbing bitterly. Eve sat them both down and held the girl until her grief was played out, while Alan and Guilfoyle stood patiently by.

Finally she emerged from Eve's embrace, her face scarred with weeping. She looked up at Guilfoyle imploringly.

"I – I can't stay in Durleyford. I must leave tonight, go back to my mother in Manchester. She knows nothing of this."

"I'll take you back to your lodgings now," Guilfoyle decided. "I'll come and see you in the morning, and together we'll speak with Mrs Dale, help you to sort something out."

"Tania." It was Eve again. "How did you find out about all this?"

The girl shrugged. "I came across my father's photograph a few months back, made inquiries at RAF Syerston. They put me in touch with several people who knew him. They in turn passed me on to others who might have information."

"Then who told you that he'd been there?"

Tania shook her head. "I can't say."

Eve wasn't going to give it up, and Alan moved alongside her and placed his arm round her shoulders. The look which passed between them was eloquent: they both knew. And Alan was filled with dread.

Eve nodded, and Guilfoyle, reading the script, took the girl by the arm.

"I think we should go, Miss Bredon." He began to lead her away, then glanced back over his shoulder. "I shan't be long," he told them. "Do feel free to wait here. There's brandy in the dining-room."

Alan and Eve exchanged a quick look. "I think it's best if I take Eve home," Alan said.

"As you wish, Cawley. Goodnight to you both. I'll be in touch."

They waited until Guilfoyle and the girl had driven away before they went out to the car and made the short journey back to the cottage in silence. Arrived there, Eve went up to the bathroom, while Alan poured them each a generous nip of brandy.

When she came down, he could see she'd been crying. "Please, Alan, hold me. I need to be held."

He sat her down on the sofa, his arm round her. She turned and clung to him, and he felt the wetness of her tears through his shirt. The time ticked by, minutes which might have been glorious hours, and still she held fast to him, and he felt both strong and helpless at the same time, as he sat gently stroking her face, her hair.

Finally she slept, and he lifted her, carried her upstairs, laid her on the bed and covered her with the eiderdown. He sat beside her and must have dozed, for he was suddenly aware of the church clock striking two.

Eve was sleeping peacefully now, and as Alan went back downstairs to make sure the bolts and windows were secure, a thought came to him.

Tania Bredon had been responsible for the shotgun incident, but it couldn't have been she who'd taken Guilfoyle's car in the High Street on Friday afternoon, because she'd been quickly on the scene with her employer, Mrs Dale.

There was someone else who wanted Eve dead, and even though he could scarcely believe it, he felt sure he knew who it must be.

For it could be no-one else.

17

Guilfoyle phoned early, before Eve was awake. He'd put Tania Bredon on a train to Manchester, having explained to Mrs Dale that she was having to return home for family reasons. Mrs Dale had supplied a reference to enable the girl to find employment elsewhere. "She'll not come back here," Guilfoyle concluded; and Alan wondered if the MP might not have given her a parting gift of money to help her on her way.

He thanked Guilfoyle for all he'd done. The MP had seemed slightly ill-at-ease, as if he was in some way to blame because the incident had happened at the Hall. The two men promised to be in touch before long.

Eve came down in her dressing-gown a little later, looking drawn. She greeted Alan with a kiss and asked for coffee, toast and a cigarette. He knew that, like him, she seldom smoked, although he always kept a packet in the sideboard drawer 'just in case'. This was one such occasion. As she sat at the kitchen table and he prepared her breakfast, Alan told her about Guilfoyle's phone call.

"I think we've seen the last of Tania Bredon," he said.

She was on edge, and he tried to put her at ease. He could tell she was grateful for his reassurance, but she was preoccupied. Neither would broach the subject first: and the name on their lips remained unspoken.

Soon Eve went back upstairs to shower and dress, and on her reappearance in the kitchen, they were startled by a knock at the back door.

Alan opened it to find Madge and Piers Fullarton on the doorstep. "We were out for a stroll," Madge announced cheerfully, "and thought we'd drop by to see you both."

He invited them in, took them through to the living-room, sat them down and made coffee.

"We ran into Gilly earlier," Fullarton said. "He told us about what happened last night after we'd left. I trust you're all right, Miss Ransom?"

Eve smiled bravely. "There's no harm done. I don't want to go into detail, but it was an old grudge dating back from the war – really a misunderstanding. And please – Piers – do call me Eve."

Madge cut in gushingly. "We've come to tell you that Piers has rented a place on the Dorset coast for the remainder of the year, with a view to buying. We're about to go down there now. I've written out our address and telephone number for you: we'd like you both to come and visit before too long."

Eve and Alan exchanged a glance, guessing that something was afoot. Madge was radiant, and Fullarton, grinning fit to burst, had lost his habitual pastiness.

"And as I can see from your faces," Madge swept on, "you know there's more. I walked out on Tony this morning, my dears. One infidelity too many, and he comes over all self-righteous when I announce that I intend to have one of my own."

Alan was delighted; Eve, probably on account of the previous night's skirmish with Madge, more restrained. He embraced Madge and shook Fullarton's hand heartily. "Don't let her bully you, Piers."

"Oh, *Alan*." From Madge.

"I'm afraid she already does," Fullarton admitted, but his demeanour was that of a happy man.

The strident ringing of the telephone interrupted their celebrations. "I'll get it," Eve offered, and made her way through to the tiny hallway.

Alan sat and listened to Madge and Fullarton excitedly sharing their plans for Dorset, conscious all the while of Eve speaking into the phone. He couldn't make out her words but understood that the matter was of some urgency.

She came back into the room looking crestfallen. Her eyes were only for Alan. Her sad eyes: for her, the turmoil continued.

"Alan, I must return home today. Mrs Parrish discovered my mother wandering around on the landing in the early hours, her coat over her nightdress. It's the Peggy saga again – she can't sleep for fretting over it. She's sure Peggy's dead – which she may well be nineteen years on – and she thinks she knows how it happened. Alan, I'm sorry, but I must catch the next train back."

Madge and Fullarton were on their feet, full of condolence. They hoped all would turn out well and looked forward to seeing them both soon. Madge jotted down their details, and the happy pair took their leave.

While they'd been there, Eve had put on a brave face. Now she collapsed into Alan's arms, and he sat her down and held her close while she shed more tears: the trauma of the previous night colliding with today's relentless reality.

Before long, she pulled herself together, went upstairs and packed her suitcase. He got her to the station in time for the midday express.

They kissed as the train screeched into the station.

"Eve, my darling. Be careful."

"I will, my love. And you too. I'll ring later."

He stood on the platform and waved her off. He realised she'd called him 'my love'; and his heart warmed to that. But he knew that danger lurked within striking distance.

Eve telephoned that evening. Between them, she and Mrs Parrish had managed to settle Stella down, and the doctor had prescribed a sleeping draught. As they spoke, her mother was sleeping like a baby.

She went on to thank Alan for the time they'd spent together, for the way he'd looked after her.

"That's how I want it always to be," he said, suddenly emboldened.

"I know." Her voice faltered: it was all she could say. "I know."

He changed tack, essaying cheerfulness, and said he'd ring the following evening.

Alan returned to the shop the next morning. Miss Gray was back, having spent a "truly lovely time" with her sister in Sidmouth. Eve's brief sojourn in the shop had resulted in a spate of orders, notably from Gerald Carbury, and Ariadne busied herself with these and the task of ensuring that the stock was arranged in the *proper* order, tut-tutting audibly on the few occasions when she discovered a title Eve had misplaced.

As the day wore on, Tony Ventnor preyed increasingly on Alan's mind. Tania Bredon had gone, and Tony would take Madge's defection badly.

Alan asked Tom Badger at lunch-time if he'd seen him, but the landlord shook his head. He made inquiries of two or three of his regulars but drew a blank. Perhaps Tony was burying himself in work in an effort to put off the inevitable. But as Tony and work had ever been uneasy companions, it seemed more likely that he'd sought solace in drink.

He called in at the Coach & Horses on his way home. The lads from the factory were in playing darts, but Tony wasn't among them. Alan finished his pint and went back to the cottage, deep in thought.

At some time, he knew, there would have to be a confrontation. For it was Tony's name that he and Eve had left unspoken, the matter of Tony which she'd plainly not wanted to discuss and which Alan had been reluctant to raise. There were questions which needed to be asked, answers which had to be given.

The phone rang as he was finishing supper and still pondering what to do.

"Al?"

"Tony! I was wondering where you'd got to. No-one's seen hide or hair of you all day."

Ventnor chuckled drily. "That would have been difficult. I've not stirred from here. Listen, we need to talk. Can you come round?"

"Tonight?"

"Now would be a good time."

"I'm on my way."

He drove there deep in thought. Bayes Wood was a secluded, rambling Edwardian property which had belonged to Tony's father, a wealthy banker. Tony had inherited it soon after the war and done very little with it. He'd flitted from job to job as the fancy had taken him, but had been left so well off that he didn't need to work.

As he made his way down the track, Alan spotted Tony's shooting-brake. It had been left sprawled across the forecourt, the driver's door hanging open. It gave him some idea what to expect.

He pulled the Morris Minor up alongside, got out and cautiously crept up the steps into the echoing hallway. It had been a fairly dull day, yet there wasn't a light on in the house. To Alan's right, a wide staircase curved away towards the upper floor, while to his left a door stood open, offering a glimpse into the dining-room.

A long mahogany table stretched almost the length of the room. At its far end sat Tony Ventnor, although the light was so dim that Alan could only just pick him out. Lining the walls either side were framed photographs of Tony during his RAF heyday. Alan knew them well, having had them pointed out on several previous occasions. Tonight they seemed like shadows, or like ghosts mingling with the shadows, inconsequential mementoes of a time which seemed so long ago.

Alan felt apprehensive as he crossed the hall and entered the room. Tony looked up and saw him.

"Why, Mr Cawley. Fancy seeing you here. Grab a glass from the sideboard and come and join me."

Alan hesitated. Ventnor looked a mess. He lolled at the table in his shirt sleeves, unkempt, unshaven, his jacket slung over the back of a chair. Before him stood a half-empty bottle of scotch and a glass. An empty bottle rolled around on the floor at the side of the room, while behind him in the corner was propped a shotgun.

The gun worried Alan: it should have had no purpose there. "No thanks, Tony." He fought to keep his tone light. "A bit early for me."

"Suit yourself. You don't mind if I do?"

He didn't wait for Alan's reply before refilling his glass. The hand holding the bottle was unsteady, and Alan wondered if Tony had been drinking all day.

He raised the glass as if it was his first. "Cheerio." But all he took was a swig. Then he set the glass down, looked up at Alan and grinned ruefully.

"I'm in a hell of a state, old pal. I don't know if she might have told you, but Madge has left me. And d'you know what? She's gone and run off with that snivelling ruddy poet, a spineless shit who lost his nerve during the war. I mean, he lost his bloody *nerve.* And there she was, banging on to all and sundry for as long as I can remember about my medals, and what a brave chap I was and how proud she was that I'd done my bit in that bloody war — I mean, I *ask* you! Well, good riddance to the cow. Ungrateful isn't the word, after all I've done for her. Anyway, she's gone for good, and I shan't waste another thought on her."

He picked up his glass again. "C'mon, Al, we're pals, you and I. Let's drink — oh well, to something or other. But above all, let's drink. Here -." He pushed the bottle along the table. "Pitch in."

Alan ignored it. "No thanks, Tony."

"'S up to you. In my humble 'pinion, staying sober never did anyone any good."

"Tony, why do you need the shotgun?"

"Eh?"

"The gun. In the corner there, behind your chair?"

Ventnor flicked it a glance. "Oh, that. Well, why not? The bitch might come back and try to bump me off, so's she inherits this pile. Wouldn't put it past her. That reminds me. Must see old Kedwell this week, change my will. Leave it to a dogs' home or something. No, I need the gun, Al. It's lonely out here. Lonelier still now, and you never know who might walk in. Need to have something to hand in case of – intruders."

Alan didn't like the emphasis on the last word nor the whole brooding atmosphere of the darkening room. He'd been cautious before; now he was on his guard.

"Why did you ask me here tonight, Tony?"

Ventnor shrugged, paused a moment before replying. "Wanted to talk, I suppose. About Madge. Why should she suddenly decide to walk out on me, Al? Why?"

"Because of your involvement with Tania Bredon?"

"*Tania?*" Ventnor spluttered and set down his glass. "That conniving whore? And *involvement?* My dear old pal, whoever – except Madge, of course – reckoned there was any *involvement*? She *used* me, the little tart, and I never saw it coming, not for a minute. Well, she told me the other night, quite bluntly, that it was over. Not, you'll understand, that anything had really begun. She was cold. Al. A blonde icicle in a pretty frock. And I, poor sod, was simply a means to an end." His face crumpled in a private and unpleasant smile. He sipped from his glass, his gaze all the while fixed on Alan's guileless face.

"I called her conniving, didn't I? Well, she was. The little cow would do anything to get what she wanted. But, you know, bad as she was, Tania wasn't the worst I've known. Oh no, not by a long chalk. Because there's one who'd beat her hands down for connivance, for using and rejecting people – men in particular – every day of the week."

Alan shifted position. He guessed what was coming and felt more uncomfortable still. He wanted to be away from there, but knew that this had to be faced; and better now than later.

"Shall I switch a light on, Tony? It's getting dark." He reached across and flicked a switch. Nothing happened.

"Must've fused," Ventnor grunted. "Leave it, Al."

"I can -."

"I said leave it! And sit down, for the love of Mike. You're making me nervous. Oh, before you do, grab yourself a glass and join me in a drink. At least make an effort to be sociable."

"No thanks, Tony." He pulled out a chair halfway down the table, gingerly lowered himself on to it.

Again the shrug. "Suit yourself. But by the time you've heard me out, you might need one." Ventnor leaned an elbow on the table and wagged a lecturing finger at his guest. "Mr Cawley, I have to warn you, because someone should. All that glisters, my dear old pal, is not gold."

Alan opened his mouth to protest, but Ventnor swept on. "Let me finish. I'm going to tell you a story: about a sweet young thing with a heart of pure stone. It was back in the war, you see, and this brave girl had been parachuted in to help a fearless resistance group hamper the Jerries in the push to D-Day. But the group was compromised. *Someone* was passing information to a notorious collaborator, who was passing it on to Jerry.

"And, do you know, because she was so sweet, brave and especially pretty, no-one suspected her. It was easy enough for her, because she had every man fawning over her. And she betrayed them all, even that blinkered idiot Marius, who was always so protective of her.

"She implicated a man called Emsley. We'd escaped together from a train wreck, as I believe I've told you, and were taken in by Marius's group. They promised to get us back to England. Well, she was clever enough to organise a rumpus in which poor Emsley got shot – by her, I hasten to add. And the night we were at the rendezvous with the plane about to land, she nearly scuppered me into the bargain. I had to knock her unconscious and take her with me, otherwise we'd all have been dead meat. Oh, except her, of course. Once the dust had settled, she'd no doubt have been rewarded generously by Herr Kommandant."

Alan's head was spinning as he tried to take all this in, and he covered his eyes with a hand. Alive to his confusion, Ventnor ratcheted his voice up a few notches, driving home nail after wounding nail as Alan fought to think clearly.

He was glad he'd taken no drink, because that would have befuddled him even more. Tony would have preferred it that way: it would have made his task easier.. Three times he'd suggested Alan should join him, and Alan was relieved that he'd refused.

He clung now to a redeeming thought which neither his confusion nor Tony's aggression could chase from his mind. He was thinking of Saturday evening, forty-eight hours before, the assault on Eve by Tania Bredon, and the glimpse he'd had of Tony Ventnor backing away into the shadows, a look of horror on his face as he realised what he'd set in motion. Tony, for all his braying superiority now, frozen in a moment of abject helplessness and guilt, oblivious to the fact that he'd been seen.

Alan removed his hand and stared boldly into the other man's gloating face. He caught a flash of apprehension in Tony's eyes: this wasn't the reaction he'd expected.

Another recollection came to him: Tony greeting Eve with a kiss on her arrival at the Hall that evening: a traitor's kiss. He'd known what he was about, known that Tania Bredon had murder in her heart.

Alan felt rage welling up in him, as he realised how close the woman he loved had come to death that evening. And all through the fault of this man, whom until now he would have called a friend.

He suppressed his rage, forced it down, down, for it must have no place there. He too, now, was flirting with death. He had walked into a trap, and it was only by keeping a clear head that he would be able to extricate himself.

"No, Tony," came his firm response. "You were the traitor, not Eve. She told me about Emsley: how gullible he was, how sullen, how he never fitted in. I suggest that he shared with you everything he'd been told about the false rendezvous, and you passed that information on to Bosquet. In other words, *you* set him up. And when, a few weeks ago, Tania tracked you to Durleyford, you immediately recognised her likeness to her father and latched on to her. She was young and pretty, so everyone thought it was just Tony being Tony.

"She was burning for revenge, and your priority was to get yourself off the hook. So you convinced her that Eve had been the traitor. That could only have come from you, and Eve would never deny that she'd killed Emsley.

"In her innocence, Tania believed you and made an attempt on Eve's life. Or at least she thought so. She shot at Madge in my garden, having mistaken her for Eve. She used a rifle which had gone missing from the pigeon shoot. I'd guess you'd stolen it on her behalf.

"And I suspect that you killed Rennie. He was a private detective of sorts. Did he have something on you? Of course, we don't know who he was working for, but I dare say he was up for a spot of blackmail. What did he have on you, Tony?"

Alan settled back in his chair, wondering what reaction he'd get and expecting Tony to bluster, protesting his innocence.

But he simply stared back, a hand stroking his chin, a quirky half-smile on his face, as if he was surprised by what Alan had just said, and by the very fact that it had come from him.

Ventnor topped up his glass and took another drink. All the while Alan could sense his mind working. Yet when he spoke, he denied nothing.

"I never knew who employed Rennie, but he had to be stopped. He couldn't give two hoots for his client, because he had his own agenda, and I could tell that once he got his claws in he wouldn't let go.

"I told him we'd come to some arrangement, which was just what he wanted to hear. I pretended that he'd unnerved me – said that Madge mustn't know at all costs. You should have seen his eyes light up – he thought he'd got me.

"I asked him to meet me in the woods up at the Hall very early that Saturday morning. Of course, he couldn't resist: this was pay-day with a vengeance. He arrived at the spot we'd arranged and walked right into the noose. A strangled squawk, and that was that. I hung him in a clearing, where either Harris or someone from the shooting party would spot him." He chuckled lewdly. "Gussie, as it happened. Poor old Gerald, bet it spoiled his fun."

Ventnor drank again, staring levelly at Alan over the rim of his glass, serious again.

"And yes, I betrayed them. That is, I passed on the information. Marius was no slouch, and after Emsley had copped it I think he was coming round to suspecting me.

So I couldn't take any chances. But I wasn't the only one passing things on. Eve and I only just got out. Someone must have alerted Jerry to that final rendezvous.

"But anyway we made it. And by the end of the war, I was a Wing Commander, a hero decorated several times over. So how do I match that up with being – as you call it – a traitor? Well, what I did wasn't for Germany. When you analyse it in the cold light of day, you'll understand that I never betrayed my country."

18

"Why did you do it?"

Alan was scarcely able to believe what he was hearing, and incredulity echoed in his gasping words. Ventnor was sitting there smugly, alcohol-fuelled, and admitting to the murder of Rennie, to inciting the murder of Eve Ransom, a woman he'd professed to love, and to the betrayal of a band of brave men who'd been fighting not only for their country, but for his freedom as well as theirs. It was despicable beyond words, but further words were something of which, at that moment, Alan was incapable.

When he'd first arrived in Durleyford, it had been Madge and Tony who'd befriended him, making sure he got to know everyone. There'd been a little wishful match-making on Madge's part, but it had been kindly meant. Alan had come to like and respect them, for they eased him through his first few months in a strange town. He'd been grateful for that, and they'd remained friends ever since.

And now this monstrous revelation. He fought to make sense of it; but he couldn't, because he knew it defied sense. He wanted to summon up rage, an ungovernable rage which could hardly be sated by lashing out and beating this man before him to a pulp. He screamed inwardly at the enormity of Ventnor's crime. His head whirled madly.

But he held back, kept his anger simmering. He held back because he had to; had to remain reasonable, sane, in control. Because he knew that tonight his life depended upon it.

"*Why?*" Ventnor laughed bitterly. "Do I really need to tell you *why*? Are you saying you don't know what it's like to fall deeply and, damn her, hopelessly in love? Eve was all I wanted: nothing else mattered. I *begged* her to return to England with me. London had recalled her, and she was set to disobey, for her principles, for France, for Marius and his band of ragamuffins. Dedicated? I'd call it damned downright irresponsible. There was danger all around. Jerry frequented the village shops and bars, and I know that Bosquet wasn't alone in passing them information. Added to that, Marius was reckless and it was only likely to be a matter of time before he got them all killed.

"I decided that there was no way I was going to leave her. But even then, with Jerry closing in and the whole set-up crashing down around her ears, she wouldn't go. So I knocked her cold and took her by force. Saved her life, and she never forgave me. Once we reached home, she avoided me, did so for years. I searched and searched for her. In fact, it's only in the last year that I succeeded in tracking her down."

"Perhaps she knew." Alan found his voice, was surprised by its coldness.

But Ventnor shook his head adamantly. "It's because she's incapable of giving love in return. She's a woman with a heart of stone."

"And what about Madge?"

"What about her?"

"You were married to Madge before you got shot down in France, before you'd met Eve. She knew that and told me. I'd say, Tony, that it's you who have the heart of stone, for doing all you've done, and for the way you'd have abandoned Madge if Eve hadn't rejected you."

Ventnor looked pained. "I never *loved* Madge. It was a marriage that simply arose out of the war – convenient for us both. And she played me for a fool. She was penniless, you see. And I was pretty well off, particularly once my parents had gone. Oh, she gave herself airs and graces then, and I soon found I was hitched up to a walking gin palace. No, it had no right to have lasted so long. We should have called it quits years ago."

"You led her quite a dance for her pains." The bitterness was with Alan now.

"Do you think she didn't ever play around?" Ventnor snapped back, his eyes flashing. "That she never played the whore, the way she's doing now?"

"And all of a sudden you're the injured party, Tony? Listen to yourself trying hard to justify your actions. You can't convince me. Because none of what you did was for Eve. It was all for you."

Ventnor stared back at him throughout a long silence, his eyes hard, his mouth set grimly. Alan held his stare. He was hard put to do so, but he dared not look away nor drop his guard.

He was more than ever conscious of the gun. He had to remain strong, or else fear and foreboding would overwhelm him, and he would be lost. He knew why the house was in darkness, the gun within Ventnor's reach. *Intruders*, Tony had said; Tony who'd never given a thought to intruders at Bayes Wood in the years Alan had known him. His heart was racing, and he struggled to stay calm.

Ventnor seemed to have sobered up, although how he'd managed that was a mystery to Alan. But now he pushed his glass away and wasn't slumped in his seat.

There was an air of superiority about him, and those cold eyes flickered with a lively amusement born of malice.

"Y'know, Al, it's a mystery to me how you and Eve hit it off so well. I've seen her in action: a gutsy fighter, focused, single-minded. And I look at you and see something totally different. What about your war record? Not exactly glowing, was it? Stuck up there somewhere in Jockland: not what I'd call flirting with danger. But then, your Dorothy did that. She lived and worked in the thick of it, with bombs raining down all around her. She died a heroine, and in my opinion, chum, you let her down. You stood aside and let the girl you loved fight the real war in your place. Where do you keep your medals, Lance Corporal Cawley?"

Alan was choked, unable to speak. Memories of Dorothy caved in upon him, reminders of his guilt. Guilt didn't really come into it: he'd been a serving soldier for practically the duration of the war and had had no say in where he was to be posted. He knew Ventnor's accusations were unjust, the product of a warped and embittered mind; but even so they hurt.

He knew he had to fight back: for Dorothy, for Eve, for himself.

"I met Eve six months ago, Tony. She knows all about my war, and she'd be the first to say we don't all have to be heroes. Besides, the war's over. It ended sixteen years ago.

"That's where you're wrong, old pal," Ventnor sneered. "It's never ended. And I doubt it ever will."

It wasn't only the gun that was on Alan's mind. Bayes Wood was secluded: half-a-mile down a rutted track surrounded by quiet country lanes. Silence set in again, and he took it upon himself to break it, desperately striving to keep his tone light.

"Tony, do you mind if I use the bathroom?"

Suspicion clouded Ventnor's face, as if he'd guessed that Alan knew what he had in mind. "Upstairs," he murmured. "As you know."

"Thanks."

Alan rose laboriously to his feet and pushed back the chair. He doubted the wisdom of it but had no choice than to turn his back on Ventnor. His heart pounded, his legs struggled to bear him up. But there was something in his favour: the lights were out. Whether they'd fused or Tony was bluffing didn't matter: Alan had the advantage of the gathering gloom.

Ventnor's chair scraped back: he too was on his feet. Alan willed himself not to turn his head. He sensed that Ventnor had moved to the corner to pick up the gun and guessed that if he were to confront him now, Ventnor would shoot.

"Are you visiting the bog or what?" Ventnor growled.

"Just going." Alan moved forward, his legs leaden. Necessity spurred him on. Step by slow step he left the dining-room, began to cross the hallway.

"Y'know, Al, I liked you."

Alan tensed. Ventnor's voice sounded far closer than he'd expected. He must have moved the length of the table to stand at its nearest end, in all probability propped against it, given the volume of scotch he'd consumed.

"You were a decent, unassuming bloke, nothing spectacular or loathsome about you. But it was a bad day for us both when I introduced her to you. At one point I even felt I could live with you taking her from me."

"She was never yours, Tony."

"You what? Speak up, you're mumbling."

"I said she was never yours. Madge was yours. You neglected her, and now she's walked away."

"Madge is an ungrateful cow. After everything I did for her." He chuckled long and unpleasantly. "And I should say, Mr Cawley, that you did a lot for her too. A shoulder to cry on, or maybe something more? What was she doing in your garden the other day? And what a pity that cold little bitch couldn't shoot straight."

Alan kept his voice level. "If you're suggesting that Madge and I were carrying on, you can forget it. You have my word of honour on that."

"Honour?" Ventnor uttered the word as if it were entirely new to him, then snorted. "Pah! Straight up the stairs, second on the left, old pal, in case you've forgotten. That's the place for honour."

Alan was certain he'd be shot if he started to climb the stairs. Ventnor was directly behind him, and he could only guess that he was probably five yards away, leaning back against the table because he needed its support. Before him, the wide staircase beckoned, some seven or eight yards distant. To his right, about the same distance away, the front door stood open. He remembered he'd inadvertently left it like that and was glad he had: it might just save his life.

Because if he made a sudden bolt for it, keeping low, he was sure Ventnor would fire high, leaning back as he was. Alan knew there was one way to test that theory, and that he had to act right away: it was the only chance he'd get.

Without further thought he threw himself to the floor, scrabbling across on his hands and knees. Ventnor swore, his words drowned by the colossal boom of the gun. The ceiling above Alan was ripped apart, and plaster rained down upon him. He couldn't let it deter him. The open doorway still seemed miles away, but he continued to blunder towards it.

He expected a second shot, lower, at any moment. None came. And then he was out of the doorway, on the steps and trying desperately to make it to his feet.

Alan fell down the steps, regained his balance and started to run. Darkness was closing in early, and he was glad that the day, unlike so many which had preceded it, had been dull and overcast.

But he'd not gone two steps before a vast shape loomed up before him and he clattered into it, bounced off and sprawled on the gravel at the man's feet.

He struggled to get up. The man was huge. All Alan could make out was a broad, bearded face, and a body swathed in a thick coat from which sprang a pungent, earthy smell. Recognition kicked in: *he knew this man from somewhere.* But there was no time for further thought. He watched helplessly as a massive arm swung back and smashed into him.

The blow lifted Alan off his feet and sent him spinning backwards. He crashed into an immovable object – his car, as things turned out – and his head rang as he made violent contact with it.

From the doorway, a second shot sang away into the night. Alan struggled to his knees, but already his senses were fading. He saw the figure of Ventnor on the steps, realised the huge man was lumbering purposefully towards him. He heard Tony's voice, distant, emasculated, full of fear.

"No! It can't be! Not *you*! Stay back! Don't make me shoot!"

Again the gun boomed, and Alan yelled out. But he was already falling, a long, spiralling descent, through darkness into a further darkness blacker than the hateful night.

* * *

He supposed, as his senses began their slow return, that he might be in heaven. Darkness and silence surrounded him, broken only by the sound of her sweet voice swimming effortlessly around him, breathing life into the pit of death.

But why was *she* there? How had she got there, and how could she have known where he'd gone?

"Oh, my darling Alan. You're safe. Thank God, thank God!"

He was seated on the ground, propped against his car door, and Eve was beside him, her arms enfolding him, her face close to his, showering him with tender kisses.

He reached back deep into the nightmare, retrieving images of Tony, the gun, the huge man who'd swatted him out of his path. He remembered now where he'd seen him: the man who'd accosted Eve, the man he'd followed.

"He saved my life," he stuttered. "That man who met you the other evening at Mile End station. But who is he? And what did he want here? And Eve – why are you here?"

"It was only when I returned home this evening that I learned he'd left. Rennie had been working for him – taking his money for the most part. But there was a communication from Rennie which got delayed. It had only just reached him. And I knew, Alan, *knew* where he'd come. Mr Guilfoyle was at the House. I contacted him, and he brought me here and called the police."

From where he sat, Alan had a view through to the hallway, now ablaze with light. A man lay sprawled across the bottom stair, a shotgun abandoned beside him.

"Eve! Is – is that – Tony?"

"Yes, dear," she whispered. "I'm afraid Tony's dead."

He sat and clung to her. An ambulance came tearing down the track on to the forecourt, its bell ringing frantically, and skidded to a halt. The ambulance men hurried into the house to re-emerge a few minutes later with someone on a stretcher. Guilfoyle strode behind them, grey-faced and authoritative, a uniformed police sergeant beside him.

Eve cried out and rushed over to them. Left to fend alone, Alan hauled himself up by the door handle and hobbled after her.

"There's no hope, I'm afraid, Eve," he heard Guilfoyle say.

Eve was in tears. The man's gigantic hand folded over both of hers, and Alan caught a glimpse of the bearded face he remembered from London, now pale and diminished.

"*Tu me pardonnes, petite?*" the man croaked.

She sobbed her reply. "*Oui. Avec tout mon coeur.*"

His gaze limped past Eve and lit upon Alan. "Look after her," he murmured.

The men loaded their burden into the ambulance, got in and drove furiously away.

Eve, watching, lurched forward as if to follow. But Alan, stepping past Guilfoyle, came up behind and placed firm but tender hands upon her shoulders.

"Who *is* he?" he asked gently. But he already sensed what her answer might be.

She turned her tear-ravaged face towards him. It was pained and sad, but not desolate, for he glimpsed there some undercurrent of relief, some stray hint of absolution.

"His name was Marius Delattre." Eve's voice was scarcely above a whisper. "He was my husband."

19

With the war over, she became Eve Ransom again. But to them she would always remain Yvette.

She returned to Calombes in March 1946 and was shocked by what she found. The only young men in the village had been those who'd not been old enough to fight; schoolboys then, but adolescents now with sad, grey faces. And for the most part the women recognised and shunned her.

She found Anselme helping in his mother's bakery. He at least made her welcome, but the last year of the war had not been kind to him. Still in his teens, he was a young man grown old, his once lively face pale and haunted. He and Pierre had fled the village after that terrible night, and the two of them had joined a group of resistance fighters in the Limoges area.

"They seem to blame me," Eve lamented. These had been the people among whom she'd lived and worked, the people for whom she'd fought the war, her countrymen and women whom she'd striven to help liberate. She thought her heart would break; and yet she could understand why they felt that way.

"They blame me too," Anselme said with a shrug, as he offered her bread and chocolate and drew heavily on a cigarette. "They blame us both because we lived, because we didn't have the guts or grace to die alongside the others."

"So were they all killed, Anselme. *All?* Yes, but I feared it must be so when I heard the firing. It went on so long — seemed so final."

"There is no-one left, Yvette. Marius and all his brave companions perished that night. Only Pierre and I survived, and he bought it a few months later." He paused, gazing at her oddly, then laughed mirthlessly. "Oh, but it must be nothing. Just that there was a rumour..."

"What?" She leapt upon his hesitation, frantic for some small scrap of redemption. "Anselme, please — tell me."

"You remember old Francine, always in the corner of the bar knocking back her *cassis*?" He grinned. "Always turning it into a cognac whenever anyone offered to stand her another?"

"The farrier's widow? But didn't everyone reckon she was -?"

"Mad?" Again the laugh. "Oh, you bet. Completely off her rocker. That's why no-one paid too much attention to it. But according to my mother, Francine always maintained that one man had survived the ambush and made his way back to Calombes. He was badly hurt, close to death, and she tended him for weeks, kept him hidden in her cellar. Once his wounds had healed, he was taken away on a wagon at dead of night, far away to safety. Francine would never say who took him; and that's partly why she wasn't believed."

"But do you know who he was?" Her heart pounded with expectation. "Or who took him?"

Anselme shook his head gravely. "You knew old Francine: full of stories, and seldom a grain of truth in any of them. My mother hasn't found a soul who saw hide or hair of this man. Everyone scoffed at Francine whenever she mentioned it."

"I must talk to her. Please – where can I find her?"

Anselme's young face was downcast. "You will find her in the churchyard, Yvette. A heart attack before Christmas. I'm sorry."

"But is there not still Gaston? I seem to remember that Francine was his cousin? She might have confided something to him."

"Alas, he suffered a stroke back in the autumn and has been unable to speak since. He's with his daughter in Noiret, but he scarcely knows her let alone anyone else, poor old fellow."

"Then there is no-one left." She pushed back her chair and got wearily to her feet. "Thank you, Anselme. I pray that God will always be with you."

"And with you, Yvette."

It was almost a ghost village, like so many once the war was over. Shorn of its menfolk, the women disgruntled, impoverished, embittered, the children slipping fatherless into turbulent adolescence. Marius, Fernon, Armand, Gaspard, Pierre and so many others: Calombes had been drained of its life's blood.

She left there with a heavy heart; and never went back.

* * *

Eve returned to London, to a city slowly getting back on its feet after the ravages of war, its scars and open wounds all too apparent. The Three Bells had survived, although much of the area around it had not been so fortunate. Her mother was short-handed in the pub, for the dependable Sam Perkins had moved across London with his family. So she pitched in and helped Stella for a while, until she was in a position to employ new and reliable bar staff. And before long she'd moved into teaching, running evening classes in French at a local college. Eve's life was beginning to settle down, but her heart had been torn by what had happened in Calombes, and their faces were always before her.

Two years later, London hosted the Olympic Games, and Eve, who'd been a keen athlete during her schooldays, went along to Wembley Stadium to watch some of the track events. As she came away one evening, she ran into George Bazeley.

Bazeley had been the man she'd replaced as wireless operator at Gaston's farm. He'd been wounded in a skirmish and had lost the use of an arm, which had resulted in his having to be flown back to England. Eve had met him while undergoing training at Wanborough Manor, and he'd been so impressed with her ability that he'd recommended her for service in the field.

A good-natured Lancastrian, Bazeley had travelled down to London with his wife and small son to see some of the Games. He'd heard that Eve had acquitted herself well and invited her to join the family for tea so that they could talk about old times and exchange news of former colleagues. Many they'd known and trained with hadn't made it back. Some had been traced to various concentration camps, where the trail had gone cold. But Eve was lifted to learn that their circuit organiser Jimmy Petworth, alias Fréderic, had survived the rigours of Ravensbrück and was back in England trying to pick up the threads of his life again.

And there was more.

Bazeley had heard of Eve's timely escape from France and saddened to hear what had befallen the resistance group.

"We were betrayed," she told him. "Marius had planned the attack on the bridge at Meniers to create a diversion so that Tony Ventnor and I could get away safely. He'd put word around that it was a bridge farther afield at Marronvert that would be attacked. But someone put the Boche right on that. Marius' group was ambushed and wiped out."

Her voice faltered as she finished the sentence, and her eyes were cast down, so that she didn't witness the look Bazeley exchanged with his wife.

"Sorry, lass. Did you say they were wiped out?"

"Yes. Every one of them perished."

Again the look was exchanged. Eve saw it this time and, puzzled, glanced from one to the other.

Rose Bazeley reached across and patted her hand. "Not all, my dear," she said. "One man survived. We've seen him."

Eve couldn't believe her ears, stared back openmouthed in astonishment. "Seen? But who did you see? And where?"

"It were last year," Bazeley said. "A village in the Dordogne. We went over to catch up with one or two old friends. Oh blimey, what were the name, love?"

"Oh, I'm not sure," Rose said. "Something 'les-Bains', that was it. Valmy. Valmy-les-Bains, ten miles or so from Nevers."

"We were passing through and stopped off at a café," Bazeley resumed. "Littl'un here needed the lav. That's where we saw him, coming out of a baker's shop. At least, I could've sworn it were him."

"But *who*, George, *who*?" Eve tugged at his sleeve impatiently.

"Why, the big lad. Marius. I'd worked with him three months, didn't reckon I could mistake him. Although perhaps after all it were his twin. 'Cos you see, he didn't recognise me. Looked right through me when I spoke to him and walked off wi'out a word."

"George puzzled over that for days," Rose put in. "We thought we must've been mistaken after all."

"But I'd still back my original instincts," Bazeley said firmly. "I knew Marius well enough. And that were him I saw in Valmy."

They finished tea and, with the usual promises to keep in touch, exchanged addresses. Much as she'd warmed to the Bazeleys, Eve couldn't wait to get away from them. Her heart was singing, bursting for sheer joy. Marius *alive*! And she was in no doubt as to what she would do next.

These were the summer holidays, and she had no teaching commitments. At the Three Bells that night, she explained to Stella that an old friend had turned up unexpectedly in France, someone she'd not been in contact with since her time there during the war, and that she'd be going over the following day.

The journey to Valmy-les-Bains was long and slow, and she endured it with mounting impatience. It turned out to be a small village, but even so Eve was unsure where to start. She decided to ask for guidance and entered the tiny church, knelt at the altar rail and bowed her head in prayer.

It was a warm day, and the church was beautifully cool. She couldn't be sure how long she'd been there when she was distracted by the rustle of a garment close by.

"*Yvette?* But surely it must be you – old Gaston's niece?"

She looked up in amazement to find beside her the spare, stooped figure of Father Bernard, who'd been priest in Calombes and the surrounding villages during her time there.

Anselme's words came back to her. Francine had insisted that one man had survived the ambush; that once his wounds were healed, someone had smuggled him out of the village in a wagon.

Tiredness and annoyance fled from her. She stood, smiling, and took hold of his outstretched hands. "Father."

"My child, what brings you here?"

But even as he spoke, perhaps before, the wise old priest already knew; and she had no need to reply.

"I believed they were all killed. But when I came back to Calombes, Anselme told me he'd heard one of them might have survived. And then only days ago, I met a man in London who'd worked with him. He was convinced he'd seen him here in Valmy."

The words poured out in a torrent, and Father Bernard guided her to a pew, sat with her, smiled, nodded and listened patiently.

"Marius survived," he said at last, once she'd run dry of words and sat beside him breathless and trembling in expectation. "Come, dear child, and I'll take you to him. But be warned. He has changed. He was badly hurt and remembers nothing of that fateful day and nothing of what went before. And understand that he will not know who you are."

Bernard took her to a small terraced house in an alley off Valmy's main street. He explained that he'd moved from Calombes to live with his elderly aunt, his only surviving relative. Francine had been very religious, and she'd informed the priest that she'd been looking after a wounded man. She'd sworn that she'd told no-one else.

"We couldn't move him until the last days of the war. His wounds were healed by then, but he wasn't safe in Calombes. There were people who couldn't be trusted. If word had got out, not only would he have been given away, but there would surely have been reprisals."

Marius had been shot several times. But Francine, mad or otherwise, had been a nurse in her younger days and had never lost her skills. She tended and bound up his wounds, helped him along the slow path to recovery.

"She performed wonders," Bernard said. "But, as you will see, my child, there were wounds she couldn't heal."

He ushered her into the house. The old lady, Bernard's Aunt Marie, was confined to her bed in the attic, scarcely making an appearance downstairs, and the priest had allocated one of the lower rooms to Marius. They found him occupying an armchair beside the fireplace. There was a book in his hand, a battered history volume, but he paid it no attention. Instead he was staring listlessly into the cold, black pit of the grate.

Bernard gently called his name, and he turned. A vague smile crossed his face as he recognised the priest.

"He remembers nothing of Calombes," Bernard had explained, as they'd made their way there. "He knows me only because I've been with him from the first time I saw him at Francine's, and he's got used to me. I warn you now, Yvette: he won't know you."

The moment she saw him she burst past the priest, ran across and knelt beside his chair, taking his hands in hers.

"Oh, Marius, I'm so glad you're safe. Look at me, my dear. Don't you remember me? Little Yvette from old

Gaston's farm. I was his niece, wasn't I? And then there were Fernon and Armand and Gaspard. Can't you -?"

She broke off abruptly as George Bazeley's words came back to her. *"He didn't recognise me. Looked right through me when I spoke to him."*

Which was what he was doing now. She searched frantically in those clear dark eyes for some hint of remembrance, of recognition. But all she saw was vacancy.

Bernard laid his hands on her shoulders. "His memory has gone," he whispered. "He must have suffered a fall too that evening, struck his head, for there was a large contusion there. If you look carefully, just beyond the temple, you will see the scar. Francine guessed he'd been struck a tremendous blow, one which would have killed a lesser man."

"But what can be *done*?" she asked, turning her tear-stained face towards him. "Will his memory ever return?"

The priest shrugged. "Who knows? I spoke with a doctor some months ago. He believed that some sudden jolt of memory might act as the key to unlock his mind. But our dear Marius is in the hands of God. He is a prisoner, and we must not cease to pray for his release."

* * *

She became Yvette again. She wrote to Stella, informing her that she'd found the friend she'd been seeking. He was sick, and she was remaining indefinitely in Valmy in order to care for him. She rented a room above the *patisserie* and within a few weeks had taken on some pupils for English lessons to help pay her way.

Under Father Bernard's guidance, she returned to her long-lapsed Catholic faith. Not a day passed when she didn't visit the little church and kneel and pray to the merciful God that He would restore Marius and make him whole again.

The village knew Marius as the priest's nephew who'd been wounded in the war. His experiences had left him not quite right in the head. Bernard had, ever since their arrival in Valmy, encouraged him to walk round the village, visit the shops, the church, the bar, all the time introducing him to the villagers, stimulating conversation, seeking something which might provide that key.

Yvette took on these duties now. "My niece from Calombes," Father Bernard explained to everyone they met, and they would share a private smile. "My child," he said to her one evening, "with my aunt, nephew and now my niece, I don't believe I've had so many relations in my entire life."

She accompanied Marius everywhere. They must have been a strange spectacle: the huge, bearded man led obediently by the hand of the frail girl.

His days grew brighter. They would often walk for miles, through woods, across fields and streams, watch the farmers at work, the children fishing or sailing their makeshift boats on the pond. Yvette recalled Marius once telling her that he'd worked as a carpenter before the war. She asked if he'd make a boat for the village boys.

He made several. They weren't particularly good, but she watched him become absorbed in the work, the old smile occasionally crossing his face, the old skills shedding their rust and being put to good use.

But still that vacancy remained, that emptiness in his eyes. He called her Yvette, because she'd told him that was her name. And he only knew her as Yvette from Valmy: he couldn't remember Calombes, nor the Yvette he'd known there.

In the evening they'd sit over their supper, and she'd roll out her memories of their months together at the farm. Old Gaston in the hen-house, how they often had to help him up from his knees; Fernon, cursing liberally at anything that moved, his passion for cognac, the way he thumped his brawny fist on the table in a show of temper. And Armand at the garage: Marius had once said that he and Armand had attended the village school together, friends for as long as they could remember, always up to their pranks, often soundly rated and beaten by Mademoiselle Ferrier the schoolmistress.

These and many other memories she'd relate. He would smile at some, laugh at others. But she could tell that he was unable to recall them. They were simply amusing anecdotes; nothing in which he had ever had a part.

Sometimes, exhausted and in tears, she would pour out her misery to Father Bernard. The old priest would listen patiently while she ranted and raved, and then would take her by the hands and say gently: "My dear Yvette, you are making such a difference in his life. He is smiling, laughing. Why, he even put up a shelf for me in the study the other day. Not quite straight, I grant you, but good enough. My child, I can see the difference in him. Yesterday he sat staring at the fireplace; today, with you, he is *alive.* Let us pray that his progress continues apace."

Several weeks passed, but progress remained slow; and sometimes she would despair, wondering if there was any progress at all.

One evening, Yvette returned from giving a lesson to find Bernard cluelessly examining an old wireless on the kitchen table. It was his aunt's, the only pleasure left to the ailing old lady.

The priest was shaking his head. "The thing's packed up," he said. "I can't get it to work. I'd better go up and read to her this evening, but it'll be a poor substitute."

Yvette hung her bag on the back of a chair. "Let me take a look, Father," she offered. "I knew my way around these during the war. There's probably a loose connection somewhere."

She sat at the table and fiddled around with the set. After a while she managed to get a reception and called through to Father Bernard, who was sitting with Marius in the living-room.

Both men appeared in the doorway. The priest's face broke into a smile. "Ah, Heaven be praised," he exclaimed. "That lets me off the hook tonight. Bless you, dear child. Aunt Marie will be delighted."

And then he found himself forcibly bundled aside as Marius burst into the room. Bernard and Yvette stared at him aghast, for his face was suddenly animated, and he was gesticulating towards the wireless and then the girl.

"You are calling London?" he cried. "Yes – tell them the airman must go back. And you too, Yvette. I insist, for there is danger all around. The damned Boche are everywhere. Gaston!" He whirled round, calling through to the living-room, voice echoing with the old irresistible command. "Fetch Fernon and Armand." He turned back to her, fiery and purposeful. "Tell London we need more explosives, more ammunition. And it's urgent – tell them it's urgent. It's about time we gave those bastards something to think about." He stood for a moment, panting, exhausted, his gaze darting round the room. "Come, Yvette, you must hurry, and get that wireless stowed away. You never know who might be prowling around the farmyard."

Yvette knew she had to humour him. She lifted the heavy set off the table and lugged it through to the cupboard under the stairs.

"Have no fear. Marius," she said on her return. "No-one will find it."

She spoke calmly, although her heart was leaping. For his sake, she knew they would have to take things slowly. He was looking disoriented and anxious.

The sight of Bernard seemed to disturb him further. "What's the priest doing here? Has someone bought it? Where are they all? Fernon, Armand, Gaspard: why aren't they here? Dear God, don't tell me the Boche have rumbled us already?"

He was becoming extremely agitated, but Yvette hushed him to silence, calmed him down, while Bernard pulled out a chair and between them they lowered him gently on to it. Yvette knelt at his feet, taking his huge, calloused hands in hers.

"Marius, my dear. I am Yvette, but we are no longer at the farm. The war is over at last, and we are at peace. But you were badly wounded, and the good Father Bernard, the priest from Calombes, brought you here. We are at his house in a village called Valmy, not far from Nevers."

"Valmy." Marius uttered the word as if it were entirely foreign to him. "And you are Yvette, and this the good Father. But where are the others? What has happened? I was wounded, you say?"

"Yes. And you received a massive blow to the head which caused you to lose your memory. But tonight your memory has reawakened. My dear, you must rest now. No more tonight. But tomorrow – tomorrow we will try to recall some more. Oh, Marius!" She had fought hard but couldn't contain her joy, leaping up and flinging her arms around him. "You have been restored to life. Praise God! Praise God!"

He was still in a state of confusion, and Yvette knew she must tax him no more that evening. It was getting late, and she could tell that he was tired. She suggested that they call it a night, knowing that Marius would have no trouble in dropping off. Though how she would ever sleep she didn't know, for she was so keyed-up inside, teetering on the precipice of happiness, impatient for the morning when, well rested, he might be up to making further progress.

She took him through to his bedroom and sat beside him while he slept. After a while, Bernard tiptoed in with some cocoa for her and offered to take over the vigil. Smilingly she refused: this was her place, her mission to see through to its conclusion.

She awoke with a start, must have fallen asleep in the small hours, her mind electrified with thoughts, for now the fingers of dawn probed impatiently through the gaps in the curtains. When Marius awoke some little time later, Yvette didn't feel tired at all, because she saw at once that light of recognition in his eyes, followed by a broad, slightly shy smile. "Yvette. It's you."

"Yes, Marius. Your Yvette. Let me prepare you some breakfast, my dear."

They sat round the table and talked for a long time, almost oblivious to Father Bernard dashing to mass and here, there and everywhere to visit his parishioners. Scenes and faces were coming back to Marius: his old compatriots, the British airmen, and how Yvette had saved his life. He remembered Yvette and Ventnor setting out to meet the plane, but after that his mind was blank. He seemed to understand that his old friends Fernon, Armand

and the rest had met their deaths, but could recall nothing of the circumstances. His next memory was of Valmy, Father Bernard, Aunt Marie and the kind young woman who kept trying to reawaken his memory of the past.

"There will be more, I am certain of it," the old priest enthused, as he and Yvette sat late that night over their cocoa. "We must continue to encourage him, help him remember the full picture so that he will be whole again."

Over the days and weeks which followed, they sought to do just that, Yvette sitting with him in the bar, walking with him through the fields and lanes, bringing back to him the circumstances of his former life, restoring its jigsaw puzzle piece by small piece.

Gradually he began to recollect who he was: the boy, the young man, the carpenter, the resistance fighter. The final memory of all that time, which she succeeded in coaxing from him, was of the band of fighters making their way over to the bridge at Meniers.

"I can see their faces now. We were crammed in the back of the grocer's van – what was his name? – Levert. Fernon, Armand, Gaspard – some others, but I can't recall their names. Levert dropped us off, and we made the last kilometre or so on foot. We'd been joking – Fernon as bawdy as ever. I got them to shut up; then, with the bridge in sight, a barrage of fire. Someone went down. We started firing back, and I bawled to everyone to scatter. Fernon yelled, "The bastards are everywhere!" I remember making it to the bridge, and there was gunfire all around and – well, that's as much as I remember. Valmy, and the good Father, and you, Yvette – those are the next things."

He was philosophical about the betrayal: every day they'd flirted with death, and one day your number was bound to come up.

"Bosquet would have passed the message on. He was shot at the end of the war, you say? Well, I can't feel sorry. But who told Bosquet? Pah! It might have been anyone. One of the boys blabbing when he'd had a skinful? That's how the bastard did it a lot of the time, you know. Ply them with free booze to see what he could get out of them. Unless -?" His face grew dark.

"Unless what, Marius?"

"You say, *chérie,* that Armand was charged with telling Bosquet that we were going to destroy the bridge at Marronvert? Well, I'd stake my life on Armand passing that message on. We'd known each other all our lives. Dear God, we were like brothers. Armand would've done that for sure. But what if someone who knew the real target was Meniers heard him say that? And sold us out deliberately."

Yvette reached across and took his hand, tried to distract him, change the subject. For his eyes blazed, and his mouth was set grimly. This was the Marius of old, but she didn't want him upsetting himself over the betrayal. Nothing could be done now. And he smiled back, squeezed her hand: the cloud passed. But his words had set her wondering.

She spent so long with him, days and evenings, and he became so dear to her, that it seemed inevitable that she should fall in love. The whole village, not least the wise old priest, had marked them down as lovers long before they actually were.

And indeed, hadn't she been in love with him before, during those dark days of war? He was in many ways a rough man, but towards her he'd never been less than a true gentleman, always shielding her from the crude advances of some of the other group members.

And she'd been the one to bring him back to life through her persistence, gentleness and devotion. For almost five years Marius had been imprisoned. Yvette had set him free, and he was overflowing with gratitude, which turned effortlessly into love.

Within a year of her arrival in the village they'd married, an ecstatic Father Bernard conducting the service. She invited the Bazeley family over for the wedding, for George and Rose had set her on the path to Valmy and Marius. Her mother came too, overjoyed to be back in France, where her heart had always belonged, and Yvette asked her if she would consider selling the Three Bells and come and live with them.

But Stella was comfortable in London now. The pub had been her husband's, and she felt duty bound to run it as best she could. Her staff were loyal, and she had many friends. It was only right that Eve should build her own life in the country of her birth.

She and Marius moved into a cottage at the end of the main street. He'd slowly begun to rediscover his old skills and had found employment with the local cabinet-maker, while Yvette – to him she must always be Yvette – continued to teach English and help at the local school.

She was glad, later, that there were no children in the marriage. Village life suited them, and they were happy to jog along at its undemanding pace. Marius made friends in the village and enjoyed their company in the bar two or three nights a week. His memory, apart from the period between Meniers and Valmy, was greatly restored, but he would not speak of the war with his friends. Those recollections were too painful, their wound a deep cut which would never heal.

20

Yvette kept in regular touch with her mother. However, she became concerned when several weeks passed without a reply to her latest letter. She and Marius had now been married six years, and Stella had visited them on holiday every year. She greatly approved of her son-in-law, often remarking on how kind and thoughtful he was.

Yvette wrote again. Within the week a reply came back from Rhona Parrish, a good friend of her mother's.

Stella had fallen ill. Mrs Parrish had realised that certain issues had started to confuse her and felt that, as she was now into her sixties, the responsibility of running the Three Bells was getting too much. Yvette explained the situation to Marius and, with his approval, wrote back to say that she would return to England to assess the situation.

Once there, she was shocked at the state of her mother's health, believing she must have suffered some kind of stroke. Stella didn't need a lot of persuading to put the pub on the market, Yvette oversaw its sale and, with Mrs Parrish's help, found an apartment in Bethnal Green, where she nursed her mother back to health.

It was an arduous task. Stella became virtually housebound and, with time to dwell on her memories, her mind began to ramble over things which had happened long ago, before and during the war.

Yvette wrote to Marius informing him that it might be several months before she could return. When she did, Stella was somewhat improved, and she left her in Rhona's care while she went back to France with the aim of asking her husband if he might allow her mother to come and live with them.

All in all, she had been back in England for close on a year.

* * *

But when she returned to Valmy, she found that much had changed. She was shocked to learn that during her absence Father Bernard had caught a severe chill and died that winter.

This was a devastating blow, for ever since she'd arrived in the village eight years previously the old priest had been her mentor and friend. Why had Marius not let her know? Might it have been that, knowing she was preoccupied with her mother, he hadn't wanted to upset her? But to arrive in Valmy and learn the news now was even more upsetting. She'd communicated with him every fortnight, and although he was no great correspondent she'd received the occasional reply, in a schoolboy hand. The written word had never been his strongest suit, less so since his recovery, and she might have been prepared to gloss over that. But not to have informed her about Bernard, a man who'd been a staunch friend and support to them both, was a glaring omission.

The news of the priest's death was broken to her by Solange, the *patisserie* owner from whom she'd rented a room when she'd first come to Valmy. Although Bernard had been well into his seventies, his death had come as a shock to the whole community, especially as his Aunt Marie had predeceased him by less than three years.

"I asked Marius to let you know," Solange told her. "He assured me he would, and when you didn't show up for the funeral, he shrugged and said the letter must have got lost in the post."

Yvette shook her head in dismay. "I shall have words with him," she said. Although to be fair, he was prone to the occasional lapse of memory; hardly surprising after all he'd been through.

"Before you go." Solange grasped her arm as she was about to leave. She smiled kindly and led Yvette into a room behind the shop, sat her down and offered her a drink.

Yvette declined, knowing straight away that something was amiss. "What is it?" she asked apprehensively.

"Marius has missed you," came the simple reply. "And with the good Father no longer around, he has – well – been less communicative."

Yvette nodded. "I feared that might happen. I'd hoped to be back much sooner, but my mother was in poor health for so long. I was afraid he might retreat into his shell."

"He can be a bit gruff at times," Solange admitted. "But he doesn't lack for friends. He's in the bar most evenings."

"Ah!" Yvette gasped in exasperation. "I might have known – the bar."

"Those lads are fine," her friend reassured her. "Martin, Claude, Philippe – he's known them for years, and they're a decent bunch. But another man has joined them of late. I don't like him. He's been lodging with the widow Parmentier for several weeks now. Someone who knew Marius back in – where was it? – Calombes? An old friend."

Yvette was immediately distrustful. She had at that moment no idea who this old friend might be, but she sensed right away that he was a bad influence. Marius had made a miraculous recovery, but there was about him a slowness of thought, a legacy of the trauma he'd undergone, and she felt he might be easily influenced.

She thanked Solange for her warning and returned home. Marius wasn't there and, as it was well past seven in the evening, she guessed he'd be in the bar. She went along, curious to discover the identity of her husband's 'old friend'.

Marius spotted her as she walked in, came over and embraced her fondly.

"*Ma belle Yvette.* I didn't expect you back today."

"I wrote last week to say when I'd be home."

He laughed and threw up his hands in mock despair. "Pah! You know how I am with letters, *chérie.*"

"Indeed I do. It's only today that I've learned about poor Father Bernard."

Marius contrived to look puzzled. He reeked of *pastis* and was swaying slightly. "But did I not write?"

"If you did -." She laid heavy doubt on those words. "I'm afraid I never received it."

"Then all I can do, *chérie,* is apologise. I was sure I'd informed you. But you know that I am - ."

"Bad with letters. Yes." In spite of herself, she couldn't be angry with him. There were times when he seemed so like a child, and he had suffered horribly. She relented and hugged him briefly. "Yes, dear. Of course. I know."

"Then you will join us now for a drink? Some champagne, perhaps? To welcome you home."

She shook her head. "Alas, I must return to the house to unpack. Prepare some supper. Have you eaten?"

Marius shrugged. "Lunch-time, perhaps."

"Then I'll get you some. Will you come now?"

"Ah, *petite*, but I am with my friend. We talk about old times. You remember him, perhaps?"

She had been aware of a figure sidling along the bar towards them, his identity obscured by her husband's huge frame. Only now did he come fully into view.

And Yvette's heart sank. The man was Gérard, Fernon's younger brother, a man she'd ever disliked and distrusted. He'd haunted the bar in Calombes, a crony of the late, unlamented Bosquet.

He was old now, probably over seventy, grey-haired, stooped and smiling slyly.

"Ah, the little English girl. But how you have blossomed with the years, pretty one. My friend Marius has chosen well."

She ignored his outstretched hand. "I was born in France, *m'sieu.*" she replied with asperity. "It has always been – will always be my country."

Gérard shrugged. She didn't like his smile. "*Pardon, madame.* But I was overjoyed when I learned that my old friend Marius had survived the war. My first thought was to come down and see him for myself. I am happy that all is well."

Yvette stayed for a while and joined in the conversation, but only out of politeness. She couldn't help feeling that Gérard's prolonged stay in Valmy spelt mischief. The barmaid, Giselle, told her later that some of Father Bernard's old parishioners from Calombes had travelled down to Valmy for his funeral and had learned about Marius. It explained how word had reached Gérard.

She returned to the house, prepared and ate supper and sat up a long time awaiting Marius' return. It grew late and still he didn't come, so she went to bed only to be awoken by his reeling into the house and knocking over furniture.

He burst into the bedroom. "Ah, Yvette, *chérie,* my beautiful wife. It is so good to have you back. Let me welcome you as a good husband should."

She was immediately on her guard but could see from the state of him that she had nothing to fear. He was blind drunk, falling over twice as he took off his clothes. He lurched towards her, then, as she took evasive action, collapsed face down across the bed and began to snore violently. She put on a dressing gown and went downstairs to spend the rest of the night in an armchair.

In the morning he was contrite, apologising for his unacceptable behaviour. But she'd been gone so long, and he'd wondered if she'd ever come back. He knew he'd started drinking too much, but that had been because he missed her. She kept him on the straight and narrow.

Yvette read between the lines. She suspected Gérard of putting it into his head that she might not return, and even though in the old days before she'd left for England Marius' usual cronies could be a bad influence, there was nothing malicious about them. She couldn't say the same for Gérard.

And of course this was not the old Marius, the fierce resistance fighter of thirteen years ago. His body and mind had suffered, he was slower in speech and thought and, she feared, easily led.

Once a week she met up with Solange and Giselle for coffee and pastries. Giselle was scathing about Gérard. "That man is a snake and no true friend to your husband. Always he goes on about the war, and people who died. He feeds your husband lies, tricks him into drinking more than he should."

In the days ahead, she began to find Marius less communicative; and neither did he ease up on the drinking. She stormed into the bar one evening, determined to corner Gérard and give him a piece of her mind. But he slithered out of the confrontation, and Marius, to her great annoyance, defended him and tried to placate her. Not wishing to make the scene uglier than it already was, she turned on her heel and went home.

By the next morning, Gérard had moved on. She was thankful at least for that. But the damage had been done, and Yvette feared that she would be unable to repair it.

Previously Marius had shown her great tenderness, allowing her to take the lead in their love-making, and she'd marvelled at how such a big, clumsy man could be so gentle. Now he took her whenever the mood was upon him and, fuelled by drink, could be unfeeling and brutal. Only in the morning, when he found her weeping, would he apologise for having hurt her and vow to be more thoughtful in future.

But the main content of their conversation was the war. Always the war, until she was sick of it. And he would grow angry, because she wouldn't listen to him. She imagined Gérard in some distant bar, celebrating his success. He had helped restore much of Marius' wartime memory and freely ladled it with bitterness.

One evening Yvette arrived home to find Marius waiting for her. He was already well into the *pastis*. He didn't greet her, ignored her attempts at conversation and sat staring sullenly into his glass.

"What's the matter?" she asked.

He didn't look up and took a while to reply, waiting until she was on the point of turning away. "It is time for the truth, Yvette. Tell me. Was it you who betrayed me?"

She pulled out a chair and sat down across from him, staring at him unflinchingly until he made eye contact.

"Marius, I solemnly swear: I did not betray you. Why would I, when you'd always been so kind to me? You and the boys were my family, and France is the country of my birth, the country I love. My dear, who suggested this? Was it Gérard?"

"It may have been."

"In other words it was. Then let me tell you what he's tried to do. He's jealous that I am your wife and has tried to sow distrust between us because he is a hateful man. The man who betrayed you passed information on to Bosquet. Was not Gérard a friend of Bosquet?"

His answer was swift and violent. Rising, he lashed out and caught her on the side of the head with the back of his hand. The force of the blow knocked her off her chair and sent her sprawling on the floor. As she got slowly to her feet, he was standing over her, his face like thunder, his eyes wild.

"You went back to England for a whole year. To do what? To nurse your mother? Pah! It was to run to your lover – the brave airman for whom you betrayed us all."

She thought he was about to strike her again but refused to cower before him. She stood her ground and stared back defiantly, the top of her head barely reaching his shoulder. "Ventnor was not my lover. You are my husband, and did you think I wished to be away from you for so long? If you believe me guilty, then I feel sorry for you. Everything I have ever done for you was out of love. Everything your *great friend* Gérard did for you was out of spite."

They stared each other out, Yvette wondering when the blow would come. It never came. Marius turned and walked out, presumably to the bar. He didn't return home that evening.

While Yvette lowered herself into a chair and sat for a long time, weeping silently and trembling uncontrollably.

But there were other evenings when he returned. Other occasions when, rolling drunk, he'd lash out at her over the slightest thing. Only her nimbleness saved her from serious injury; but there were blows which landed and marked her, and no amount of excuses could hide the truth from her friends.

She tried desperately to reason with him, but he was beyond reason. She'd known for some time that he wasn't the man alongside whom she'd worked and fought, the man she'd admired. Nor even the man she'd brought back to life, the gentle giant she'd married.

Solange and Giselle were her only support. The new priest, a much younger man than Bernard, was of no help. She suspected he was homosexual, and he began from the viewpoint that wives should obey their husbands and that, because Marius had been driven to lay a hand on her, the fault must lie with her.

One afternoon Solange came scurrying round to her house. Yvette was sporting a black eye and wondering where it would all end. Her friend helped her make up her mind.

"Yvette, he is in the bar with a group of farmers. They've been drinking since lunch-time, and Giselle has sent me the message that Marius has passed out. My dear girl, I beg you to take your chance. My Jacques has the cart harnessed. Pack your things, and he'll take you to the station at Nevers. Quickly, quickly, go! If you stay much longer, Marius will kill you."

Yvette had reached the point where she could have no second thoughts. She hastily packed her suitcase, picked up the money she'd earned that week and the few francs she'd laid aside for an emergency and followed Solange from the house.

Jacques was waiting and, after a tearful embrace from her friend, Yvette set out for the station, for a train to Paris and thence to England.

* * *

Alan made more tea, poured and brought it over to where Eve sat, the little living-room quiet and dim, lit only by the standard lamp in its corner.

As he handed over the cup, he saw the strain of the past weeks clearly in her face. She sat, eyes closed, her head resting against the chair-back. Yet he'd sensed relief too in the unburdening of the soul which he'd just witnessed.

He sat down opposite, reached across and took hold of her hand. Her eyes opened at his touch, and a gentle smile warmed her face.

"That happened almost three years ago," she resumed. "I swore then that I shouldn't return to him. I settled with my mother in Meadowside Court, found myself a job at Parkway Language College and began to build a life again.

"But the past wouldn't let me go. One day, over a year ago now, I ran into Tony Ventnor. No, I didn't run into him at all, it's just that he made it seem that way. He'd never have admitted it, but he'd been looking for me for years. He hadn't found me because I'd been living in France for eight of the previous nine years; and during the year I'd spent in London nursing *Maman* I used my married name, Delattre.

"Tony was obsessed with me, showering me with gifts, inviting me here, there and everywhere. I took care never to rise to the bait, because I knew where it would lead. It wasn't that he was at all repulsive, just that -." Her voice fell, and she clung tightly to Alan's hand. "Somehow, Alan, I suppose I knew what he'd done. His plan had been to fly out from France with me. He knew that I didn't need much of an excuse to disobey orders, so he decided he'd give me no choice."

"Then he – Tony -?" Alan fell silent. For he already knew what Tony had done; had worked it out in the dining-room at Bayes Wood earlier that evening. And he couldn't get the words out now because he realised that Eve, object of Ventnor's overwhelming desire, held herself to blame for the deaths of all those men.

"When Marius accused me of betraying them," she whispered, "in a sense, he was right." She gathered herself with an effort, took refuge in her tea.

"I turned Tony down time and again," she went on. "And still he kept showing up, the proverbial bad penny. Earlier this year he came to Meadowside Court, and he had Madge in tow. She must have known he was up to something and refused to be shaken off. I saw suspicion in her eyes: she thought we'd been lovers, that we still were; and Tony did nothing to persuade her otherwise.

"They were staying up in London for a few days, and he suggested we meet for dinner. You know Madge: she wasn't going to take that lying down, so she suggested we make it a foursome and invite you to travel up and join us."

In spite of herself, Eve chuckled. "At first I felt relieved. I'd be safe in a foursome. And then I thought: what if this man's another version of Tony? But as soon as I met you, my mind was set at rest.

"Poor Alan. I must have seemed so indecisive, always keeping you at arm's length, even when I wanted us to be more than friends. But as you've learned, my dear, I'm Catholic, and while Marius was alive I couldn't divorce him.

And I knew he was still alive, because I've kept in touch with Solange.

"She wrote a month ago to tell me he'd left Valmy. His drinking got worse, and he lost his job. Then he seemed to come to his senses. He sobered up and put the word around that there was a job he had to do. People must have lent him money so that he could get to England.

"I knew he'd come looking for me. I couldn't go anywhere, not with my mother housebound, so all I could do was wait and pray.

"When he found me, things didn't turn out as I'd feared. Solange had said that there was something purposeful about him. He apologised for ever thinking that I might have betrayed him; apologised too for the way he'd treated me. On leaving Valmy, he'd sought out Gérard, determined not to let him pull the wool over his eyes.

"It's my own belief, and has been for a while, that it was Gérard who sold us all out – including his own brother. But it was Tony Ventnor who passed him the information in the first place. Threatened by Marius, all Gérard wanted was to save his own skin and, as he told it, he'd overheard Tony talking to Bosquet. Once more that evil man wrought havoc; for in blabbing to Marius, he effectively sealed Tony's death warrant.

"Marius came to London in search of Ventnor. His command of English was poor to say the least, so he employed a private detective to find him. The detective was Stanley Rennie. As you'd guess, he had his own agenda and tried to blackmail Tony. But that didn't mean he intended cutting Marius out. The details he'd sent him somehow got delayed, with the result that it was only today that Marius got hold of Tony's address. And I didn't get Marius' message until I arrived home from college this afternoon. I realised right away where he'd gone.

"Of course, Tony got rid of Rennie without knowing he'd sent the message. He was more concerned with Tania Bredon. He'd noticed her likeness to her father long before I did and decided he'd better get in first. I don't know how she tracked us down, but she was bent on revenge. Tony was as unctuous as always in the company of an attractive woman and clearly worked hard to avoid suspicion. He made me out to be the traitor, and in any case it had been I who'd killed Emsley, and I would never deny it. But what he hadn't reckoned on was that Marius was still alive and closing in."

Alan sat contemplating her for a long time. Then he reached across and pulled her to him. "I'm sorry about Marius," he said. "I'm sure he loved you and was grateful for everything you'd done. Like us all, he was vulnerable and listened to the wrong advice."

"I'm sorry too," Eve said. "And sorry that he's dead. All I can do is remember him as he was: a good, brave man. And that leaves you and I, Alan. Please, my dear, bear with me when I say I need to be indecisive a while longer. Until everything has been sorted out and time has healed."

As she slept in the room above him, and he maintained his thoughtful vigil well into the early hours, Alan knew that he could put up with her indecision and would do so stoically.

But the suspicion lurked at the back of his mind that they weren't in the clear yet. There were still issues to be resolved. At that moment he didn't know what they were; but knew he had to remain vigilant.

21

Later that week, Eve and Alan attended the inquests on both men, and each gave evidence.

Eve, in a dark two-piece suit, hat and veil, stated in a quiet, clear voice that she'd married Marius Delattre four years after the war, having served with him in a French resistance group during 1944. The group had been betrayed and, it was believed, wiped out while trying to destroy a railway bridge near Meniers in May of that year. Under orders from London, Eve had escaped back to England, along with Tony Ventnor, whom the group had been sheltering.

Unknown to her, Marius had survived the attack but suffered a severe head wound and memory loss. A woman in the nearby village had nursed him, and the former village priest had helped him escape to Valmy-les-Bains, a village in the Dordogne.

After the war Eve had traced Marius to Valmy and helped restore much of his memory. They had married, but six years later she'd gone back to England to nurse her sick mother. On her return to Valmy, she discovered her husband had turned against her, believing that she'd betrayed him and his compatriots. He'd abused her a number of times, until finally she'd had enough and returned to England.

Eve had heard nothing from Marius for two years, until in the July just past he'd sought her out in London. He had little money, as he'd paid a private detective to find 'the

English airman'. Marius was now convinced that Tony Ventnor, and not Eve, had betrayed the group.

The local police inspector went on to explain that the private detective in question had been a man named Stanley Rennie. He'd taken Marius' money and located Ventnor. He'd attempted to blackmail him, demanding money for his silence, but, as Ventnor had admitted to Alan Cawley, he'd lured Rennie to the woods at Durleyford Hall and killed him, staging it to look like suicide.

However, unknown to Ventnor, Rennie had already sent a communication to a post office in Bethnal Green. But he'd badly mis-spelled Marius' surname, and when the Frenchman had first called for the letter, it couldn't be found. As soon as it turned up, some days later, Marius headed for Bayes Wood. He left a terse message at Eve's apartment: *'I have found him.'* She only got this on her return from work that afternoon and, fearing the worst, contacted Kelvin Guilfoyle, who was up in London that day. They motored down but arrived too late. Marius had succeeded in throttling Ventnor but had been shot by him in the process, later dying from his wounds.

The story appeared in the national press but, fortunately for Eve, the real reason for the betrayal was glossed over. There had been a 'long-standing mutual distrust' between the resistance leader and the decorated war hero, and while Eve was mentioned as 'the estranged wife of Marius Delattre', there was no speculation as to whether she'd been a factor in the quarrel.

The matter was pushed further aside as it was overshadowed by news of the death in a plane crash of the UN Secretary-General Dag Hammarskjöld, and a series of gruesome murders on the south coast. Even so, Alan couldn't help wondering if Guilfoyle hadn't had a hand in playing it down.

Whatever the answer, he was glad for Eve's sake. She'd borne up well during the inquest, drawing on a reserve of inner steel; but even so he knew how much she must be hurting inside.

And then there were the funerals to attend. Tony was buried next to his parents in Durleyford churchyard. The church was packed, for Tony had been a popular man. Many of his old RAF colleagues turned up to pay tribute to him, and a brief testimony was given lauding his courage and reliability in the most perilous circumstances.

Madge confided to Eve and Alan that she was glad once it was over. The Ventnors' marriage had been on the rocks for some time, but she'd been touched by the esteem in which Tony had been held and the support she'd received. Piers Fullarton, ever the gentleman, remained unobtrusively in the background, in case people talked. But once a decent period of mourning had been observed, he was determined that Madge wouldn't be alone.

Marius' funeral was simpler and far quieter, at a small Catholic church in Stepney, with Eve, Alan and Guilfoyle the only mourners. Eve was distraught, and Guilfoyle took his leave soon afterwards so that Alan could comfort her.

Alan took her back home. Rhona Parrish had kindly taken Stella next door to her apartment, so that she wouldn't be in the way.

Once Eve had recovered her composure, she poured out to Alan a tale of guilt. Tony Ventnor, Marius, even Rennie: she felt the blame for their deaths lay at her door, that she'd been the catalyst sparking the long, grisly chain of events.

Alan surprised her by his firmness. He emphasised that in no way was she to blame. Rather it was the war, its blood-spattered course, its haunting, harrowing aftermath. His father's words came back to him once more: *to finish the journey.* It was Eve's duty, and his and everyone's. Life, despite its pain and the tricks it played, was the path they were bound to take.

She thanked him then for all he'd done: for his companionship, dependability and patience. But – and she knew he wouldn't want to hear this – she needed to be alone, at least for a while.

Eve had been right: it was the last thing he'd wanted. But he knew he had no choice. He couldn't begin to understand what she'd been through these past weeks, with Marius in London hungry for revenge; and her sure knowledge that Tony Ventnor had been the traitor, allied to the fact that she couldn't bring herself to give him away.

There was, however, a silver lining; and from it Alan took some comfort. At least she'd be spared the account of the inquest in the *Durleyford Advertiser*; and more importantly the gossip and tittle-tattle which would arise from it, the covert, knowing nudges, looks, and grim, triumphant smiles. As for himself, he remained sternly silent over the matter. He knew it was a subject Ariadne Gray was aching to raise with him, but he sensed that his unapproachable air was enough to deter her.

So he gave Eve his consent. And she smiled, because she saw his reluctance. They kissed tenderly, and he clung to her, clung, knowing that all too soon he would have to let her go. She walked with him to the end of the street, promised she'd telephone soon, waved him goodbye. And when he looked back for perhaps the twentieth time, she was gone.

* * *

Two weeks passed, and he heard nothing from her. Every time the phone rang, in the shop or at the cottage, he pounced upon it. But the voice at the other end was never the one he was so desperate to hear.

He toyed with the idea of phoning her, but always dismissed it. She would contact him when she was ready, and he knew in his heart that she'd be as good as her word.

One Tuesday evening he returned home, cooked a little supper and settled down to watch the *Tonight* programme. That had become his routine: a bite to eat, some television, some reading. Into October, and it had been a busy period in the shop, ordering course books for local schools and evening classes at the technical college. Being Alan, he'd immersed himself in work and found he needed the evenings for relaxation.

The phone rang, and he snatched up the receiver hopefully.

"Durleyford 85."

"Alan?"

"*Eve?* Oh, Eve, I've been waiting -."

"Alan." Her voice was dull, ragged. He could tell she'd been crying. "Please – can you come up to London?"

"Why, of course. I'll catch the early express -."

"No – come right away. There'll be a train soon, won't there? I'll meet you at Paddington."

He glanced at the mantelpiece clock. "I can catch the eight-thirty. Eve, darling, what's wrong?"

"It's my mother. Oh, Alan – I'm afraid she's dead."

* * *

He assured her he was on his way, stopping only to switch off Cliff Michelmore in full spate and throw a few things into an overnight bag, before hurrying down to the station.

The train drew into Paddington soon after ten o'clock. He'd sat and wondered throughout the anxious journey as to what could have happened. A heart attack? Brain haemorrhage? Her mind may have been prone to wander, but otherwise Stella seemed to have been in good shape.

Eve was waiting on the platform, huddled in a thick beige coat, for the nights were turning chilly. She ran forward the moment she caught sight of him, and he enveloped her in his willing arms. Her face was pale and pinched with weeping. "Oh, Alan," she blurted out. "She's dead, and I feel so awful. The times I let her get me down and wished, really *wished* her out of my life. And now..."

He calmed her as best he could and, reassured by his presence, she gave back a wan smile. "Oh, you're so *good*. Thank you for coming."

Their arms round each other, they headed for the tube and travelled across the city. On their way, Eve filled in the details of what had happened.

She'd been at work, not due home until five-thirty. Rhona Parrish looked in, as was her habit on days when Eve was absent. On this particular day she brought Stella some lunch.

"I says to her, Stella my dear, I'm out to bingo this afternoon, but here's a plate of shepherd's pie. And her old eyes lit up at that, they did, 'cos that's always been her favourite as long as I've known her.

"Anyway, I says, let's put the wireless on, the Light Programme. There'll be some nice music and a play later on. And usually, Miss Evie, that's all she wants. I called by to pick up the plate before I went out. Clean as a whistle, it was. "Did you enjoy that, dear? I asked. "Yes, Rhona, I did. Lovely bit of lunch, went down a treat." "You have a nice afternoon, then," I says. "Have a doze and listen to the wireless." And off I went.

"I come back as usual at half-four and s'welp me, there she was at the foot of the stairs. Give me such a fright, it did, and I could tell right away that she was dead. Well, I called the ambulance and police. I rang the college, but they said you were already on your way back.

"Poor soul, whatever possessed her to go out wandering, I'll never know. Perhaps she thought she was going back to help at the Bells, 'cos it's been playing on her mind so much just lately. But I felt sure she was safe to be left. Otherwise as God is my judge, I'd never have gone."

"I was suspicious right away," Eve said. "*Maman* rarely tried to leave the apartment. Rhona was right: the pub had been on her mind a lot. I lost my rag over it two days before, and she hadn't mentioned it since."

"So why do you think she left the apartment?" Alan asked.

Eve shook her head. "I'm probably being silly, because of course it may have been a whim, as Mrs Parrish suggested. But I can't help wondering if she may have had a visitor."

"A visitor? But who -?"

"I don't know. It just – made me wonder. It was one of the first things I mentioned to Mrs Parrish. I asked if she'd noticed any strangers in the building. You see, apart from Mrs Dalton on the floor below, who's housebound and stone deaf, everyone else is out at work. The building's virtually deserted for most of the day."

"What did Mrs Parrish say?"

"Oddly enough, the same idea had crossed her mind. She said it was probably nothing, but as you turn out of Meadowside Court, there's a pub, The Feathers, just a few yards down the road. The pub was shut, as it was after hours, but there was a man sitting on a bench outside, head buried in a newspaper. Rhona walked past him and only seconds later looked back to see if it was clear to cross the road. He'd left his seat and was heading off in the direction from which she'd just come."

"Could she describe him?"

"Well, she didn't get a proper look at him. He had a newspaper in front of his face, and all she noticed were a light-coloured mackintosh and dark trilby. As she'd said, probably nothing to do with anything."

Neither Eve nor Mrs Parrish had voiced their suspicions to the police: there'd simply been nothing to go on. And the police were already at Meadowside Court by the time Eve arrived back from college. It had taken her a while to overcome her initial grief and collect herself.

"Did your mother have a habit of wandering outside the apartment, Miss Ransom?" the sergeant had asked.

"It happened on one occasion, about three weeks ago. She was becoming easily confused. Things played on her mind, things which happened years ago, during the Blitz."

The police seemed satisfied that Stella's death had been an accident.

"And do you know, Alan, once they'd gone and the ambulance had taken her away, I just wandered round the flat, picking up this and that, things which had been hers, little trinkets she'd always had, and it hit me that she'd never be back to claim them, never again be in that armchair giving me the sharp end of her tongue. Perhaps I should have been relieved, but suddenly there was such a void in my life, and I simply collapsed into a chair and wept. Rhona fussed around, made me tea; and then we had a good cry together. She asked if I wanted her to stay with me, and I said no, because I knew right away there was only one person I needed beside me, one who'd console me and understand. Thank you, Alan. But – my dear, will you stay here tonight? I really don't want to be alone."

"Of course I will."

At another time he would have been thrilled by such an invitation. But this wasn't the occasion. And besides, he was troubled. Rhona Parrish's description had been sketchy, but straight away Alan had recalled the incident of a few weeks before: the man in raincoat and trilby stealing Guilfoyle's car and attempting to run Eve down. He was surprised that it hadn't clicked with her, but resolved not to mention it tonight. She had more than enough on her mind. However, it begged the question: had Stella Ransom been murdered?

Alan slept that night on the sofa. In the morning he telephoned Ariadne Gray and explained what had happened. As he'd hoped, she was sympathetic, having lost her own mother not long before. He'd left her his spare keys and invited her to close up the shop if she wished, but might have known better. Miss Gray could cope; and would do so with reforming zeal.

The following day he accompanied Eve as she made the funeral arrangements. He knew she was glad of his company, but she said little, going about her business with something of a dazed air. She'd taken Stella's death badly, believing herself to be at fault. He did his best to reassure her that wasn't the case.

Alan cooked them a meal at the flat that evening. He intended catching a late train back to Durleyford, but again she asked him to stay. Once they'd eaten, she poured them both cognac, came to sit beside him and laid a tender hand on his arm. "You've been such a comfort to me."

With the plates cleared away, Alan made coffee while Eve poured more cognac. "A nightcap." Had he imagined it, a glimpse of invitation in her eyes, in the shy smile which accompanied her words?

He'd settled himself in one of the armchairs, expecting her to sit opposite. Instead she came and perched on the arm of his, moving effortlessly from there to his lap. She set down her glass, prised his from his grasp and set that down too before snuggling into his eager yet slightly bewildered embrace.

"Please just hold me," she said. "I need to be held. And you're such a rock and comfort to me after all that's happened."

He felt that he should warn her now that the danger hadn't passed. But he didn't want to spoil the moment, nor heap more worry upon her after a trying day.

He tried to answer her and found he couldn't speak. But the words were on his heart, and he was sure she could somehow read them.

And besides, their faces were so close that he resolved the opportunity shouldn't be lost. They kissed, long, wonderingly and passionately, and once more she was clinging to him.

This was the moment, the time, too, for him to take charge. Struggling to his feet, he gathered her in his arms and carried her through to the bedroom. She didn't resist. He closed the door and set her down on her feet, heard her in the room's glorious darkness stepping out of her clothes.

A moment of apprehension. "Eve – I -?"

Her touch reassured him. "I asked you to stay. I need you beside me."

"Oh, darling Eve, I'm so in love with you. You've no idea -."

Her finger at his lips stilled him, quelled his lingering anxiety. "My darling, you've been so patient with me. It was borne in upon me today that if you walked out of my life, I should have no-one. I don't know what I should do."

He wondered afterwards, as he lay there in the stillness and Eve slept peacefully beside him, quite what *he* would do if he should lose her. He could scarcely bear to contemplate it. And yet he sensed that someone was lurking in the shadows along the way, waiting for the opportunity to strike; wanting her dead.

* * *

They were both mature people, he just turned forty, she in her late thirties, and the following morning, as they rose, breakfasted and talked about the day ahead, he felt they might have been married to each other for years.

Eve had decided she would go into work that morning, to keep her mind occupied. Alan wondered aloud if she wanted him to stay, but she urged him to return to Durleyford.

"You have a business to run," she laughed. "Otherwise Miss Gray will take over – if she's not already done so."

His anxiety returned. "But will you be all right alone?"

"Mrs Parrish lives just along the corridor."

He wanted to warn her to be careful, but felt that by doing so he might worry her unnecessarily. She seemed to read his mind.

"And yes, darling, fretful, worrying Alan, I'll be *careful*."

Their parting was almost light-hearted. He took the tube with her to Oxford Circus and accompanied her to the college. Stella's funeral had been arranged for the following Tuesday, and he promised to be at Meadowside Court in good time. They parted with a kiss. It was Thursday, and Tuesday seemed weeks away.

Alan waved until the front door of the college had closed behind her. Then he returned to the Underground and made his way to Westminster.

He knew that Kelvin Guilfoyle had a flat in Gressendon Mews, because he'd occasionally had books sent there. He was glad to find the MP in residence. Manners admitted him, surprised at his visit.

"I've been staying up in London for a couple of nights," Alan explained. "But I need to consult Mr Guilfoyle on an urgent matter and took the chance that he might be here rather than at the Hall."

"I'm sure he'd be delighted to see you, Mr Cawley," Manners replied. "Bear with me while I have a word."

He disappeared through a doorway and re-emerged seconds later. "The master says to come through."

The master was practically at his manservant's shoulder. "Cawley! This is a pleasant surprise. Have you breakfasted? Then at least let Manners bring you coffee. Come this way."

He led Alan through into a long, dim room cosy with mahogany furniture, two chesterfields and a gleaming radiogram with a stack of 78s on the carpet beside it. He showed him to a seat and installed himself opposite. Manners brought in coffee and quietly withdrew.

Alan came straight to the point and told him what had happened to Stella Ransom. Guilfoyle was taken aback by the news.

"Although I believe Eve mentioned that she was ailing, rather troubled in her mind. Was she in the habit of wandering?"

"That's just it, sir," Alan replied. "Not to any great extent. And this is why I've come to you. I suspect foul play."

Guilfoyle took a moment to consider this, sipped his coffee and set down his cup. He sat back and folded his arms.

"And what does Eve think?"

"I need to find the right moment to tell her my suspicions. It's not now. Also I think she may still be in danger."

"But surely the business with Miss Bredon is done and dusted?"

"I don't think it's linked with that. Although I'm sure it relates back to something which happened in the war." Alan didn't say as much, but the feeling was growing within him that some of Stella's ramblings might hold a clue. And if so, could that have been why she'd had to die?

"Any idea what it might have been?" Guilfoyle asked.

"I'm not quite sure. But of one thing I'm convinced: our late friend Rennie was involved in there somewhere."

"Ah!" Guilfoyle looked more enlightened. "You may have a point there, Cawley. Since the poor fellow breathed his last on my property, I had Manners contact his old chums' network and dig up some information on Mr Rennie. He was a sergeant in the RAF, stationed at Northolt for most of the war. Ground crew, I believe. Although he was never in France and never remotely connected with

SOE, so there's no reason he should know Eve, nor she him. He had a reputation as a bit of a Mr Fix-it and was heavily into black market goods. The powers that be had their eye on him, although by all accounts he did his job well enough."

Guilfoyle promised that he and Manners would do more digging and contact Alan with any results. He would also send Eve his condolences and, schedules allowing, attend Stella's funeral.

Alan thanked him for his support and headed off for Paddington with a view to arriving in Durleyford by lunch-time.

22

S tella's funeral service was held in a cold, drab church in Stepney on a dull October Tuesday, and she was buried next to her husband in the adjacent cemetery. The service was well attended: neighbours and old acquaintances for the most part, some dating back to the early 1930s, when Hubert Ransom had brought his wife and daughter back to England.

Rhona Parrish, a staunch friend over many years, had organised a tea in the church hall after the burial. Kelvin Guilfoyle joined them there, and Alan was amused by the sight of the angular Rhona performing an awkward curtsey as she served him tea and cake.

"That's Mr Guilfoyle the MP over there," he heard one of the neighbours whisper reverently. "Isn't he handsome? Just like his photograph."

Alan had returned to London on the milk train that morning to be received at Meadowside Court by a grateful, smiling Eve. He knew the hurt hadn't gone away: she still blamed herself for her mother's death. But she looked trim and confident in her dark suit and veil, and he sensed both strength and purpose in her manner. For his own peace of mind he'd phoned her every night since he'd returned to Durleyford, when they'd conversed easily about nothing at all; and she'd spoken teasingly every time of having been *careful*, assuring him that Rhona was most attentive and wondering how much Alan was paying her to stand guard.

Once everyone had been served by the industrious Rhona and her band of helpers, Eve, with Alan at her shoulder, went round the hall to thank everyone for their support. As she came upon an elderly man sitting in a corner and leaning on his walking-stick, a broad smile on his weathered face, she took a step back in surprise. "Why, it's Mr Perkins, isn't it? Sam Perkins?"

The old man stretched out a hand. "Hello, Miss Evie. Good to see you again. Reckon the last I saw of you was in the Bells, when you was in your smart uniform off to fight in the war. This young man your husband?"

"Oh, this is my —er, friend, Alan — Alan Cawley."

"Pleased to meet you, Mr Cawley." Sam reached across to shake hands. Alan, for his part, was gratified by Eve's intimate smile.

"Mr Perkins was a great help to *Maman* in the Three Bells," she explained. "Those war years were busy, so many people in the services based in and around London. I was away for much of the time, and Sam was the only person she could rely on."

"Yep. Moved all the way across to Putney after the war," Sam said. "Ran a pub off the Fulham Palace Road for several years. Come back over this way last year to live with my daughter." He turned to Eve. "I was real sorry to hear about Stella, my dear. She was a lovely woman, and by God she had some pluck to run the Bells all them years after Hubert died. But Mrs P. tells me she was getting mightily confused towards the end."

"Peggy preyed on her mind," Eve said. "I hardly knew the girl and didn't particularly like her. She was unreliable, wasn't she? Gave *Maman* a lot of grief."

"Whew! I should think she did." Sam chuckled. "A flighty piece, our Miss Peggy Neal. In my opinion, Stella had no need to be so good to her. But during the war you counted yourself lucky to get what staff you could."

"My mother always blamed herself. She got it into her head that Peggy was dead, and that she was in some way responsible. She rambled a lot during the last few weeks. Something about some officer: that he'd done Peggy to death, and she knew who he was."

Sam Perkins was shaking his head. "Stella had no cause to blame herself, Miss Evie. Take it from me, young Peggy was no better than she should have been. She'd got in with this cocky young officer, and they were dealing in black market goods. They were both on the fiddle, and it's my opinion that she stuck to most of the money she took. That evening she disappeared, the officer chappie were in the Bells looking for her. Poor Stella had her hands full. Cor blimey! I never seen such a crowd. Reckon they must've all got a forty-eight hour pass for the same time.

"Well, our Peggy had a room upstairs. Bless Stella, as if it weren't enough to give the girl a job, she give her board and lodgings as well – that woman had a heart of gold. 'Course, soon as Stella's back were turned, Peggy cleared off upstairs with her officer friend. Stella kept calling and calling for her, but she never come back.

"Well, I wasn't supposed to be on duty, but I'd nipped in for a quick pint – huh, some hopes! – saw the crush and pitched in to help behind the bar. Dear Lord above, I never seen Stella in such a taking, and I was glad I wasn't the wrong side of her. She was adamant she'd sack the girl next time she showed her face. But that was the last we saw of her.

"No, Stella sent me up to fetch her once things had quietened down a tad. But Miss Peggy had cleared out, and her officer along with her. Then the air raid sirens kicked off, and we all headed for the shelters."

"Was that the night of the bomb?" Eve asked. "Kingsland Street?"

Sam chuckled throatily. "You're right, Miss Evie. Blimey, that were a night and a half. They were well on their way by then, though. And we discovered later that Peggy had packed a suitcase, so she wasn't figuring on coming back. No sign of the officer's mate neither. Some big-mouth sergeant he was. In the Bells quite often, doing his wheeling and dealing. You take it from me, the place was a sight quieter once he'd cleared off *and* a sight more law-abiding."

Both Eve and Alan had been listening intently to Sam's recollections. But then Kelvin Guilfoyle approached them, apologising for the interruption. He had to be going, as the House was sitting that afternoon.

They thanked him for his support, and Eve walked with him to the door. Once he'd left, her attention was quickly claimed by Rhona and a clutch of neighbours, no doubt inquiring about the reason for the MP's presence. One or two curious glances were directed towards Alan and, guessing that he might soon become the centre of attention and not wishing it, he asked Sam if he'd like another cup of tea, fetched one for them both and installed himself next to the old man.

Alan found himself intrigued by Sam's story. He was also glad that Eve was out of earshot for the moment, as he felt there was more to come.

"Did you know the sergeant's name?" he asked.

Sam took a slurp of tea. "I must have heard it, but I'm blowed if I can remember it. I only ever recall people referring to him as 'Sarge'. Anyway, the whole boiling of 'em had left before Kingsland Street got flattened. And when we come back from the shelters, everywhere had gone real quiet. Kingsland Street was a triumph for the wardens: two or three casualties, but they'd got everybody else out. There was one young girl got crushed by falling masonry – and y'know, I think that's where Stella might have got confused. She got it into her head soon after that it was Peggy. But it turned out to be some young WAAF – half a mo' and the name'll come to me. Got it: Eileen Brayson, rest her soul. We heard that the body was identified later by her cousin."

Sam was well away now. A quick glance assured Alan that Eve was still occupied, and he nodded for the old man to continue.

"And there was another funny thing happened that night. There was this sleazy hotel a couple of streets away – oh come on, what was it called? Something like The Beeches. Well, like we all did, soon as them sirens sounded, everybody headed for the shelters. When the owner got back, she checked through the rooms and got the shock of her life, poor mare. Blowed if there wasn't this Squadron Leader chappie propped up dead in bed, run through with a paper-knife. He'd had a reputation by all accounts for seducing young women. Seems he'd tried it on once too often.

"Next day the police come along to have a word with Stella. Apparently she'd learned he was in the area and had been along to see him early on the afternoon he got topped. Had a right old ding-dong, according to the owner. Really told him what she thought of him.

"Now, I don't know what it was about, and Stella never mentioned it. My guess is he'd been a bit too attentive to young Peggy. To begin with, I think Stella was a suspect. But he cashed in his chips early evening, well after opening time, and there'd been sixty or seventy witnesses who could say Stella had never left the Bells. If she had, there'd have been nobody serving, 'cos our Miss Peggy had slung her hook."

"Did they find out who did it?" Alan asked.

"Well now, that's the funny thing." Sam was warming to his tale. "It turned out that the old chap on reception saw this young WAAF come flying down the stairs and out the door quite early in the evening. He never got a good look at her, but it was generally reckoned she was this Eileen Brayson, the girl who died in the bombing. The police made inquiries among her WAAF colleagues, and they'd heard her mention this Squadron Leader by name."

"Who was he?" Alan was caught up in the old man's story. He supposed he was seeking some clue which would link Stella's ramblings to her death and the danger threatening Eve. He could hardly believe Sam's next utterance.

"Oh, he was another of 'em caught up in the wheeling and dealing. Quite a stash he had, back at his RAF base. And him a Squadron Leader! Who'd have thought it? Name of Catterick."

"I reckon I bumped into her back in the war. If she asks where, tell her it was Catterick. Catterick, eh? I'm sure she'll appreciate that."

The words had been Rennie's, uttered that evening he'd accosted Alan outside the Star. They came back now to hit him with sledgehammer force. He leaned back in his chair, unable at that moment to speak. Sam Perkins, oblivious to his shock, was happily chuntering away. But Alan paid him no attention.

His eyes met Eve's. As luck would have it, she'd made her escape from the inquisitive neighbours and was returning to where Alan sat with Sam.

She'd heard the name, because for a brief moment she halted abruptly, as if rocked by its familiarity. A shadow passed across her face. Of what? Of doubt, anxiety, fear? But she collected herself well, alert to the fact that Alan was watching her; knowing in all probability that he had seen her reaction. She joined them, her features breaking into a nervous smile.

"Sorry about that. Talk about the third degree. They wanted to know all about Mr Guilfoyle. Oh, and you, of course." Her hand reached out, and he grasped it impulsively. He felt her fingernails digging into his flesh, as if she were clinging to him for dear life.

"Oh, we've found plenty to talk about." Alan grinned back with false joviality, knowing he could say nothing here and now; knowing too, for absolute certainty, that that mention of Catterick would prey on his mind, haunt each waking moment. "Nothing wrong with Mr Perkins' memory," he added.

"Talked too much, I expect," said Sam. "But it's been so good to meet up with you again after so long, Miss Evie, and to chat to your young man here. God bless her, we shan't be forgetting Stella in a hurry. A right good woman, she was. We could do with more of her sort in the world."

Fired up, he went on to recount a couple more anecdotes, while Eve and Alan sat together hand in hand, listening patiently. Before long, Sam's daughter arrived to fetch him, and by that time the gathering had started to break up.

Alan helped Eve and Rhona tidy up afterwards. Eve had arranged to take the rest of the week off, and he'd persuaded her to come back with him to Durleyford. Ariadne Gray had been a godsend, running the shop in his absence, but Alan felt he ought to take over the reins again and give her a few days' break. Eve had agreed to help him in the shop.

The pressures of the day had made her quite emotional, and Alan could tell that she was very tired. He decided he wouldn't broach the subject of Catterick that evening. But she'd heard Sam speak the name, and Alan was sure she'd think back to when he'd raised the issue with her at the cottage, the evening after the discovery of Rennie's body in the woods at the Hall.

"Catterick? But isn't that an army base? I was never there."

Eve slept on the train and, back at the cottage after a bite of supper, excused herself and went early to bed. As was his custom, Alan sat up late, looked in on her and was glad to find her sleeping peacefully.

He returned downstairs and telephoned Guilfoyle at his London flat. The MP had just got back from a late sitting at the House.

Alan recounted Sam Perkins' tale, while Guilfoyle listened with interest. A suspicion was forming in Alan's mind, regarding the cousin who'd identified Eileen Brayson's body. Guilfoyle promised to put Manners on to it the following morning.

But there was another suspicion: one which had taken root and wouldn't go away. On account of it, Alan slept uneasily that night.

If Rennie were to be believed, *Eve had known Catterick.*

According to Sam, the general view at the time had been that the WAAF seen fleeing from the hotel had been Eileen Brayson, soon to die in the wreckage of Kingsland Street.

But he was left with the uncomfortable thought that in those days before she joined SOE, Eve had been a WAAF.

23

He continued to keep his own council. He knew that her mother's sudden death and all the stress of arranging the funeral had taken a lot out of Eve, and she was exhausted.

Nevertheless she readily accompanied him to the shop the following day, and he believed the steady, undemanding nature of the work would prove therapeutic. And there was a bonus: during her previous spell Eve had made friends with Cicely Kedwell and the Prendergast girls, and all three called in at different intervals to have a chat with her.

In the forty-eight hours since Stella's funeral, however, Eve hadn't referred to 'Catterick' or Sam Perkins' story. It created a barrier between them. Alan supposed it was understandable, but Eve was lacklustre, and each evening after supper she would plead tiredness and retire early to the spare room.

And still he let things lie, in the hope that she'd feel able to confide in him when she felt the time was right.

That time came sooner than he'd anticipated.

* * *

Thursday was early closing day in Durleyford, and late that morning, with business slack, Alan sat in his office typing up orders, while Eve was putting away stock in the shop. Suddenly the tranquillity was shattered by the sound of a horrendous crash. Startled, Alan leapt to his feet and dashed out, overturning his chair in his haste.

In the middle of the shop, a tall, free-standing shelf unit housed dictionaries and other weighty reference books. But the unit no longer stood, for it had collapsed spectacularly to the floor.

Alan's wild gaze raked the shop: Eve was nowhere in sight. Desperately he called her name, repeated it more loudly, finally rewarded with a feeble cry. She was pinned beneath the fallen shelving.

"Oh, my God!" He looked up sharply at the exclamation. Gussie Prendergast stood in the open shop doorway, her hand at her mouth. "Alan – whatever's happened?"

"Gussie! Quickly, I need your help. I don't know how this shelving's collapsed, but Eve's underneath it."

Gussie rushed in, and between them they lifted up the unit. Eve was at the bottom of a mountain of books, but when they finally got to her, Alan was relieved to find that she'd had a lucky escape with probably no more than a few bruises as a legacy.

Alan and Gussie brushed her off and helped her over to a chair. While Gussie hung the 'Closed' sign on the door and then went into the office to boil a kettle for tea, Eve explained that she'd been putting books away on the unit, when suddenly it had lurched towards her. She'd tried to take evasive action, but the cascade of books had knocked her to the ground. Fortunately they'd cushioned her from the full weight of the unit, which was made of oak.

Alan wrapped his arms round her, held her close. "Oh, my darling, thank goodness you're all right. I'm sorry about what happened. That unit's so heavy, I was sure it was secure -."

"Alan." Eve placed a finger to his lips. "My dear, it wasn't an accident. There was someone on the other side of the shelves. He pushed it."

"Pushed it! But I didn't think there was anyone else in the shop -?"

"Neither did I. But someone was there, a man I think. He must have been lurking around for a while. No-one's been in since Miss Pomfret left ten minutes ago. We'd have heard the bell."

Gussie was just then returning with the tea and overheard what Eve had said. "Someone ran out of the shop just as I came along," she said. "He was in a hell of a hurry – left the door wide open."

"Did you get a good look at him?" Alan asked.

Gussie shook her head. "He had his back to me and dashed off down the street. All I glimpsed were a light-coloured mac and a dark hat pulled down on his head."

Alan felt Eve's grip tighten. The description was vague, but they both recalled that it fitted the man Rhona Parrish had seen walking towards Meadowside Court on the afternoon of Stella's death.

He didn't want to make too much of the incident in front of Gussie and was glad that Eve was on the same wavelength. Indeed, she passed it off as an unfortunate accident: the man couldn't have known she was there and made himself scarce when he realised he'd upset the shelf unit.

Gussie nodded, accepting the explanation, although to her credit she was more concerned about Eve.

Eve was clearly shaken, and when Alan declared that he was going to take her home, she made no objection. With Gussie's help, he righted the unit and replaced the books, then closed up early. They thanked Gussie and headed back to the cottage.

Once there, he made more tea. He could tell Eve was struggling to keep her composure, and she glanced up imploringly as she took the cup from him.

"I thought it was all over." she said. "But it's not, is it? Oh Alan, tell me, *please*. What is it I'm supposed to know that's such a threat that someone wants to *kill* me?"

Alan sat down beside her and faced her earnestly. "I don't believe your mother's death was an accident," he said.

"Neither do I now. The man -?"

"The man's no coincidence," Alan went on. "But there's something else, isn't there? At the church hall the other day, I had a long chat with Sam Perkins. He told me about a Squadron Leader named Catterick, who'd been stabbed to death in a hotel called The Beeches on the day Peggy disappeared. I caught the look on your face when Catterick's name came up. You knew him, didn't you?"

She smiled wanly. "Yes, Alan. I denied it before, when you mentioned it, because it was a brief episode in my life which I didn't want to inflict on you. But yes – I knew Clive Catterick."

She set down her cup and faced him squarely. There was an air of resolution about her again. The time for evasion was past, and Alan, to his great relief, sensed a dark cloud lifting.

"You remember I told you that my fiancé, Stewart, was killed in a mission over Belgium? Well, Clive Catterick was his CO, and it was he who came and broke the news of Stewart's death to me. He visited me again shortly afterwards and brought flowers. I was staying with my mother at the Three Bells at that time. He was so kind and seemed so genuine.. And of course I was very young and vulnerable. I fell head first into his trap. Once he'd got me into bed, he was ready to move on. I – I was a fool. I thought he cared for me. Soon after, I visited him in the room he always used at The Beeches. He was in bed with another woman. I fled from there back to the Bells – I remember the woman laughing at me. I was hurting so much, I just cried and cried.

"*Maman* went there the next time he was in the area and confronted him. She told me afterwards that it was actually on the day he was killed. She went there, burst into his room and, in front of the girl who was there, told him exactly what she thought of him. The police came and questioned her, and she made up a story about an unpaid bar bill. Fortunately for her, at the time he met his death she was serving at the Three Bells with a pub full of witnesses, and they left her alone after that."

Alan nodded thoughtfully as he took this in. "Sam Perkins told me that, early in the evening, the receptionist at The Beeches saw a WAAF leaving in a hurry."

Eve smiled. "And you thought that might have been me? Well, you weren't alone. My mother was worried sick about that too. But at the time it happened, I was over eighty miles away at RAF Lyneham, where I was stationed. All right, maybe someone covered for me, and I went up to London. As you've learned, Alan, I'm certainly capable of killing. But I didn't go there. On that you have my word."

"Which is good enough for me." He pulled her towards him, and they kissed. As they drew apart, her expression was one of gratitude.

"Thank you, Alan. You don't know what that means to me."

They sat in silence for a few moments, hand in hand.

"Another thing I learned from Sam," Alan continued. "The WAAF who died in the bombing of Kingsland Street was a girl called Eileen Brayson. She'd come to the Three Bells to see a man known as 'Sarge' – who I'm sure was Rennie – and the officer who was upstairs with Peggy. Sam said it was generally supposed that Eileen Brayson had killed Catterick. And that it was all to do with competition over the sale of black market goods. After his death, the police found a stash at Catterick's quarters."

Eve pondered this for a moment. "I didn't know Catterick that well," she said. "But I think someone must have planted those goods in his quarters. From a few comments he made to me, he was on the trail of whoever was doing the dealing. And I remember Stewart telling me how much his CO was against that sort of thing."

"Where was Catterick based?"

"Northolt, just west of London."

"So was Rennie."

"Then what if Catterick was on to Rennie? Eileen Brayson – possibly by accident – killed Catterick and then - ?"

"Went to Rennie for help. In which case she played right into his hands."

Eve frowned. "How do you mean?"

"Well, if she was out of the way, that tied everything up nicely. She wasn't around to defend herself, and once he'd dumped some black market goods in Catterick's quarters, Rennie was in the clear."

"She was *murdered*?"

"I don't know, Eve. But it's a possibility. Rennie's out of the picture, so now we need to identify the officer."

Eve's grip tightened. "So you're saying that the officer - ?"

"Is the man who's trying to kill you, and who in all likelihood pushed your mother down the stairs."

She looked at him aghast. "But who could it possibly be?"

"That's what we have to find out."

* * *

At supper, they puzzled over the identity of the officer who'd been upstairs at the Three Bells. Rennie had been an RAF sergeant, so they presumed the officer was RAF too, although it didn't necessarily follow. Sam Perkins had said he'd never seen him, so they had nothing to go on.

But they concluded that to an extent they had some idea of Eve's enemy: a man now in his forties or fifties. It was vague, but they were determined to remain alert; with the result that neither of them slept well that night.

The next morning they returned — in Eve's case resolutely — to the shop and set to work as if nothing untoward had happened. Alan put the reference stock back in proper order and posted off a clutch of customer orders, while Eve served customers, dusted and tidied round.

In the middle of the afternoon they received unexpected visitors: Madge Ventnor and Piers Fullarton. They'd clearly enjoyed a slap-up lunch at the Coach & Horses, but that wasn't the sole reason for their exuberance.

"I've found a buyer for Bayes Wood," Madge announced. I can't tell you what a relief that is. To be frank, I've not been able to set foot inside the place. I thank my lucky stars that Piers has been on hand to do that for me."

"I just want it sold and consigned to the past." Fullarton was unusually forthright. "And once that's done, I intend making an honest woman of you, Margaret Ventnor."

Madge winced. "Oh darling, how I *hate* that name. Please, please, stick to Madge, or even "Oi, you over there.""

Fullarton grinned. Alan had never seen him so carefree: a different man altogether from the one haunted and scarred by the war. "We're on our way down to the place I'm renting on the coast. Madge has persuaded me to make an offer for it once the sale of Bayes Wood has gone through."

"Honestly," Madge gushed, "you'd both love it. We're just off a main road, but a bumpy track runs down the side of the house, and at the end there are fantastic views across Lyme Bay to Golden Cap."

"Sounds idyllic," Alan said.

"Well, we think so." Fullarton exchanged glances with Madge. "Listen – er, Eve, well actually both of you. Here we are, all jolly and everything, and we realise things have been pretty bloody for you recently. Madge and I wondered if you'd like to come and stay the weekend with us? I realise you've got the shop, Alan. But why don't you come down on Saturday evening and stay over Sunday?"

"And Eve, dear, there's nothing to stop you travelling down with us this afternoon," Madge went on eagerly. "That's if the two of you can bear to be apart for so long?"

She'd caught Eve's uncertainty; as had Alan. "Why not, Eve? Everything's more or less up to date here. Madge, Piers, would you excuse us for a moment?"

Both smiled graciously, and Alan ushered Eve into the office.

"I really think the change of scene will do you good," he reasoned. "Particularly after yesterday. And if someone comes looking for you, I think he'll be hard pressed to get past Madge."

It drew a smile from her. "I'm sorry, Alan," she said. "But Madge has actually hit the nail on the head. I don't want to be apart from you. And yet -?"

"And yet what?"

"My darling, don't you have misgivings about me? All my chequered history, the way I've tried to avoid being truthful with you. The Catterick business, Marius, Valmy..."

"I won't hear another word," he said firmly. "Your history – which I don't think is chequered at all – stems from one thing: the war. I can't say how much I admire you for the way you came through it."

"You're biased."

"Maybe I am. But I'm right too." He wondered if this could really be Alan Cawley speaking. If love had made him bold, perhaps he should get used to it.

"Darling Eve, go with Madge and Piers. I'll get directions from them and be with you tomorrow evening."

"I shan't feel properly safe until then. Or completely happy."

They were oblivious to the office door softly opening.

"As soon as the tender leave-taking is at an end, perhaps we'll be on our way?"

It was Madge, grinning mischievously, and they leapt guiltily apart. Fullarton had gone to fetch the car, which he'd parked down the street and, as it was virtually closing time, Alan locked up and returned with them to the cottage, where Eve put a few things in an overnight case. He went upstairs to help her pack, equally relieved and alarmed to see the black wedge of the gun in her suitcase. Once again she was prepared to be tethered in plain sight.

"Look after her, you two." It was a plea, a prayer. They promised they would.

"May God go with you, Alan." Eve's parting words, whispered as they kissed goodbye.

"And with you, dearest. Above all, with you." He stood at the gate and waved them off up the lane. "And be watchful," he murmured, as they passed from sight. "Always – be watchful."

* * *

Alan had plenty of time for his thoughts. Without her that evening, the cottage seemed cold and empty, and he could find no solace in his books. He was worried about her, but told himself to buck up. She was safe with Madge and Fullarton at an address which few people knew about, and within twenty-four hours he'd be with her again. Besides, in the day ahead he needed to knuckle down and get some work done.

But he found little consolation there. The morning's trade was unbelievably flat, and Alan applied himself to the tasks in hand, although with little appetite.

Around midday, Manners came into the shop. Apparently 'the master' had a book waiting for him, which he wanted for Sunday.

"He's still in London, then?" Alan inquired.

"Yes. He'd intended collecting it himself as he usually does, Mr Cawley. But the House overran a bit last night, and as he wanted to drop in on Mr Fullarton at Lyme this afternoon, he sent me back on the train. It's a present for a nephew who's coming to the Hall for lunch tomorrow."

Alan reached for an invoice, so that he could enter the book to Guilfoyle's account.

"Oh no, sir," Manners protested, "I'll pay by cheque. The master realises he's run up a bit of a bill, so he's asked me to settle up."

Alan would have been happy to put the book on account but accepted the manservant's offer.

He watched as Manners, tall, ascetic-looking and perennially correct in suit, tie and bowler hat, wrote the cheque in a flowing hand, tore it out and handed it to Alan. As Alan blotted the ink, he had to look twice at the signature.

"That's odd," he chuckled. "I always thought your name was Manners?"

The manservant's face creased in an unusually wide grin. "Oh, bless you, no, Mr Cawley. As you can see, it's McManners, and there's a story to it. I was Mr Guilfoyle's batman during the war, and there was an adjutant, Bob McMinn, in the same squadron. Well, we were both known as 'Mac', and the master used to get mightily confused. One day he called us both to his office. "Now look here, you chaps," he said. "We've got to do something about this. McMinn, I shall call you Minns, and McManners you'll be Manners, so get used to it before I go off my chump." And to this day, sir, Manners it's remained. Funny old things, you know, Mr Cawley, names."

Alan put the book in a bag, and the manservant wished him good day. He hesitated as he reached the door. "Oh, sir, I knew there was something else, and the master told me specifically not to forget it. Eileen Brayson's cousin – the one who identified the body? Well, sir, you'll be surprised to learn that it was none other than Stanley Rennie. Quite a coincidence, sir, as Mr Guilfoyle remarked, and as I'm sure you'll agree."

"Yes, Mr Manners. A strange coincidence. And thank you for letting me know."

He wished Manners good morning and was left alone with his thoughts. He was glad to be alone, because he was preoccupied. He remained in that state as he closed the shop for lunch and wandered across to the Coach & Horses for his usual sandwich and half of best.

The thunderbolt hit him as he was halfway through these, and he thudded his tankard down on the bar with such force that Badger whirled round in alarm.

"Whatever's the matter, Mr Cawley? You look as if you've seen a ghost."

"Something like that, Tom," Alan mumbled distractedly. "I'm sorry. I've really got to dash."

And dash he did, or as fast as his confounded leg would allow. He didn't return to the shop. The 'Closed' sign would remain in place for the rest of the day. Instead, he hurried back to the cottage, got into the car and drove.

May God go with you, Eve had said. "And with you," he replied solemnly. "Oh, my darling, above all may He be with you."

Funny old things, sir, names. Manners, not an hour since.

And it had been Rennie who'd identified the dead girl from Kingsland Street.

Alan doubted that he'd been her cousin. And he doubted now that the girl had been Eileen Brayson.

24

Madge had given him written directions, but even so he managed to take a couple of wrong turnings, cursing vehemently each time he realised his mistake. He drove at speed, expecting at any moment to find a police car on his tail. If that had been the case, he'd have taken it along with him. For he knew without any doubt that this was a matter of life and death.

She'd described the house well: just off a main road a few miles west of Lyme Regis and down a gravelled track which gave on to the coastal path. A little way down stood a newly-whitewashed thatched cottage with mullioned windows. Alan turned the car in at the gate and drew up next to the Triumph he recognised as Fullarton's.

Fullarton, alerted by the scrunch of gravel, was at the door as Alan got out of the car. A smile of welcome flickered on his face.

"Why, Alan! We didn't expect you so soon. We're waiting on Gilly. He's supposed to be coming down from London but must have got delayed."

"Piers, I'm sorry." Fullarton's smile vanished as he recognised the look of anguish on Alan's face. "I must see Eve. I believe she's in danger. Is she inside?"

"No, she and Madge went for a walk along the cliffs — down the track there and turn left over the stile. They — Alan, wait!"

But Alan had turned and hurried off. He didn't look back, although he was aware of Fullarton standing at the gate, staring after him in bewilderment.

He clambered over the stile and followed the footpath which skirted a field. As he rounded the next bend he had a view of the sea, the tide charging in and the white breakers crashing madly against the jagged cliffs.

A figure was running towards him, and Alan gasped as he recognised Madge. He rushed to meet her, caught her, dishevelled and tearful in his arms. *Where was Eve?* He suddenly felt numb, and the words belched harshly from his parched lips.

"Madge, where is she? *Where is she?*"

"Oh, Alan, I couldn't save her." Madge was distraught. "I tried, Alan, I tried."

"But what's *happened?*"

She turned and pointed towards the headland, some half-a-mile distant. "We were walking along the coastal path – up there through the gorse. A man attacked us – he started to grapple with Eve. I tried to pull him off her, but he dashed me to the ground. Then he – he just flung her over the cliff and ran off. It was the same man, Alan. The light raincoat and dark hat – *the man who attacked her in the shop.*"

His voice was hoarse as he held her away from him. "Madge, fetch Piers. Phone for the police and an ambulance. I'm going to see if I can reach her."

Madge stared at him in disbelief. "But she *fell*, darling. Fell all the way down. Oh, Alan, I'm so sorry. But she's gone. *Gone.*"

"Fetch Piers!" he barked and thrust her aside. He stumbled on, almost tripping in his haste, turning once to make sure Madge was on her way. The half-mile stretched out, seeming more like ten. At last he reached the gorse and, blundering through it, came upon a patch where the long grass beside the path had been flattened, showing signs of a struggle. He moved haltingly towards the edge, felt an awful emptiness in the pit of his stomach, his head starting to swirl.

He looked down, saw the wild sea surging against the rocks far below. It was a long way down: no-one could have survived such a fall. His heart sank, and he felt his senses departing. He made one last, gigantic effort, bracing himself to prevent his listless body pitching forward.

And then he saw her.

It was a splash of pink, incongruous in such a landscape. It suddenly dawned upon him that it was her blouse, one he'd seen her wearing the other day.

Hope rose frantically within him. He sank to his knees and peered over the edge. Probably some twenty feet down, a bush jutted out from its anchorage on a narrow ledge. Eve was lying across it: it had broken her fall.

He bawled out her name, and then again: but there was no response. He turned as he heard the sound of urgent footsteps swishing through the tall grass. Madge, Fullarton and Kelvin Guilfoyle were hurrying towards him.

"She's down there!" Alan cried. "A bush has stopped her fall. But I think she's unconscious."

"Then we need a rope," Guilfoyle declared. "Fullars, do you have one back at the house?"

"I'm pretty sure there's rope in the garage -."

"Then fetch it now, man. It needs to be good and strong. Madge, you'd better go with him. Telephone the fire brigade."

The two of them needed no further bidding. Guilfoyle, in shirt sleeves and baggy corduroys, face glistening with perspiration, sank heavily to his knees.

Alan pointed out where Eve lay. "I'm going down," he said.

Guilfoyle looked up sharply. "I think we should wait for the rope," he replied. "There may not be much in the way of footholds."

Alan jabbed an impatient finger at the bush. "She's very light, but I doubt that bush'll hold her for long. Here, give me a hand. I'm going down."

Guilfoyle stared at him levelly, then nodded curtly as he made up his mind. "Take care."

Alan tore off his jacket and crawled to the edge of the cliff. He'd done some rock climbing during his army days, but that had been before he'd smashed up his leg. He found purchase for his left, but the injured right felt fragile and he winced as he put his weight on it. He gritted his teeth but couldn't prevent himself grimacing with the effort.

"This is no good," Guilfoyle said reasonably. "We should wait for Fullars."

"I've got to try!" Alan snapped. "That bush could give way at any moment."

"I'm damned if I'll let you." The cold steel of command sounded in the MP's voice. Without warning he reached down and grabbed Alan's forearms in either hand. It was useless to struggle: if he wriggled out of Guilfoyle's grip, Alan knew he'd plummet on to the rocks below.

Sweating and heaving, Guilfoyle hauled him back over the edge of the cliff, and both men lay panting for breath.

Alan recovered first: he was furious. "You've no right -" He began.

"Every right," the MP snarled back. "Unless you're such a damned fool that you want to kill yourself. That won't help Eve."

Alan had struggled to his feet. The fire in his eyes caused Guilfoyle to get to his. Fuelled by anger and resentment, Alan advanced towards him, hands balled into fists. Guilfoyle was the bigger man by far, and Alan no fighter; but at that moment he was ready to fight.

And then his reason broke in: *what purpose would violence serve?* Guilfoyle was right: it wouldn't help save Eve.

Alan let his hands drop to his sides. "I −I'm sorry," he muttered.

The MP reached out and patted him consolingly on the shoulder. "There's no need," he said. "I'd have felt the same in your place. As would any man worth his salt."

They turned on hearing approaching footsteps: Fullarton, a coil of strong rope looped over his shoulder and Madge, slightly breathless, trying to keep up with him. "Fire brigade's on its way," she panted.

"Let's have that rope." Guilfoyle was his usual decisive self. "Here, Fullars, tie it round my waist."

Alan was quick to intervene. "No, sir. It must be me. With respect, we'd have difficulty supporting your weight."

"But Alan's leg will do him no favours." To Alan's surprise, it was Fullarton who spoke, and with unaccustomed authority. "Sorry, Alan. But if anyone's going, it'll be me."

"Piers, *no!*" The outburst came from Madge, and she rushed across and grasped his arm. "Not *you.*" She was pleading with him, fear rampant on her face.

But there was in Fullarton a determination which Alan had never suspected. The man had suffered horribly in the war, broken in body and spirit by the gruesome experience of Dachau. Perhaps here was the ghost of the man who once had been, the idealistic young pilot going boldly off to fight the war.

"My dear old Madge, look at me. I'm skin and bone, as light as a feather, and for certain a better bet than Gilly or Alan. I'll go."

There was no mistaking the admiration Guilfoyle had for his friend. "I say, old man, is this advisable?"

But his manner was almost tongue-in-cheek. He knew the quality of a man; and he had known Fullarton long before his time of suffering.

Fullarton held out the rope. "Do the honours, Gilly. And make a good job of it, or Madge will haunt you for the rest of your life. Anchor the other end to that post, and you and Alan take the strain."

"Me too." Madge was determined not to stand idly by.

"The more the merrier." Fullarton seemed almost light-hearted, and Alan noted the wild gleam in his eye: the gleam of pride, the pride of a man proving to himself that he was still the blood relation of the man who had been.

They secured the rope and lowered Fullarton down the cliff, the angry sea swirling dizzily below. "More play, you chaps," Fullarton called out; and then again: "More play. Steady as she goes, now. I'm there."

From where he was positioned on the rope, Alan couldn't see what was happening below. But relief washed over him as, after what seemed an age, Fullarton's voice again rang out: "I've got her! Heave away, chaps! Pull us up."

Both Eve and Fullarton were lightweights, but even so Guilfoyle, Madge and Alan had to pull on the rope for all they were worth to bring them up. Fullarton struggled to find purchase on the rock face, finally succeeding to make the ascent of the last few feet easier.

He laid Eve gently on the grass, before sinking exhausted to his knees. Madge ran to him, her face a mask of tears, and revived him with her kisses and endearments. Alan stumbled over to where Eve lay and knelt beside her. As his shadow fell across her, her eyes flickered open. "Alan? Wh-where am I?"

"Safe, my own darling. Safe." She was bleeding from several cuts and abrasions caused by her collision with the bush. He asked if she was hurting badly and was rewarded by a brief shake of the head, before she closed her eyes again.

He gently gathered her up in his arms and headed back towards the house, stopping only to thank the others for all they'd done, and particularly Fullarton for the brave act of rescue he'd carried out. They followed along behind him, Madge arming the exhausted Fullarton.

Police, ambulance and fire brigade arrived in quick succession, the latter sent away once news of the rescue had been confirmed. The ambulance crew treated the cuts Eve had sustained, and the local doctor was called in to prescribe rest and a sedative.

A police sergeant from Lyme took down details of the attack. Madge provided a description of the fugitive and she and Alan confirmed, having previously agreed their story, that they knew of no-one with an obvious grudge against Eve.

The sergeant's opinion was that the attacker might well have been a vagrant, whose motive was robbery; and that he'd panicked when he'd met resistance from the two women. Eve herself was able to recall very little, only that she'd been set upon from behind, had tried to retaliate but had been caught off balance. She believed she might have been unconscious when she went over the cliff.

Once the sergeant and doctor had left, Madge insisted that Eve should rest. The ordeal had taken a lot out of her, and Eve didn't resist. Alan took her through to her room, while the other three remained in the lounge, fortifying themselves with malt whisky.

The sedative had relaxed her, and Alan sat beside the bed and held her hand while she slept peacefully.

The afternoon was drawing to a close when Alan, whose eyelids had begun to feel heavy, jerked awake at the sound of the bedroom door opening stealthily.

The large frame of Kelvin Guilfoyle filled the doorway. "How is she?" he asked in a whisper.

"She'll be fine, Mr Guilfoyle," Alan replied. "Thank you for all you've done today, and please accept my sincere apologies for my behaviour earlier."

The MP waved it away, smiling warmly. "The name is Kelvin, Alan. I think we know one another well enough by now." He nodded towards Eve. "I'd count it as a privilege to be there, you know. At the wedding." He withdrew, softly closing the door behind him.

Eve's eyes flickered open. "Alan, who was that? Mr Guilfoyle?"

"Yes."

"What was he saying?"

"That he'd like to be invited to the wedding."

"Oh? Is there going to be one?"

"A word from you and there will be."

"Then hadn't I better say that word?"

"Only if you want to make me the happiest and proudest man on God's earth."

She smiled. "I've given you plenty of chances to walk away from me. I'm not giving you another. The answer's yes. And bless you for all the faith you've had in me. I shall try never to let you down."

"Oh, my darling Eve. You're here with me and safe. That's all I care about."

He took her in his arms, his heart bursting with pride. He knew without doubt that he'd obtained a pearl of great price, and that no moment in his life, should he live to be two hundred, could be filled with greater joy than this.

* * *

But there were still shadows. They didn't speak about the shadows, not while they had such happiness to share. Alan couldn't bear to spoil those beautiful moments, willing them to go on and on. But he knew that if he didn't, the shadows would never depart. There would always be the threat of danger.

"Eve, forgive me for bringing this up again. But the man who attacked you – did you get any sort of glimpse of him?"

"I saw nothing, darling. I was struck from behind, as Madge tried to fend him off." She gasped at the look on his face. He was pale with shock, with more than that – sorrow, regret – as he took this in.

"Alan, whatever's the matter?"

He gripped her hand. There was a grim set to his mouth as he replied. "Then it's as I feared."

"But what do you mean?"

The door swung slowly open again, and Eve fell silent. Madge appeared, carrying a steaming mug.

"Ah, I see the invalid's on the mend. Who wouldn't be with such a handsome doctor and his engaging bedside manner? Eve, dear, I've brought you some soothing cocoa. It'll help you to sleep."

Eve sat up in bed and held out a hand. But Alan reached over, intercepted the mug and set it down on the bedside table. "I'm afraid she doesn't want it, Madge."

Madge laughed harshly. "Surely a bit early to play the overbearing husband, Alan?" she remarked tartly.

"I don't think it'd be good for her."

Eve's hand crept into his. She threw him a puzzled glance, then, frowning, fixed her attention on Madge.

"Oh?" Madge picked up a pack of cigarettes, extracted one and lit it with a lighter from the pocket of her slacks. She sat down on the dressing-table stool, crossed one leg over the other and languidly blew a puff of smoke across the room. "And how have you managed to arrive at that bold conclusion, my dear Mr Cawley? Is there something you want to tell me?"

"Yes, Madge. But sadly it's nothing you don't already know."

Madge took a long, thoughtful drag on her cigarette. "Try me."

"All right. Let's go back to the war, to the East End of London, when a randy squadron leader named Clive Catterick seduced a young WAAF named Eileen Brayson. I think part of his plan was to persuade her to help him find out more about a thriving black market scheme being run by another RAF officer and a sergeant, a man called Stanley Rennie, who was known to all and sundry as Sarge.

"I don't know exactly what went on, but as a result Eileen stabbed Catterick to death as he lay in bed. She panicked and ran off. She knew Sarge frequented a nearby pub called the Three Bells and went to him for help. She got more than she bargained for: he helped her all right.

"The officer running the scheme with Sarge was in a room upstairs with Peggy Neal, a barmaid at the pub. Peggy was an intermediary in the scheme, selling goods on. And now I'm guessing at what happened. Peggy was greedy and tried to hang on to the money she took. From what I've heard of the girl, she might already have spent it. The officer had come for his share, and she couldn't or wouldn't pay it. There was a scuffle, the officer hit her too hard and found himself upstairs with a dead body for company. He was at a loss for what to do and called to Sarge for help. Sarge came upstairs, bringing Eileen with him.

"Luck was on their side. Eileen confessed to having killed Catterick. Just what they needed to hear: they'd help her if she helped them, and of course she had no choice. She dressed in Peggy's clothes and packed a suitcase. They put Eileen's uniform on Peggy, along with Eileen's identity cards.

"They probably didn't have any definite plan in mind. Put the body in the river perhaps, and hope it'd be there long enough for the features to be obliterated? Again luck played a part. They made their escape through the pub's back entrance, no doubt with Peggy's body wrapped in a blanket and slung over Sarge's shoulder.

"And then a bomb dropped on nearby Kingsland Street. Once the dust and smoke had cleared, their best option was to bury the body under the rubble. When it was discovered, the dead girl was identified as Eileen Brayson, whom the police had wanted to interview in connection with the murder of Squadron Leader Catterick."

Madge calmly stubbed out her cigarette and reached for another, lit up and took a long drag. Her laughter was light and teasing.

"Your man is quite a storyteller, Eve," she said. "You really must get him to write books as well as sell them."

Alan glanced at Eve. She was sitting bolt upright in bed, clutching his arm. She was pale and tense, but her eyes smouldered.

"It was you, wasn't it?" she murmured. "You're Eileen Brayson."

Madge smiled ruefully. "No, darling. I'm Madge Ventnor. I *was* Eileen Brayson, and I took the only way out when it was offered. If I hadn't, there'd likely have been two bodies buried in the rubble.

"Yes, Clive Catterick seduced me, and you're right, Alan. He knew Tony was in league with Rennie, knew I had – what shall we say? – *feelings* for Tony and wanted me to get close to him so that I could bring him proof of their dealings. Tony was already the great war hero, and Catterick envied him, I think, wanted to bring him down.

"Catterick was an arrogant man. Once he'd got me to roll over for him, all I was good for was to do his dirty work. I lost my temper. He started laughing at me and I saw red, picked up a paper-knife from the dressing-table and..."

She pulled on her cigarette again. "Well, of course, then I panicked. I got out of that place as quickly as I could and went straight to Tony and Sarge. They were my only hope. But if you think I haven't been punished for what I did, don't forget I was hitched up to Tony for almost twenty years. There can't have been many fates worse than that."

"Do you mean to say that the RAF officer at the Bells was Tony?" Eve asked. "And that he killed Peggy Neal?"

"Yes, he did. It was an accident. She lashed out at him, and he hit back. He didn't mean to hit her so hard. My God, he turned to jelly. Rennie was the only one who kept a cool head. If it hadn't been for him, we'd both have been in the soup. So Tony and I were rather thrown together. I think that's partly why we married, simply so that we shouldn't let one another out of our sights, bound by the secret we shared. Wing-Commander Ventnor, as he eventually became, threw himself wholeheartedly into the war after that and emerged from it a hero. What a pity he ever made it back from France."

"Ironic, isn't it?" Eve mused sombrely. "Marius employed Rennie to seek out the man he'd known as Antoine, and Rennie found the man who owed him a tremendous debt."

"He tried to fleece Tony of every penny he had," Madge said disparagingly. "He'd misjudged his man: Tony wouldn't take that lying down. If he hadn't topped Rennie, I'd probably have done so myself."

"Let's go back to you, Madge," Alan resumed. "You couldn't afford to be recognised. That's why you killed Stella."

"*No!*" A gasp from Eve.

"Yes," Alan confirmed. "Your mother may have rambled a lot, Eve, but there was some truth in what she said. Remember, she'd been to confront Catterick on the day he died. There was a girl with him. I'd guess that was Eileen, and Stella saw her then and when she came to the Bells to see Sarge and Tony. Stella recognised Tony too. If Rennie was a frequent customer, Tony would have been as well. And she remembered those faces. You told me that Madge and Tony came to your apartment not all that long ago, and she berated them. It was because she recognised them from the war."

"But she did the same to Mr Guilfoyle," Eve protested.

"A man of military bearing. Remember she was reliving those war years. Possibly she'd confused him with Catterick."

Madge worked languidly at her cigarette. She seemed almost light-hearted, as if she was enjoying this. Alan knew that was far from the case. He could see fear in her eyes, eyes which restlessly scoured the room.

His heart went out to her. He'd liked Madge, owed her a lot, but there was no way he could condone cold-blooded murder. He ploughed resolutely on.

"A few weeks back, you and Piers came to the cottage to tell us you'd walked out on Tony and were moving to Dorset. While you were there, Eve had a phone call from her neighbour Mrs Parrish. Eve told us that her mother was in a state. She'd started fretting over Peggy again, and I recall Eve using the phrase *'she thought she knew how it had happened.'* That really set alarm bells ringing. You couldn't afford for Eve to take Stella's ramblings too seriously. It might set her thinking."

Madge stared back boldly, attempting to brazen it out. "So I killed Eve's mother too? Can you really see me dressed as a man in light raincoat and dark trilby?"

Alan's stony expression forced her words to tail away. "You gave yourself away, Madge, on the cliffs this afternoon. You said that the man who pushed Eve over the edge was *the man who attacked her in the shop.* We never spoke to you about the incident in the shop."

"But Eve must have mentioned -?"

Eve shook her head. "I said nothing, Madge. Just that the shelves collapsed."

"That first time in Durleyford High Street," Alan went on. "When the man stole Guilfoyle's car and tried to run Eve down – well, that couldn't have been you. You were on the scene almost immediately afterwards. But I suspect it was Tony, and that the raincoat and hat were his. He was conspicuous by his absence that day.

"But Meadowside Court and last Thursday in the shop were another matter. You'd got to the stage where you had to remove Eve in case Stella had passed on her suspicions.

"And earlier today, there was no man on the cliffs. Just you and Eve. You attacked her from behind."

"And you came flying out of nowhere, game leg and all to save your damsel in distress," Madge sneered. "So by what feat of deductive reasoning did you work out that it was all down to me?"

"Because of something Piers said," Alan replied.

"Piers?" Madge was suddenly unnerved. "But what did he say? How – how could *he* have known?"

"It was a chance remark. When you came into the shop with him yesterday, he referred to you as Margaret. But his wasn't the only one. Earlier today, Manners called in. We were in conversation, and he said something like "funny thing, names." Well, both Peggy and Madge are contractions of Margaret. It set me thinking, and the thought crossed my mind that you might have assumed Peggy Neal's identity. And there I'd been believing Eve was safe with you. When I'd given more thought to Sam Perkins' story, a number of issues began to make sense."

Eve stared at Madge in bewilderment. Madge, on the other hand, remained outwardly calm. With a quirky smile, she stubbed out her cigarette and rose to her feet.

"I suppose it was good while it lasted. But in my defence – well, what can I say?" For a moment her features convulsed, and Alan thought she would give way to tears. "Oh, Alan. Dear Alan. If only things had turned out differently."

Alan stood too, concerned, and took a pace towards her. "This is all conjecture, Madge. Nothing can be proved. Listen, we -."

She shook her head, stifling a sob. "But I – I *know*." She looked across the room at Eve. "And I'm sorry, my dear. Believe me, please. I'm sorry." She smiled wanly, then turned and strode purposefully from the room.

Fullarton and Guilfoyle were in the lounge. They heard Fullarton call out. "I say, old thing, where are you off to? Madge? Madge – come back!"

"Dear God." It suddenly dawned upon Alan that Madge had made her decision, and that he knew what she was about to do. Eve was on the same wavelength, scrambling out of bed and flinging a cardigan round her shoulders. She was right behind him as they hurried from the room.

Ahead of them came the slam of the front door, the fierce gunning of the Triumph's engine, the sound of its tyres mashing the gravel as it tore away up the track.

Fullarton and Guilfoyle ran after it, with Eve and Alan stumbling along in their wake. The car swerved across the main road, picked up speed and was lost to sight for a matter of seconds before the tortured squeal of tyres rent the air.

By the time Eve and Alan reached the scene, the other two were there. In the fading light they saw the Triumph, its bonnet crumpled against a thick oak tree, black smoke billowing from its engine.

Guilfoyle stood at a distance, hands dangling uselessly at his sides, his face drawn, powerless, as he stared at them unseeingly. "I – I'll call for help," he stuttered, and turned and blundered past them.

Fullarton knelt beside the car. The driver's door had sprung open, and he held fast to the limp arm which hung down beside the seat. He turned towards them a face of utter misery, of total devastation: a man broken by the war, miraculously healed and within the space of minutes broken again.

Tears coursed freely down Eve's face. "Oh, Alan," she whispered. "Will this war *never* end?"

"One day it must," he answered haltingly through his own tears. "Surely – one day."

He clung to her then as he would for the rest of his days; clung because he couldn't bear to let her go, someone honest, sane and true in a dizzying world.

And he clung too, grimly, to his father's faith, as he raised his beseeching gaze to heaven and prayed that the answer to her question might come from there.